I0762524

back stab bers

back stab bers

a novel

eliza jabore

BANTAM • NEW YORK

Bantam Books
An imprint of Random House
A division of Penguin Random House LLC
1745 Broadway, New York, NY 10019
randomhousebooks.com
penguinrandomhouse.com

Published by arrangement with Little, Brown Book Group Limited. First published in the United Kingdom by Sphere, an imprint of Little Brown Book Group in 2026.

Hardcover ISBN 979-8-217-09536-0
Ebook ISBN 979-8-217-09537-7

Printed in the United States of America

1st Printing

First U.S. Edition

BOOK TEAM: Production editor: Loren Noveck • Managing editor: Saige Francis • Production manager: Ali Wagner • Copy editor: Madeline Hopkins • Proofreaders: Wes Alspach, Deborah Bader, and Adele Starrs

The authorized representative in the EU for product safety and compliance is Penguin Random House Ireland, Morrison Chambers, 32 Nassau Street, Dublin D02 YH68, Ireland. https://eu-contact.penguin.ie

To my daughters—

may you know many adventures

back stab bers

one

"This was the best decision I ever made. I feel so alive!" Florence Marsh sent that message to her brother a little over five years ago, on June 17, 2019. She was never heard from again.

According to her wilderness permit, Florence had planned a seventy-eight-mile loop hike of the Bones Hollow Trail through Olympic National Park in Washington.

Despite the case being closed after the death of Wendy Whitmore in 2018, Florence is believed by many to have been the ninth and final victim of the Bones Hollow Hunter. The eight other hikers' bodies were each discovered naked, pinned against a tree with an arrow through the heart and a single tooth missing. But Florence Marsh's body was never found.

Who was the Bones Hollow Hunter, and why do people suspect Florence was his ninth victim?

These are the questions we explore together on episode nine of Serial Killers USA: The Bones Hollow Hunter. *As always, my sweet Little Savages, I'm your host, Laurie Wolff. Let's dive in.*

"Why are we listening to this?" I asked again, like I had at least once a day. Laurie Wolff's husky voice had serenaded us almost constantly since we started hiking the Bones Hollow Trail three days ago.

"Why wouldn't we?" Zoe grunted, the exertion of hiking the rugged terrain audible in her voice. The two-foot-wide trail moved steadily downhill through the old-growth forest in a series of switchbacks. Giant evergreen roots and moss-covered rocks and boulders protruded onto the muddy path, threatening to trip us with every step. "We're literally *in* the Hunter's old stomping grounds. It's no different than having a guidebook, Jade; we need to be prepared. He's dormant, not dead. Besides, it's great research for when I start my own podcast one day. And I catch something new every time I listen to it."

"Me, too," Stefanie said, breathing heavy. She always took her cues from Zoe. We both did. "And noise is good. It keeps the bears away."

The Hunter's victims all had a few things in common, Laurie Wolff continued. *Young women between the ages of twenty and thirty-five hiking the Bones Hollow Trail alone. Aged thirty, Florence Marsh fit this profile.*

I looked to my two best friends, aged twenty-eight. "Noise also attracts," I said.

According to Florence's wilderness permit, she expected to take two days to reach Bones Hollow Valley, where she would rest for one day before hiking back. Her family says that she easily trekked twenty miles a day, regardless of terrain, and would have finished the loop in that time frame with ease. A torrential rainstorm rolled through on her second day. Being the experienced hiker that she was, it is believed that Florence knew to shelter in place and wait for the weather to pass.

"You're supposed to shelter in place? Shit, I wouldn't have known that." It was mid-July and yet the cool, misty air chilled the sweat on my neck. Goosebumps prickled my flesh. "Seriously, guys, I can't listen to this anymore. All I'm hearing is that a super-experienced hiker bit the dust in some gruesome way and now we're following in her footsteps. If *Florence* got killed out here, what the hell kind of chance do we stand? We've never been backcountry camping like this!"

"We've camped before," Stef said, defensive.

"Yeah, at campgrounds in state parks. A little different than hiking across the wilderness for eight days, don't you think?"

"We all pop our cherry sometime," Zoe said. "Stop worrying so much."

"C'mon," Stef said. "You know that telling our sweet baby Jade to stop worrying is like telling a fish not to swim." She blew me a kiss.

I smiled, snarky, and flipped her the finger. "I'm not a worrier, I'm just sensible. And Zoe would probably be dead without me by now."

"That's probably true," Zoe said with a sigh. "But that's why I love you so much. I need someone who helps me question my impulses. Even if it drives me fucking crazy." She weaved her arm around my neck for a quick hug, nearly toppling us both.

The ball of aggravation that had knotted my stomach softened now. Zoe and I often said that we balanced each other out.

I brought her back down to Earth while she challenged me to reach for new heights. It was one of the reasons we were such good friends.

Stef snorted, laughing. "Oh my god, remember when she stopped you from picking up that snake?"

"She wasn't just going to pick it up," I reminded her. "She was going to push it into that glass bottle! Idiot."

Zoe tossed her hands into the air. "It didn't seem so dumb at the time! But okay, fine. That one was venomous. You saved my life. I freely admit it."

"I would've thought most people knew that, like, basically everything in Australia is poisonous. But you're welcome."

"Well, we all know I'm not most people," Zoe said with pride.

Laurie Wolff went on: *The search party never found a single item that belonged to Florence. Not even her grandfather's antique silver compass, which she never left home without. She vanished without a trace. Plenty of other hikers in Olympic National Park go missing, but normally they leave evidence behind. So, was she just another unfortunate traveler, like the police and the park rangers want us to believe? Or was she the next victim of the Bones Hollow Hunter? Well, my Little Savages, what do you think?*

I stared into the rich coniferous forest around us. Wide cedars and firs reached their needlepoint noses up to the clouds. Mammoth trees, ferns, and white-flowering hemlock stretched as far as the eye could see, every inch of rock and earth dripping with emerald moss. The forest vibrated with scuttling critters and birdsong. Eagles soared overhead in clear blue sky. Out of sight, we heard a stream bubbling through the undergrowth down to Bones Hollow, where we'd camp tonight.

Everything around us felt so alive, in a way that was both

magical and unsettling. I couldn't shake the feeling that, somewhere out there, predators lurked behind this vibrant greenery. Bears, cougars, or worse. Some invisible beast could be hunting us right now.

Shadows moved behind a wide cedar. A twinge of panic momentarily coiled tight around my lungs. Okay, maybe my friends were right; maybe I did worry too much. But that was why our annual adventures together were so good for me. Stef and Zoe loved to push me out of my comfort zone, and I got to challenge myself.

Between April and September for eight consecutive years, the Bones Hollow Hunter pierced one unlucky woman through the heart with his bow and arrow and left her body posed in the exact same way. Florence Marsh fit his profile, and her family has always maintained that she was too experienced a hiker to go missing, not to mention without a trace. They are convinced that the Bones Hollow Hunter was involved. But if the Hunter killed her, why hadn't he positioned her body?

There are some of us that agree with the Marsh family. The police might want to tie this case up with a nice little bow, but not everyone is so convinced. Perhaps the Hunter isn't dormant at all.

I hated this podcast. I couldn't understand why my friends liked it so much.

"Don't you guys think it's tacky, though?" I said, panting between words. "How Laurie Wolff uses those cheesy intros to every episode, like, just get on with it! No one who has decided to listen to this stupid serial killer podcast chooses to start with episode nine. And don't even get me started on her ending credits song. I mean, 'I Think We're Alone Now,' really? It's so disrespectful to the actual victims. Just like calling her fan base 'Little

Savages.'" I paused to catch my breath. "Not to mention that it's outrageously annoying that we've come out here to enjoy nature and can't unplug for even half a day."

"Oh my god, fine!" Zoe stopped and reached into her backpack's side pocket. "If you're not going to stop complaining." She switched off her phone. As none of us had signal out here, Zoe had taken the liberty of downloading the full season of *Serial Killers USA: The Bones Hollow Hunter* before we left. "Happy now?"

"Yes," I said. But then I wasn't so sure. The silence was at once blissful and foreboding.

A thick branch snapped somewhere in the dense foliage, loud like a bone cracking. I screamed. On instinct, my friends screamed with me. Laughter immediately followed. Our backpacks threatened to catapult us down the sloping trail, and we anchored ourselves against one another, giggling uncontrollably.

By the time I caught my breath, my knees felt ready to buckle. I unclipped my waist belt and the chafed skin on my hips stung with relief. I hefted my backpack, the size of a small child, onto the ground and sat atop it. The others followed suit. We rubbed our sore calves and shoulders, kneading impenetrable knots. I checked my watch to see that it was nine A.M. and we'd been hiking for two and a half hours.

"Did you think it was the Hunter?" Stef said, still laughing. "When you screamed, I won't lie, for a second I thought it was him."

"Oh, please, we both know what you're scared of, Stef," Zoe said. "All that hocus-pocus bullshit and evil spirits."

"Don't play," Stef said, serious now. "It's no joke. We're hiking toward an ancient burial ground."

"Rumored," I pointed out. An important distinction.

"I'm just saying," Stef said, looking around for invisible ears. "Be respectful."

Wiping sweat from my brow, I restrained myself from taking a swig of water. Streams and creeks were plentiful in this forest, always audible nearby, but it took time to refill our hydration packs using the tiny filter pouch in Stefanie's backpack. She carried purifier tablets, too, but it was best to reserve those. Zoe had said we were about seven miles from Bones Hollow, and if we were careful we wouldn't need to refill our hydration packs until tonight. I watched as Stef tipped her bottle to her lips.

Leaves rustled behind us. "Relax," Zoe said, seeing the tension in my shoulders. She massaged them now. "It's probably just the bear."

We'd seen a beefy black bear eating huckleberries in a meadow on our first day. All three of us had frozen. Stef and I clung to each other, unable to move until it had shuffled all the way across the meadow and out of sight. Even then, I was nervous to go on. I imagined it turning to see us and giving chase, its lumbering gait too fast to outrun. But Zoe had said, "Black bears rarely attack humans unprovoked, don't worry." How she knew this, I couldn't be sure. But then Zoe had a way of sounding confident in just about everything she said, justified or not.

"Why would you say bear?" I asked. "It's not funny."

"You're right. It's probably a cougar. Except, wait, you'd never hear a cougar."

I rolled my eyes. "I seriously hate you sometimes."

"Oh, come on." Zoe put her arm around me. "You've got nothing to worry about. We're out here in one of the most beautiful places on Earth. Breathe it in; enjoy it! If anything tries something—a bear or a cougar or the *Hunter*," she wiggled her fingers like she spoke of the boogeyman and not a real-life serial killer who had prowled this trail, "there's three of us. Strength in numbers, girl. We're perfectly safe."

We'd been friends for seventeen years, since middle school, and I could still never tell if Zoe was tough as nails or just the best poker-faced bluffer. Nothing seemed to faze her. Maybe that was why she could listen to true crime podcasts like they were lullabies while I lay awake at night envisioning an arrow through my heart. Zoe often talked about starting her own program one day; she saw it as her chance to be a real-life hero, solving cold cases. Whereas just imagining the gruesome research involved in such a project terrified me.

"Thanks," I said. My friend was right. We were surrounded by breathtaking beauty, nature so untouched and pure, it was like stepping back in time. I needed to appreciate this experience.

Zoe squeezed my shoulder. "You want to see her again, don't you?"

Stefanie nodded emphatically. "Yes, yes, yes."

Zoe reached into her shorts pocket and withdrew a three-and-a-half-inch folding knife she'd affectionately named Ripley. "Here she is." She unfolded it and passed the knife to me.

Ripley's weight in my palm momentarily soothed my nerves. I traced the ridge of its black handle. But when my eyes came to the serrated blade, I had to admit to myself I'd never be able to use a knife, even if I was in danger. But it was reassuring Zoe had it.

I passed it to Stefanie and she smiled, switching it between her hands before twisting the blade in the air, stabbing at the nothingness. "Is it weird that just holding this makes me feel like a badass? Maybe this is what the Hunter feels like." She sliced at a dangling fir branch.

I cringed at the thought of the killer with this knife. But, at the same time, I understood what she meant. Having the knife meant we stood a chance against a predator like him.

Zoe had the map spread across her lap. The pink streak she'd dyed into her pale blond hair fell from her ponytail into her eyes; she tucked it behind her ear, then again when it fell once more. The small black tattoos that littered her arms looked like a map in and of themselves, and they were in a way. A map of everywhere we'd gone together, a new one for every trip. She'd designed each one herself. A jaguar for Costa Rica. A seashell for Sicily. She'd told us that she planned to get a wide cedar for the Bones Hollow Trail. Stef had admired her ink for years now and said she was finally ready to take the plunge. Naturally, she planned to get the same cedar that Zoe would design.

Zoe glanced at her compass as Stef continued stabbing the air. Another branch cracked in the forest, but this time I didn't scream. I searched the trees and the endless expanse of gray-brown trunks and branches and the vibrant greenery for any trace of movement, for the shadow of antlers passing by in the thicket. Or worse, steam off a bear's large snout or the glint of a predator's eyes.

I silently repeated my mantra:

1. The Hunter's victims are always single female travelers. We're a trio. We don't fit the profile.

2. He hasn't killed anyone in years, even if you believe he killed Florence Marsh.

Though, I supposed if he *had* changed his methods for Florence, there might be a whole trail of other missing women no one had even linked to him, since the police had stopped searching . . .

Damn it, Jade, don't think like that. Cling to the mantra!

There was nothing to be afraid of. We were out here to conquer fear, anyway. To look the wilderness in the face and prove that we could hack it. We could do this. Together.

The Bones Hollow Trail was full of dualities. It was punishing and rewarding all at once, and not just physically. We hadn't seen another hiker since we first set off three days ago and the isolation made me feel both soothed and vulnerable. The three neatly stacked rocks that marked the trail were the only indication that any other soul had once stepped foot here. I was terrified of seeing another face, and yet, at the same time, I longed for it.

"That detour I told you guys about is coming up," Zoe said, looking at Stef. They'd been trying to sell me on a detour to a hidden waterfall since day one. It was supposed to be spectacular, an untouched gem in the wilderness unlike the rest we'd seen. Obscured by a canopy of moss, secluded and unmarred by regular pedestrian traffic.

"Think how nice it'll be to shower in a crisp, clean waterfall all to ourselves," Stef said, pleading. "Come on, come on, come on. We've got to do it."

The blisters on my feet pulsed at the thought of a half-day hike farther downhill, which was where Zoe had told us it would be, in a hidden gulch surrounded by forest. It would mean an eventual half-day hike back up this same terrain. But I couldn't argue that the picture they'd painted of this secret waterfall sounded rather majestic. Besides, it would be a good spot to replenish our water supply and wash away this thick coat of grime from my skin.

"You just want to wash your face again," I said to Stef. She was the only one of us who had brought an actual skincare "regimen" with her; two different lotions, one for morning and one for night. Such a waste of packing space.

"You're just jealous of my flawless complexion," she said. "And, actually, I'm much more interested in washing this swamp crotch." She plucked the black spandex bicycle shorts from between her butt cheeks. The three of us laughed.

"Okay, that does sound nice," I said, keenly aware of the sweat pooling between my own thighs. "Can we please just move now?"

We saddled up again, feeling mildly revitalized. There was a spark in Zoe's and Stefanie's eyes that I drew fervor from. They'd been excited about this waterfall since we started the trail. I'd seen a few anecdotal references to hidden waterfalls when I looked up Bones Hollow, but I'd left the majority of the research to Zoe. This entire trip had been her idea, and she had a knack for finding hidden treasures. Knowing her, it would probably be the most beautiful thing we'd ever seen in our lives.

Every year, we saved money to go on an adventure together: backpacking all across Europe, touring the ancient ruins of Southeast Asia, exploring the jungles of South America. It was an unbreakable pact we'd made when we were young, that once a year the three of us would travel someplace new together. Though we were active and enjoyed the outdoors, we'd never hiked for such a distance through unmaintained wilderness like this before. It was Zoe who had convinced us that we needed this challenge. That we could trek for eight days alone through the wild, carrying only the necessities on our backs. Her confidence was so infuriatingly unearned and yet so unwavering that one couldn't help but feel swayed by it. I loved that about Zoe. Most of the time.

The Bones Hollow Trail had been chosen for its isolation. She said there was hardly anywhere else we could go in the country where we'd be surrounded by such a vast, ancient forest, still almost completely untouched by man. Of course, Stef had been the one to discover the trail's spiritual history, a burial ground rumored to be in Bones Hollow Valley. More people had mysteriously vanished from this trail than any other in the Pacific Northwest, even without taking a serial killer into account. Most conspiracy sites attributed this to Sasquatch, but Stefanie had found the one website dedicated to hauntings and sent us all a link. I'd never been too worried about ghostly apparitions. I was much more afraid of the proven, tangible dangers that existed in the world.

Still, the Bones Hollow Trail had already lived up to Zoe's promise. On the first day, it had given us a stunning view atop a grassy peak overlooking Mount Olympus and a range of glaciers. Then it wound us through a gorgeous wildflower meadow, by breathtakingly blue lakes, and past crystal-clear rivers. The astounding beauty of this rugged wilderness made up for the stress of its potential threats. The air here in the old-growth forest smelled clean and moist, like cedar and pine and moss. Each breath was revitalizing. And, sure, I longed for a margarita on the beach at least once a day, but the experience had already made me stronger, and not just physically.

My patience with little inconveniences like blisters and pebbles in shoes expanded every day, built up like a new muscle. My pathological need for structure—which had shackled me back home—melted away here, cleansed by the pure forest air.

Even the spiders that normally sent me screaming when I was alone in my apartment no longer fazed me. Yesterday, Zoe saw me brush a disgusting eight-legged monster from my shoulder like it was nothing more than a ladybug. I didn't even yelp. She gave me a knowing smile. She knew better than anyone what an achievement this was for me.

The first time Stef invited us to her parents' cabin on Lake Michigan for the weekend was the summer after eighth grade. That night, as we all curled into sleeping bags on the den floor, our stomachs full of popcorn and bubbling with Cherry Coke, I glimpsed a large spider skittering across the ceiling. I jolted upright like I'd been stunned by a cattle prod.

I'd never spoken of my crippling arachnophobia, and I wasn't about to then, so when Stef asked what was wrong, I'd said I needed a drink of water. But I already knew I wouldn't sleep that night. I would sit, terrified, until dawn, staring at the ceiling with bloodshot eyes like a sentinel, waiting for the arachnid to descend.

"Hey, will you stay up with me for a while?" Zoe had whispered when Stef eventually left to pee. "You're a better listener. I love Stef, you know that. But her mom is, like, perfect in her eyes. She doesn't get the stuff that goes on in my house. The way a parent can let you down. Not the way you do."

It was true. Stef had a way of dismissing Zoe or me when we tried to talk about our mothers. Mine was overbearing. Zoe's was a secret pill fiend. Stefanie's was her *best friend.* She couldn't understand.

"Yeah, of course," I'd said, my secret relief so immense I could've cried.

Once Stefanie was snoring softly, Zoe leaned in close and murmured, "I have a secret." We'd scooted our sleeping bags so close together that we were nearly nose to nose. "I knew we'd be best friends before we'd ever even said a word to each other."

"What? Why?" I'd asked in disbelief.

"Remember when Mr. Welch wanted to send me to the principal's office for asking why he even wanted to be a teacher, since he was so shit at it?"

"Yeah . . ." I muffled my giggle, remembering how cool I'd thought Zoe was at the time, saying out loud what every kid in that class already thought. Mr. Welch was the worst teacher imaginable, a bitter old baseball coach who resented every second he spent in the classroom, taking out his spite on all of us.

"You were the only one to stand up for me. 'If she goes, then I should go, too.' That's what you said. Even though we'd never spoken a word to each other." We both snickered softly.

Getting sent to the principal together was the birth of our friendship. We emerged from the office basically inseparable. Stef and Zoe were already friends by that point, so we became a fast trio.

We fell asleep that night reminiscing. I realized the next morning that Zoe never did vent about her mom. She'd never needed to. She'd known that I was scared, without my ever having said a word, and knew exactly what I needed in order to get through the night.

Though eventually I confessed the real reason I couldn't sleep that night, Zoe never once made fun of me. She never told Stefanie about my arachnophobia, either. I felt proud now, with Zoe seeing how far I'd come. Witnessing me brush the spider away like it was nothing.

But I didn't come on these trips just for the personal growth. Nothing brought you closer to someone than traveling alongside them. These annual adventures were our sacred time together, without interruption or distraction from the outside world and all its adult responsibilities. This was how we kept our friendship fortified.

"I haven't told anyone else this yet," Stefanie said, as if reading my mind, "but I think I'm gonna break up with Jeff."

Zoe and I exchanged a quick look of relief. We'd never liked Jeff. He was far too controlling, always trying to convince Stefanie that he should tag along for our travels, or she should back out of our plans last minute. Last year, he'd bought her a Caribbean cruise for the same dates as our Costa Rica trip. Stef had tried to laugh it off at the time, saying he'd simply forgotten. But Zoe and I knew the truth: Jeff was an asshole.

Still, I said, "Why? Did something happen?"

"I don't know. I just feel like he's about to propose and it's gotten me thinking. Is he really the guy I want to spend the rest of my life with?"

"Well, I'll be the first to say it. Good fucking riddance!" Zoe fist-pumped the air. "You know I've always hated the mustache. No one named Jeff should have a mustache."

"And let's be honest," I said. "Stef and Jeff? Just imagine those wedding invitations."

I could hear the release of tension in Stefanie's laugh. "I know you guys never liked him. It's okay; it's not like you hid it well."

"Um, excuse me, I listened to him talk stocks and bonds at your birthday dinner for over an hour," Zoe said. "If that's not hiding it well, I don't know what is." She stopped to give Stefanie a hug.

"Don't worry," I said, hugging her now, too. "It'll be okay. You're better off without him."

Stef swiped at a tear, frustrated with herself. "You know I hate being alone."

"You're never alone." Zoe squeezed her arm. "You have us."

We reached the end of our current trail. It continued with another switchback farther down toward the valley, but Zoe gestured toward a mossy boulder on the path, nestled into the massive roots of a fir. She consulted her compass and nodded, sure of herself. "Oh, here it is! See? This boulder looks like an egg in a wicker basket. That's the landmark. It's this way." Zoe pointed to the trees descending off-trail to our left.

"Are you crazy? You didn't say the detour was off-trail, Zoe. We'll get lost."

"Come on, where's your sense of adventure?" Stef asked.

"Here!" I gestured all around me. "Here, it's here. This is enough adventure for me. I don't need more."

Zoe slapped my backpack. "Sorry, you've been outvoted." Then she skipped down through the trees, with Stef a few paces behind her.

I skidded down the muddy slope after my friends. My backpack snagged on the branches every few paces, like the forest was reaching out to grab me.

• • •

We'd been hiking down this absurd detour for over an hour. It was nearly midday, and already it was clear we weren't hiking back up this incline before nightfall. It was too steep and too far. If we wanted to take our time at the falls, we'd need to camp there for the night—but Zoe assured us that she had read this was possible. The farther down we hiked, the more my muscles screamed and the more the waterfall sounded like bliss. But I still couldn't stop checking over my shoulder. The ache in my bones reminded me just how fragile they were. A twig crunched beneath my muddy boot and I wondered how easily my legs could make that same sound.

"No way Florence is the last victim," Stef mused as we marched along.

I resented how much the Hunter dominated our conversations. "Because she wasn't found?" I asked.

"No," she said, pausing to crouch down and massage her calves, "the Hunter totally killed her. I just mean, no way is Florence his last. Guys like him never stop. Once they get a taste for it, it's an addiction. It's only a matter of time before they kill again."

"Yeah, but serial killers have an MO," Zoe pointed out, breathing heavy. "That's part of their addiction, too. So why wouldn't she have been displayed like all the others?"

"Don't either of you think we should at least consider that maybe, just maybe, that Lars guy was guilty?"

Lars Brunner had been the only suspect in the case. A late-thirties Swiss-German national with a history of mental illness, he'd entered the country in 2011 shortly before the first victim was found, and had been traveling on his expired visa ever since. He'd been hiking the Bones Hollow Trail alone when he supposedly found the body of the eighth victim, Wendy Whitmore, in 2018 and called the police—an act that would later be interpreted as a killer desperate to be caught.

Police were immediately suspicious of the hippie-haired vagabond and labeled him a person of interest and brought him in for questioning. When they discovered that Lars was lying about his alibi for Rae Fischer's murder the previous year, and then that he had no alibis for any of the other victims as he claimed to have been traveling off-grid, they issued an arrest warrant. But they were never able to serve it. Lars Brunner hanged himself from a big-leaf maple here in Olympic National Park. It's why so many still argued that Florence Marsh couldn't be a Bones Hollow Hunter victim.

"Come on, you have to admit that it's at least *possible* that Lars was the guy," I said.

"No way," Zoe said, definitive. "They railroaded the first guy they could find. It's so obvious that Lars lied about his alibi because he was trying to cover up another crime—I've read that there was a string of robberies on the trail that year; all the hikers' guides were littered with warnings about some crazy dude with a machete. The thief was taking all their gear, sometimes even their clothes. It'd make sense if it was Lars since he was living off-grid and probably needed the supplies. So, it was either confess to armed robbery—which would have only made him look more guilty of these murders anyway—or try his luck with a false alibi. He was up shit creek. But the cops had nothing on him, no real evidence at all."

"Tale as old as time," Stefanie said, as if she knew about such things. "It's just lazy policing, plain and simple, charging the first patsy they catch. Even that detective for the case said so, when he came on the podcast. His boss basically told him that the case was closed. It's utter bullshit."

"Then why did Lars kill himself?" I asked.

"Well, he'd already been checked into a mental health facility once back in Switzerland for a suicide attempt. Maybe the poor kid decided he'd rather die than go to prison for murders that he didn't commit," Zoe said. "That's *if* he even killed himself. Tons of people don't think Lars committed suicide. Laurie Wolff clearly doesn't. She talks about a theory that the real killer is the one who strung him up."

"The Hunter case was never officially closed for a reason," Stef agreed. "He's still out here somewhere. I can just feel it."

"Maybe not. Even if it wasn't Lars, maybe the real killer is dead," I volunteered, hopeful. "Maybe Florence fought back and killed him. Or maybe it just all went so wrong that he finally hung up his hat for good. Or!" I was animated now, rejuvenated by my sudden theory but painfully out of breath. "Maybe it wasn't even the Hunter and she died of natural causes. Like a bad fall or hunger or hypothermia or any number of the other dangers out here." Strange that this seemed a hopeful situation, but under the circumstances, it most certainly did.

"Maybe it was a cougar!" Zoe said, a little too exuberantly.

How quickly my optimism could be stolen. I shuddered. "I seriously hate you."

She stopped walking long enough to plant a kiss on my cheek.

"I do," I maintained, but smiling now. "I hate you."

"There's actually a whole online community devoted to this," Zoe said.

"Why am I not surprised?"

"Most people think that the Hunter has way more victims than those found. All the other women who have mysteriously vanished from this trail, they weren't taken by ghosts or Bigfoot. They were taken by the Hunter. Some people think that he might mount the special ones on his bedroom walls." Her tone changed, lurid now. "So, if we found his place, we'd find Florence."

"I think I like Stef's evil spirits theory better," I croaked, throat dry.

Zoe's eyes gleamed, excited by the intrigue of it all. "Hell, maybe we're both right and the Hunter has been sacrificing women to the spirits."

"Don't joke about that shit," Stef said, gravely serious. "It's not—"

Stefanie didn't see the rock. Her boot caught on it and she pitched forward headfirst, the slick mud and the weight of her backpack propelling her like a bowling ball down the steep hill. She caught herself on a tree trunk just before she rolled a second time.

It all happened as if I was seated in the back row of a theater seeing it play out on the screen. I watched it, unable to move, unable to help. Her scream ripped me from my trance.

Blood trickled down the side of Stefanie's face from a cut on her forehead. Leaves and muddy clumps dangled from her loose black ponytail. She clutched her ankle, howling, and Zoe was already by her side. Slowly, she undid the laces from Stef's low-rise hiking shoe, slipping it off the heel, and rolled down her thick wool sock. Stef's ankle looked a little red and swollen; for a moment I had hope that it wasn't too bad. But then Zoe gingerly pressed two fingertips to the wound and Stefanie screamed.

"Oh my god, oh my god," I gasped, again and again. "Shit!"

"Come on, you're all right." Zoe was our coach in times of need, the one who urged us onward when our legs buckled. She eased the shoe back on, tying up the laces. "Let's get you upright."

Stefanie put an arm around each of us and we hoisted her upward. The extra weight of her with her bag was almost too much for me to bear. I steadied myself against a nearby tree, careful so that I didn't catapult forward now as well.

"Can you put any weight on it?" Zoe asked.

Stefanie tried now, breathing deep. She screeched in pain. "No! Fuck, fuck, fuck! Put me down. Put me back down."

We eased her back down onto the muddy, mossy hill. She leaned backward onto her pack, holding her face. "I can't walk. I can't fucking walk."

"This is bad," I said, turning to Zoe. "This is really, really bad."

Zoe braced herself on a mossy fir trunk, like she was trying to draw strength from it, resolve. Then she took out her map and studied it, sweat beading between her knitted brows. "We can't go back up. It would take us three days hiking the Bones Hollow Trail the way we came to get to our car. Probably longer, given her ankle. But if we keep going south now, we'll hit the falls and if we keep going south from there, eventually we'll hit an access road."

Stefanie sucked in a deep breath, composing herself. "Okay, get me up. I can do it." She bit her lip, holding back the tears, as Zoe and I gently eased her back upright. But as soon as we propped her on her feet, Stef screamed again. "Put me down!"

"She'll have to take her backpack off," Zoe said. "We can't carry her with it."

I shook my head. "No way! That's a third of our food. We'll have to divide it between us."

"I don't fucking care about the food!" Stefanie screeched. "Just get me out of this forest!" As we eased her out of her shoulder straps, she moaned. "Oh god, I think it's broken. I think it's fucking broken."

"It's not broken," Zoe said with a certainty I knew she couldn't feel. "You'll be fine. Ice-cold waterfall is all you need. You'll see. Then we'll find a way back to civilization. Everything's going to be fine. Everything's going to be fine." She kept saying it as we hauled Stefanie upright. "We'll leave your bag here and come back for it."

"Obviously we aren't coming back for her bag. She needs to go to a hospital."

"Damn it, Jade, work with me! This is a fucking crisis. We have to get her help before dark."

"Fine!"

Slowly, the three of us began to maneuver down the rocky,

muddy slope, blanketed in slick emerald moss. It hadn't been easy with just our own weight to bear, and now it felt impossible. Zoe had been right not to split up the food in Stef's backpack. I couldn't have handled an extra ounce on my knees as I remained in a half squat, half lunge down the steep hill. Sometimes one or both of us would start to stumble and Stefanie would slip to the ground, screaming. She couldn't put even a little weight on her foot, and every time it touched the earth, she cried.

"Everything's going to be okay," Zoe kept saying. "We're going to find a road. We'll flag down a car. We'll be sleeping with our heads on fresh cotton pillows in a hotel tonight." But this couldn't have sounded any less probable to me. Still, I gritted my teeth and kept silent as she continued. "Think about that hot shower you'll have tomorrow. 'Cause damn, girl, you really need one."

Stef managed a feeble laugh. "You're the ones with your pits in my face."

"God, it'll be good to wash this trail stank away."

I desperately wanted to buy into this misplaced optimism. I forced myself to imagine the hot water blast from a hotel shower that I knew did not await us. It was useless, though. We were in the middle of the wilderness, three days from where we'd started the trail, utterly isolated, and one of us couldn't walk. The only sliver of hope I could glean from the situation was that we were walking toward a crisp waterfall to filter into our dwindling hydration packs.

Shit.

"The water filter!" I stopped so abruptly that the others nearly fell like dominoes. How the fuck had I not thought of this, how the fuck had I let this happen! Oh god oh god oh god! "The water filter and purifier tabs are in Stefanie's backpack."

Stefanie's face went as white as mine felt. "Oh fuck."

"I'll run back up the hill," I decided. "I'll go and come back."

"Don't be stupid," Zoe snapped, a little too brusque. Her agitation was showing. She took a breath, and when she spoke again, it was with more poise. "Even if nothing went wrong, it would take you hours. We have our stovetop; we'll just boil the water when we reach the falls. It'll be fine."

"Yeah, seriously, it's a bad idea," Stef said. "We've all seen that horror movie before. We can't split up. That's how people get lost. Or eaten by a bear."

I hated horror movies. I never watched them. But the thought of getting eaten by a bear was enough to convince me they were right.

Carefully, we picked our way through ferns and hemlock, stepping over stones. Soft blue-green cedar needles brushed our faces. It took us another two hours to get to a place where the hill tapered into flat land. Why was it taking so long to find this waterfall? Were we lost? I longed to see the three neatly stacked rocks that marked the Bones Hollow Trail, or any indication that we were stepping foot where others had gone before.

Finally, we emerged from the dense trees and ferns, having reached the end of that treacherous downhill slope. Now we found ourselves on a section of some unmarked path that sliced through the forest from east to west. A minor step up from being off-trail, I supposed, though I couldn't tell if this thin strip of earth was a footpath made by humans or deer. We stopped here, easing Stefanie onto the ground, and both Zoe and I ripped our backpacks from our bodies. The inflamed skin on my hips and shoulders was angry, rubbed pink and raw. Drenched in sweat, I grabbed my water now and took a greedy gulp, safe again in the knowledge that we'd be able to replenish tonight.

"How much farther?" I asked. "We've got to be close now, right? You said it'd be half a day's hike."

Zoe already had her map and compass out. I didn't like the puzzled expression knitting her brows. "Um . . ." She glanced around. "We just need to keep going south. Not much farther, I don't think."

That meant veering back off-trail. To the south of the unmarked path we stood on now was another densely forested hill, sloping down seemingly forever. My knotted calves shuddered at the sight. "You don't *think*?"

"I don't really know. It's hard to tell."

"Give me the map." I hadn't demanded this since our first day, but now I did, hand outstretched. Zoe had refused when I'd asked before, insisting there was only room for one captain aboard a ship. There was no more time for those foolish games now. "Seriously, I'm not kidding. Give me the fucking map, Zoe."

Stefanie sounded a hair's breadth away from panic. "Are we lost?"

"No, we're not lost," Zoe said. "We just have to keep going, that's all. If we keep going south from the boulder that looks like an egg in a basket, we will hit the waterfall. We *will.*"

"I can't hear a waterfall, can you?" I listened keenly now. I couldn't even hear the bubbling creeks and streams that had serenaded us back on the Bones Hollow Trail. "Shouldn't we be able to hear it if it was close?"

Zoe snapped her map shut. "Can you just lay off me for one fucking minute. We need to keep walking. We'll find it."

"And then what? We wander for how much longer until we find a road, and then wait for a car to come along? There's no one out here, that was the whole point of this fucking hike! Stef can't walk!"

“Calm down, Jade. We’re camping at the falls and I can rest there,” Stefanie said. “Maybe my ankle will be better tomorrow.”

“Fat chance,” I said.

“Jade! You’re not helping!” Zoe crouched down and slid back into her shoulder straps with a grimace. “Let’s get moving.”

So, we did. We followed Zoe. Like always. We followed her wherever she wanted to lead us.

two

We kept hiking onward as dusk drew near. The forested hill was overgrown and muddy, with slick rocks and ferns and vines reaching up for our ankles. My calves ached from the strain of the descent. We didn't speak anymore, too tired to focus on anything but putting one foot in front of the other, in unison as best we could. One foot. And the next. Again and again. Our heavy breath and the grunts of exertion, the only sounds we made. Though we marched in silence, Laurie Wolff's voice echoed in my head, replaying segments from the podcast we'd listened to days before.

Virginia Appleton, age thirty, from West Texas, had grown up listening to her father's stories of hiking the Bones Hollow Trail. After his untimely death when she was seventeen, it became Ginny's dream to follow in her father's footsteps. Her mother said that she had prepared for the trip for years. Many friends had begged to tag along, but Ginny insisted she go alone. "It was her pilgrimage," her mother said.

Ginny was found on the Bones Hollow Trail on May 23, 2011. She was naked, an arrow protruding from her heart and pinning her to a tree. Her top left canine tooth had been removed. She is believed to have been the Hunter's first victim.

We were never going to find the waterfall before night. That much was clear. At this point, all I prayed for was a small patch of clearing for us to set up our tents. Or a tiny bit of flat land.

My prayer went unanswered.

"We have to stop," I said, my legs flimsy like Jell-O. "I'm done. We need to camp here."

"Where?" Zoe gestured at the forest, the trees here barely spaced wide enough apart for us to walk side by side. The sloping terrain was littered with soft, browned pine needles, but rocks and boulders jutted from the earth every few paces. She was right. We'd never be able to set up a tent here, not on such a steep, stony hill. But even so, I couldn't take another step.

"I'm with Jade," Stefanie said. "We can sleep on the tarps."

Though it was the height of summer, the evenings here were cool. The sweat on our bodies chilled in the night air and my teeth chattered. Normally, we spent our dinners comparing trail wounds like battle scars, each blister and bruise a new notch on the belt. But tonight, we had barely enough energy to force down a granola bar before collapsing. Our sleeping mats had never felt more useful. I could still feel at least one rock digging into my spine, but it was muted. Of course, Stefanie's mat and sleeping bag had been left behind. Zoe volunteered hers before I could, and I envied the body warmth they'd share tonight. She fished out some Tylenol for Stefanie, but still the simple task of sliding into their shared sleeping bag seemed like agony for her. An eerie fog enveloped us, sitting over us like a cloud. We fell asleep to a coyote's sinister song.

I dreamed of crunching footsteps, edging closer. My sleeping bag held me tight, a boa constrictor squeeze, as glowing yellow cat eyes crept in. *The cougar stalks her prey with ease, her razor-sharp talons silent upon stone,* Laurie Wolff's husky voice played in my head. *Her victims never hear her coming.* Then suddenly it was on me, but it wasn't a cougar pouncing with razor-sharp claws. It was the Hunter. He raised his bow and let the arrow soar into my heart.

I jolted awake at the first gray light of dawn, my sleeping bag covered in frosty dew and mosquitoes. My body was stiff as a board as I grumbled and cursed, swatting them all away. Sullen and sore, none of us felt strong enough to pull out our stove and try to make mushy oatmeal for breakfast. Even if we had, it would have been difficult on such a steep slope. We resigned ourselves to another granola bar each. My teeth ground the food mechanically, on autopilot, but it took effort to force myself to swallow.

She ate not because she was hungry, Laurie Wolff said in my brain, *but because she knew she needed her strength.*

I really wished I could get her damn voice out of my head.

After breakfast, we checked Stef's ankle again. It had swelled like a black and purple balloon. She yelped as we squeezed the hiking shoe back over her heel, but we couldn't tie the laces up properly anymore.

"So, we're just going to keep heading south," Zoe said, consulting her compass. "We'll hit the waterfall, and from there a road." It was like her very own mantra.

"Just admit it," I said. "We're lost. You have no idea where we are. If this waterfall had actually been half a day's hike from that stupid fucking boulder that looked nothing like an egg, we'd have reached it by now."

"We're not lost," Zoe replied, annoyed. "I may have gotten the distance a bit wrong, but I know if we keep going south, we *will* eventually hit the access road. Trust the map, okay?"

"C'mon, now," Stef cut in, strangely chipper for someone lost in the wilderness with an almost definitely broken ankle. She touched my arm. "Zoe's never steered us wrong before."

"What was it Zoe said yesterday?" I knew I was making things worse, but I couldn't help myself. "'We all pop our cherry sometime'; there's a first for everyone. If you can't read the map well enough to tell us the distance, then maybe we should have brought a fucking GPS! I told you we should have gotten one for this trip." Only Zoe could have convinced us that going old school with a map and compass was a better plan. "Why do I let you talk me into this shit!"

"Because it's Zoe," Stef said with a smirk. "Let's just stick with the plan, okay?"

Zoe put both hands on my shoulders and touched her sweaty forehead to mine. Her pink lock of hair fell across my cheek. "I promise you, it's going to be fine."

No one could reassure me like Zoe could, even at the worst of times. I took a deep, calming breath and let it shiver back out.

"We've got this, yeah?" Zoe said, a captain rallying her team.

"Okay," I said, drawing strength from her confidence. Panicking and fighting would only make things worse. Stef was right—this was Zoe. We could trust her to get us out of this mess. "Yeah."

So, we continued south. Walking shoulder to shoulder, we picked our way through the overgrown brush. Stef tried to lean on us less today, putting a little weight on her foot, hobbling more, but I could tell it was excruciating.

"It's fine," I told her. "Lean on us. We got you."

"Remember that time when Zoe made us all hitchhike in Trapani?" Stefanie laughed, clearly looking for a distraction.

"Well, yeah, because it was really annoying," I said. "We could have taken a perfectly safe, scenic ski lift up the mountain to the temple." I grunted, readjusting Stef on my shoulder. "But Zo is the only person in the world who's too scared to go on a ski lift but not even a little scared of getting into a car with a total stranger."

"I seem to remember telling you both to go ahead without me and that I was happy to hitch alone."

"Like we were going to let you do that," I scoffed.

"Did anything bad happen?" Zoe asked, feeling justified before we'd even responded. "Oh, that's right. We met a handsome Italian boy who drove us all the way to the top of the mountain. And when the temple was closed, what did our oh-so-dangerous chauffeur do? He asked us where we wanted to go and drove us all the way down the mountain to the other side of Trapani so we could see the best beach. Then he just dropped us off and left. So, I hardly think I asked you to jump off a cliff or something."

"It *was* a great beach," I admitted begrudgingly.

"God, I'd kill to be on the beach now." Stef sighed.

Zoe smiled. "Sounds like I've given us all *another* great story."

The fleeting joy this memory had conjured turned to worry in an instant. Was Zoe taking this seriously? "You know, I can never make up my mind whether you're right about these things or just infuriatingly lucky. But on days like today, I get really scared. Because everyone's luck runs out eventually, Zo. We could die out here. For real. Not hypothetically for some funny story down the road. We could actually, seriously die."

"Don't talk like that," Stef cut in, weary, pleading. "It's not helping."

We stopped now to regroup, all of us panting and ruddy-cheeked. Zoe and Stef shared some trail mix. I felt too sick to eat. Then the skies opened.

I'd almost become accustomed to these sudden downpours that frequented the Olympic Peninsula, able to whip my poncho out and have it over my head in less than a minute. Now, I wanted to scream at the sky. We should be sheltering in place, like the podcast had said all experienced hikers knew to do. What shelter could we find here? I felt my boots growing soggy and I turned, longing to hear Zoe admit that this had all been a mistake.

Instead, she gave Stefanie her poncho and tilted her face up to the rain until her blond hair had darkened, plastered against her head, pink streak pasted to her cheek. "Weren't we just saying we needed a shower? Jade, pass me some shampoo!" She cackled at the sky defiantly, shaking her head like a wet dog. I couldn't help but laugh. A weight lifted from my chest.

The downpour was short-lived, but the chill in our bones remained. Since our first day on the trail, the temperature had never passed seventy; today it felt nowhere close. The falls were still nowhere to be seen. We marched on in silence, southward down this treacherous, mossy hill, threading our way through the trees. Laurie Wolff narrated every step in my mind.

Jade put one foot in front of the other.

Jade slipped on a mud patch and nearly fell on her ass.

Jade should have never ventured into these woods.

I couldn't shake the feeling that something stalked us. I felt yellow predator eyes beating down on my neck. Every clack of our backpacks sounded like a footstep following ours. I checked our surroundings constantly, swiveling my head to and fro.

Jade Edelman, age twenty-eight, followed her two best friends everywhere. Even if it meant off a fucking cliff. She was found with an arrow through her heart and a sign that read: Big Fat Idiot.

Around ten, we stopped to eat. "Look, I don't want to fight," I started carefully, "but I think it's time you let someone else look at the map."

"No. We just need to keep going south," Zoe insisted. "We'll hit it eventually."

"At least let me look."

"No."

"Give it to me!"

"No!"

I turned to Stefanie now, incredulous, begging for backup. She'd gone infuriatingly mute, eyes turned downward. She *knew* I was right but refused to say.

"Why won't you let me see the map?" My voice was sharp, slicing through the damp forest air. "I don't understand!"

Zoe leapt to her feet now, exasperated. "Because the falls aren't on the map, okay! Happy? I read about them online."

"*What?*" I turned to Stefanie. "Did you know about this?"

She wouldn't look at me. Of course she'd known. Those two told each other everything. Obviously, Zoe had known better than to tell me because I would have argued. But Stefanie wouldn't say shit to her if her mouth was full of it. Stef always said that Zoe was the fiercest, most *alive* person she knew. It was annoying how right she was. But sometimes it felt like there was a thin, perhaps nonexistent, line between being Zoe's brand of alive and outright reckless.

I felt a burst of rage. "Are you two fucking stupid? This isn't a game! This isn't some story we'll tell about happy hitchhiking or accidentally eating acid lollipops at a music festival. We could run out of food before we find anyone. We were three days away from civilization yesterday, and that was when we were back way the fuck up there on the trail! Now how far are we? Oh god, we're going to be the next people vanished without a trace. They're never going to find us."

My cheeks blazed so hot they made me dizzy. The fir needles surrounding us spun. My stomach roiled, a volcano ready to blow. I tried to catch my breath, but I couldn't. I couldn't breathe.

Zoe was beside me in a heartbeat, holding me. She pressed a palm to my chest. "You're hyperventilating," she said in a calm, soothing tone. "Just calm down. Breathe, that's it. Breathe." She eased me onto the ground, never taking her hand away. "You've got this. You're okay."

Despite her reckless nature, even in times like these, I couldn't help but think that one day Zoe would make an excellent mother. She knew how to soothe people.

And how to convince them.

At her friend's command, Jade drew in a deep, calming breath and let it back out.

So, we continued our foolhardy southward descent of this seemingly endless hill, deep into the forest's vast embrace.

three

I had always envied my friends' figures. Zoe could look cute in anything, even the hideous beige cargo shorts she wore now. And Stef with her beautiful long legs. Sure, my wide hips and thick thighs looked great in a dress; but they didn't exactly lend themselves to baggy T-shirts and pink hiking shorts. Even though Zoe and Stef always told me it was just in my head, I was convinced that my shoulders were masculine and my nose was two sizes too large.

I'd spent far too many hours pining over Stef's tall, lithe figure. But now, I stared at those long legs, and I hated them. Why did it have to be Stef who twisted her ankle? Why couldn't it have been Zoe, with her pixie-like frame? She'd be so much easier to carry—and a tiny part of me whispered that if one of us deserved it, she did.

"Hold up," Zoe said, stopping. "Do you see that?" She pointed at the moss-draped mud we'd been trekking through.

My eye caught on the mushrooms that sprang from dark tree roots and I remembered some hippie Zoe had introduced us to at a pub in Camden—because, of course she did—who ranted to us about the sentience of fungi.

"We came from mushrooms," he'd told us, before I gave Zoe the signal that if we didn't get out of that pub I was going to scream.

Staring at the toadstools now, in this lonely, enchanted, haunting world, I wondered if they were the reason it felt like something was watching us. Perhaps they knew something that we didn't.

Like where the fucking waterfall was.

Jade Edelman had reached such a point of despair she was ready to consult the mushrooms. Thanks, Laurie Wolff.

"Do these look like tire treads to you?" Zoe asked, pointing again at the ground.

Now, I looked closer. Patterned grooves marked the earth in a steady line. They appeared from the west and carried onward. South. Just like Zoe had said.

"Yes!" Stef said. "Those are definitely tire treads. Mountain bike, maybe?"

Zoe shook her head. "Too wide. It's got to be from a motorcycle."

Joy sprung from my heart into my throat, and if not for my backpack, I could have leapt into the air with it, too. "You were right! Holy shit, you were right! It'll take us to a road, Zoe, it'll take us to a motherfucking road!"

Zoe and I grunted as we readjusted Stef's arms atop our shoulders. We moved down the hill with urgency now. Hope refueled our weary bodies, our muscles reinvigorated. The pain in my feet and shoulders was quieted by this newfound optimism. Soon, I would hear the comforting hum of a car along a busy road in the distance, or an ostentatiously loud Harley-Davidson. How ironic. The very sound I'd looked forward to escaping here in the wilderness was now what my ears yearned to hear. I thirsted for it with every droplet of sweat. The forest felt all at once less isolated, less haunted.

The three friends followed the tire trail south, into the unknown.

Maybe Zoe wasn't as unreliable as they thought.

Or maybe she was just one lucky bitch.

We'd been walking south for half an hour, following the tire tread, when we saw the animal tracks.

"Maybe it's someone's dog," Stef said.

Except there weren't any claw marks. Canines didn't have retractable claws—razor-sharp, rip-you-apart claws. These didn't belong to a dog. We were following a cougar's trail.

"Should we turn back?" I asked.

"We can't." Zoe was resolute. "Don't worry. There are three of us. A cougar won't attack us in a group."

I wanted to ask how she knew this, but I didn't. I needed to cling to the belief that she was right. What other choice did I have? We had to keep moving; our only hope lay ahead. Even so, a hollowness grew behind me. Like the wilderness at my back was a giant open mouth, waiting to swallow me whole.

As if sensing I needed a distraction, Stef broke into my thoughts. "Do you remember that guy on the beach?"

She didn't need to say where or when. Both Zoe and I remembered all too well. We'd been drinking till close at a bar in

Sicily and then wandered the beach, looking for a place to set up our tent, when we noticed a man following us.

"Zoe said that all we needed to do was act completely fucking crazy. Like we were out of our minds," Stef went on.

"Because," and then I continued in my best serious-Zoe impression, "in the animal kingdom predators want easy prey, so don't make it easy for them."

"Exactly! And it worked, didn't it?" Zoe said. "We went apeshit, throwing sand. I think you even started to drool, Jade; a really nice touch."

I laughed, remembering.

"And he left us the fuck alone," she said.

"So, like, maybe we should just act crazy," Stefanie said, swiping a sweaty lock of black hair from her eyes. "And the cougar won't fuck with us. Right?"

"We're three women who hiked off-trail in search of a hidden waterfall that isn't even on a map. We're already acting fucking crazy." I wheezed with the effort of speech. "Isn't it illegal to use a motorcycle in designated wilderness areas anyway?"

Stef snorted, incredulous. "Is that really what you're worried about right now? Babe, I think we've got bigger concerns."

"Honestly, a dude could rip through here right now in a Hummer and I'd still kiss his feet. But please be sure, Jade, to tell the owner what he's doing is illegal when we find him, right before we ask him to save our asses."

"Women ride motorcycles, too," I pointed out.

"This was a man," Zoe said, certain. "Only a man would illegally ride a motorcycle through protected wilderness."

The dark trees huddled around Jade and her friends as they followed the trail of both a cougar and an illicit motorcycle-

riding man. But would their lighthearted banter be a deterrent or the bait that brought a hunter right to them? And which kind of hunter would it be?

I groaned. "I really wish we hadn't listened to so much of that fucking podcast! I can't get Laurie Wolff's smug voice out of my head."

Zoe and Stef laughed mercilessly.

"Hey, that's actually a really good idea," Stef said. "Loud noises help scare off cougars and it's better than talking nonstop. My throat's getting so goddamn dry."

"Goddamn it," I said before Zoe could reach for her phone. "Let me guess. Outvoted?" Rolling my eyes, I handed Stef my water bottle. There wasn't much left in my hydration pack now. If we didn't reach the road soon, we'd need to find a stream to boil water.

Laurie Wolff's voice reverberated through the forest: *Harper Reed, age twenty, was on a gap year. She had always dreamed of being a doctor and planned to be a pediatrician. Last seen in her yellow raincoat, she told her family that if she could hike the Bones Hollow Trail alone, she knew she could handle anything.*

But all I could hear was, *Jade Edelman was the World's Dumbest Girl. Her body was never found.*

• • •

We'd been hiking for five and a half hours, with the motorcycle treads only sporadically in view in this steep, rocky terrain, and we'd probably covered just four miles. It was twelve-thirty when the cougar's tracks veered eastward, into the old-growth and ancient trees. Somehow this made every forward step even worse. Knowing we were behind the predator had been my only solace. Now, it had returned to the shadowy, nebulous green wilderness around me. It could have circled back to get behind us. It could be anywhere.

As I strained to listen to the trees, to weed through the forest sounds and our heavy breath for the nefarious growl, I heard a methodical hacking noise, over and over.

"Turn that off," I said, stopping. "Listen."

Thwack, thwack, thwack. It sounded too rhythmic to be anything but human.

"Sounds like someone chopping wood!" Stef said, eager.

We rushed forward, following the sound. It grew louder with each step, spurring us on faster now, so fast I tripped, nearly toppling the three of us like a house of cards. Tree branches that normally I'd have paused to pull aside scraped the side of my face. The thwacking sound stopped now, but still we carried on forward. One minute, all we could see were trees. The next, it was there. Conjured as if by our sheer collective will and desire. Manifested, as Stef liked to say when she made vision boards for our adventures.

Either that, or we were Hansel and Gretel stumbling onto the witch's gingerbread house. My stomach clenched in equal parts joy and trepidation.

The hill finally leveled out into flat land. There in a grassy gulch was a sturdy two-story log cabin. Two wide windows on the first floor were boarded up with plywood. The four smaller windows on the second story remained unshuttered, but the glass was opaque with gray dust and earth. Two thick wooden beams held up a slanted awning over the front door. A tiny stream bubbled behind the house and then continued into the dense forest that surrounded this small patch of valley on all sides.

My eyes snagged on the bloody deer carcass dangled by the

front door, dripping. Its skin was draped over a nearby tree branch like a bedsheet hung out to dry. My mind immediately went to Ripley, the sharpness of her blade. I imagined what it would take to stick her jagged edge into flesh and peel back the skin, as this hunter had done. I shuddered.

I glanced nervously around the property. Whoever had killed this deer and been chopping wood a moment ago was nowhere to be seen. I couldn't decide if this made me feel better or worse. All I knew was this cabin gave me the creeps.

"Yes!" Zoe cried. "I knew it!"

"What do you mean?" I asked.

"I read that a cabin might be here in that forum online. I wanted to surprise you with happy news." She flashed her best, most charming smile. "Surprise!"

"Oh, thank god!" Stef exclaimed. "I couldn't walk another step!"

"It used to get used by rangers and hunters, but now it's abandoned because it's in a river runoff and floods in the winter," Zoe told us.

I let out a deep sigh, waiting for the relief to sink in. But for some reason, I couldn't shake the angst that still roiled in my belly. "It would have been nice to know beforehand," I muttered, thinking of our agonizing hike here with no hope in sight and Zoe's seemingly blind faith. "But this is good." I nodded, trying to convince myself. "We can rest here, refill our water supply, and continue on toward the road first thing in the morning." With my next deep breath, the tightness in my chest finally loosened. "A very happy surprise, Zo." I offered her an approving smile. "So how far are we from the waterfall now?"

"I don't even want to think about that. Can we please just get inside?" Stef pleaded. "I'm dying to take these shoes off."

I pointed to the bloody deer carcass. "I thought you said it was supposed to be abandoned."

"Guess I was wrong," Zoe said. "It's still wet. Someone must be home."

"Even better." Stef sighed with relief. "Maybe they have a satellite phone or something and can call for help."

The angst suddenly came back full force. "This doesn't feel right, you guys. . . ."

Laurie Wolff echoed in my ears: *They found an isolated cabin in the woods, with no one around for miles to hear them scream.*

I pictured the Hunter's bow ready to greet us inside and shuddered.

"What choice do we have?" Stef asked. "I can't go any farther."

"We are going inside," Zoe said.

I couldn't argue. Mine was an indefensible position; we needed help. Zoe took off her backpack as we approached the door. I'd planned to keep mine on, just in case, but seeing the relief in her shoulders caused a reflexive reaction in me. I couldn't restrain myself from unbuckling and throwing my pack to the dead pine needles that blanketed the pale green grass.

Fog seeped through the leaves now, rolling in like a blanket over the treetops, bringing with it a chilling stillness. Every hair on my arms stood on end as the three of us wandered around the side of the cabin toward the back where the stream bubbled joyfully. The grass was littered with rusted shards of metal and old machinery, wrenches and gears strewn across the browned pine needles. But there weren't any motorized vehicles or even a single bicycle wheel. The ramshackle work shed behind the cabin might have housed one. Beside the shed, there was a neat row of moss-covered earthen mounds. When was nature ever so perfectly straight?

Zoe smiled, following my gaze. "Must be graves. Stef, we found your burial ground, after all."

"What the hell is wrong with you?" I said. "That's not funny."

"Oh, come on," Stef said, sliding an arm around my waist for a squeeze. "Lighten up. It was a little bit funny."

"I hate you guys," I said as they dragged me back around the house.

Zoe rapped her knuckles against the front door. We listened keenly for the squeak of a floorboard. The silence was deafening, ominously so.

"Well, there's no one home," I said, a little too eager. "We should keep looking for this road." It was a terrible idea, I knew; but I couldn't shake the feeling that going inside this creepy cabin was an even worse one.

"We heard somebody chopping something," Stef said. "Someone's here."

Zoe knocked again, harder this time. "I'd sooner break into this house than sleep on that tarp one more night."

As she said this, the door snapped open.

A tall man with shoulders almost as broad as the doorframe glared down at us. His cheeks were so clean-shaven they practically sparkled, and a thick pink scar stretched between the corner of his right eye and his remarkably square jaw. He'd flung the door open with all the aggression of a wild animal, but seeing us, his thin lips curved into an unnervingly charming smile.

Under different circumstances, he might've been handsome, with pale green eyes and strong biceps on full display in his bleached white tank top. Dark chest hair peeked out the top and a few charming silver threads laced through the chin-length curly brown hair he kept mostly tucked behind his ears. But given our current vulnerability, those biceps were not a welcome sight. Here was a middle-aged man wearing blue jeans and cowboy boots in an abandoned cabin in the wilderness. He didn't look like our hero. He looked like a wolf. And wolves didn't look handsome up close. They just looked hungry.

One thumb hooked under his belt, he leaned in the doorway, a real cowboy pose. His silver belt buckle was bigger than my fist. I was surprised he didn't have a holstered pistol. With his free hand, he slicked back his hair, and when he spoke, it was with a smooth Southern drawl, sweet and slow like molasses. "Well, to what do I owe this pleasure?" His voice was deep and inviting, full of warmth. He smiled, showing a row of sharp white teeth. "This must be my lucky day."

My, Granny, what big teeth you have.

"Can I help you, ladies?"

No. That's what I wanted to say. No, no, no. He may have looked and sounded charming, but he was still a lone man living in the woods staring down three vulnerable girls. Surely it was obvious that we needed to leave. I looked to my friends for support, expecting they felt the same. But Stef was exhausted, pale with relief; no way was she going anywhere. And Zoe looked fearless as always, her confidence unwavering. There was no point even asking for a vote.

"Yes," Zoe said, assertive. "We've been hiking the Bones Hollow Trail and my friend twisted her ankle. It's pretty bad. We think it's broken."

"We're trying to make it back to our car at the trailhead," Stef said. "If you maybe have some sort of car . . . or motorcycle?"

"Well, I'm afraid I can't help you there." The man nodded at her ankle. "Why don't you let me have a look at that now, sweetheart?"

A loner calling her friend "sweetheart" should have been the red flag Jade needed. She would look back on this moment and wonder why it hadn't been. That is, of course, if she lived to think about it at all.

The three of us exchanged a fleeting, cautious glance. With a nod from Stefanie, Zoe knelt and removed Stef's mud-caked hiking shoe. Stefanie grimaced, squeaking with pain, as she unrolled her sock as slowly as possible.

The man knelt to inspect the wound and whistled. "Can you put any weight on it?"

Stefanie shook her head.

"No, I wouldn't have thought so." The man clucked his tongue. "You girls have gotten yourselves into some pickle now." He stood again, running a hand through his hair. "I suppose you'll be needing the rangers."

"Oh my god, yes," Zoe said. "Do you get signal here?"

The man's laugh had a rattle, like a loose bolt in an engine. "Of course not. We're in a dead zone here, darlin'. But I've got an old radio, been left behind by rangers that used to stay here. I'll make a call for you."

"Thank you so much," Zoe said, and Stef echoed her.

"Thanks," I managed. My friends seemed to trust him. Maybe I was just being paranoid, my nerves shot from all the stress on the trail. Still, I couldn't look him in the eyes, though he stared right at me, begging me to.

"You come inside now. Make yourselves at home." The man caught my hesitant look. "I promise I don't bite." He flashed a disarming smile, baring his teeth. "But if you feel more comfortable, of course you can wait outside. Wherever you feel safest."

The tension festering in my chest loosened. Maybe I was wrong about him. Maybe this man didn't look like a hungry wolf. Maybe he was just a man who enjoyed nature and a bit of solitude, and who genuinely wanted to help us.

My friends prodded me with their stares, beckoning me forward, and I sighed. "Thank you," I said a little more earnestly this time. "We really appreciate your help."

But as I followed my friends inside, Laurie Wolff whispered in my ear, smug as can be: *The cabin looked like it'd been cut from every horror movie ever made. Did Jade and her friends turn and run like clever girls? No, my sweet Little Savages. No, they did not.*

four

The floorboards squeaked as we dragged our backpacks across the threshold: loud, like mice caught by a housecat. I glanced around the dimly lit room. I could tell by the deerskin-covered couch and homemade furniture that this man had been here for some time. This wasn't some temporary hunter's lodge for him. This was his home.

The fragments of animal bones stood out to me first. Skulls crafted into bowls and ashtrays and paperweights filled the shelves of two handcrafted bookshelves. There were several other rudimentary tables that seemed to have been built for this purpose as well. A desk stood off to the left, by a darkened hall, with a single wooden chair and a coffee table in the center of the room. A few books and magazines were stacked here and there, but mostly the shelves and table space were lined with bleached animal bone ornaments. A stag's head stared down at us from one wall with dead eyes. On another hung a large wooden bow, unstrung. My eyes lingered here.

It was clear what this man did with his time. He built furniture. And he killed things.

Plywood boards strangled any light that tried to peek through the windows. A single lightbulb dangled from a chain above the couch, offering little illumination. The cabin remained shadowed and dim, and yet it somehow seemed even larger now than it had from the outside. There was a door to the right and another room down a small hallway to the left, where there was presumably a staircase to the second floor.

Just how long had this man been living here undisturbed?

How many more dead things adorned the walls in the rest of this cabin?

"Make yourselves comfortable, ladies," he said, gesturing toward the deerskin couch.

He leaned against an interior support beam in that same cowboy pose, one thumb looped through his belt, waiting for us to sit, like a gentleman who had just pulled out a chair. My legs were limp like overcooked noodles. Zoe's and Stef's limbs clearly felt the same. We collapsed onto the couch, the deerskin coarse against our bare legs.

For the first time since we got on the trail, I fished my phone out of my backpack and turned it on. Just after one. I hadn't expected to have service, but my heart still sank when I saw the red line through the signal bars. I slipped my phone back into the side pocket with a sigh.

"The name's Jeremiah, by the way. And what can I call you

sweet rays of sunshine? I'll need something to tell the ranger." He smiled at us, full of charm, as he stared with glowing green eyes.

My, Granny, what big eyes you have. But no, stop it, Jade. Although the decorations were unsettling, plenty of outdoorsmen shared his taste in interior design. It didn't mean anything.

"We're the Meyerses," Zoe said without hesitation. "Cora," she pointed to herself, "Dora," she pointed to me, "and Nora," she gestured at Stefanie. "We're not sisters, if that's what you're thinking—everyone always thinks we're sisters, it's so funny. We're just cousins. Our mothers are all sisters."

I almost resented how quickly my friend could think on her feet, and even more so how she didn't care that her lie sounded like complete and utter bullshit.

"Is that right?" Jeremiah grinned, clearly amused as he rubbed a thumb up and down his scar. "So what, may I ask, are you doing so far from any trail?"

I suddenly found my voice. "*Cora* heard about a hidden waterfall a day's hike off the Bones Hollow Trail. Obviously, we got a little lost."

"A waterfall?" Jeremiah laughed, his cheeks lifted with mirth. "I'm sorry, I don't mean to poke fun. But someone sent you dolls on a wild goose chase. I know these woods better than anyone alive. Trust me, there are no waterfalls around here. None even remotely close."

For once, Zoe had been wrong. I knew this had been a bad idea! This was why people didn't take directions from the fucking internet! I almost turned to Zoe now to say as much, but I stopped myself. I'd get my I-told-you-so moment later. I'd make sure of it. I opened my mouth to ask him how far we were from the access road, but Jeremiah cut in.

"Well, forgive me, ladies, I've forgotten my manners now. What would my mama say? I know you must be thirsty. You want some water? Let me get you some water. I'll be right back."

Jeremiah strode to the room on the right, which I assumed was a kitchen, without disturbing a single floorboard, surprising given his stature. Even the door was silent as it swung shut behind him. As soon as he left, Zoe popped up from the couch and started traipsing about the room, thumbing through magazines and opening desk drawers.

"What are you doing?" I hissed.

She smiled, eyes glittering mischief. "Looking for clues." She pointed to the wall and whispered, "Didn't you clock that bow? Don't tell me you're not thinking what I'm thinking."

Of course I was thinking it. *Obviously* I was thinking it. But hearing Zoe breathe the fear into life, that this creepy cabin could belong to the Bones Hollow Hunter, somehow transformed it from a dismissible paranoia to a rational concern that bubbled back to me now full force. I stared long and hard at the bow on the wall. It disturbed me to consider Laurie Wolff's theory that the Hunter might still be at large.

A shiver raced along my spine. I swallowed hard, pushing these dark, paranoid thoughts away.

"Yeah, because we totally stumbled into the serial killer's cabin. Sure. Let's pretend that the odds of that seem even remotely plausible—wouldn't that be all the more reason not to get caught messing with his things? He'll be back any second. Besides," I added, "he seems really nice."

Stef eased off the couch and hobbled to one of the tables. She smiled as if this was some fun game. A humorous way to pass the time. "Ooh, he reads Nietzsche," she said, picking up a book and eyeing the spine. "Hot."

"Pretentious." Zoe rolled her eyes. "And predictable. Next, you're gonna find Machiavelli. Even worse." She lifted up a copy of *Bowhunter* magazine. "This guy is so *alpha male.*"

"Come on," Stef said. "Like you're not into it. The rugged cowboy thing works for him. He's a total snack."

"You have the worst taste in men," Zoe declared, far too loud. "He's probably the serial killer."

"Keep your voice down!" I whispered so hard my throat hurt.

Stef shrugged. "Tons of people thought Ted Bundy was hot."

"Would you two shut up?" Glassware clinked and I checked over my shoulder at the kitchen door. He'd be back any second. "He's going to hear you!"

Zoe snapped her fingers. "We should look down the hall. Jade, you distract him."

"Are you kidding?" The thought of being the decoy filled me with dread. Regardless of Jeremiah's charm, he was still a large, unfamiliar man, and there was safety in numbers. "You can't leave me alone with him. *None* of us should be left alone with him."

"Someone's got to stay," Stef said.

"You've got Ripley in the side pouch." Zoe pointed to her backpack by the sofa. "You'll be fine."

Then, like an apparition, Jeremiah materialized. He looked at my friends, caught red-handed holding his books. A torturous silence lingered for a full thirty seconds before he said, very nonchalant, "Got some old *Life* magazines if you're bored. *National Geographic,* too, I think in that desk behind you." He sounded like a stately Southern gentleman, but he looked like a rodeo cowboy with those three large glasses of water balanced in one palm. "Can't say I have much else that'll interest you ladies."

"Don't sell yourself short, Jeremiah." Zoe picked up a small skull from his desk. "I love this, what is this . . . rabbit? Is it for sale?"

Jeremiah smiled. "Well, as a matter of fact, it is. That's what I do. Everything you see here is for sale. I've got an online shop."

"And the park rangers are fine with that?" Zoe asked.

"Why wouldn't they be? They're my best customers. Helps them pretend they know how to hunt worth a shit." He smiled again. "Don't you worry now, darlin', no one's used this cabin for a long time and I know the risks. So, they don't mind my setup here one little bit. Here's that water for you."

He walked around the room, passing a glass to each of us. But though we ached with thirst, none of us dared take a sip. Never accepting drinks from men we hadn't seen pour them was a number one rule of ours.

"Best water you've ever had in your life." Jeremiah stared at us with crisp green eyes, waiting. "Oh shoot, maybe I was wrong. Ain't you dolls thirsty?"

"Maybe *you* could be a doll and drink it first." Zoe's smile was dry. She sniffed the water with furrowed brows.

"I haven't drugged it, if that's what you're implying." Jeremiah hooked his thumb through his belt loop, arm akimbo, a wounded expression knit between his brows. "I'll be honest, I'm not sure I appreciate such an unsavory accusation coming from a guest in my home, when all I'm doing is trying to help."

"Cora doesn't mean to be rude," I cut in, nervous. "She only meant, like, is the water safe to drink? 'Cause how do you even have running water out here?"

He leaned back against the wall, balancing on the heel of his cowboy boot. "Well, the plumbing was done long before I got here, but I suspect whoever built this cabin dug a line to the stream."

"So, you're telling me this water could be riddled with parasites," Zoe said, an annoyingly provocative edge to her tone. "Is it even filtered?"

I shot her a look that could wither stone. Why was she antagonizing him?

"What?" she said aloud to me. "We have a right to know."

"Yes, it's filtered." Jeremiah sucked his tooth. "Look, ladies, I don't know what hospitality is like where you come from, but for me, I hold it quite sacred."

Said the man living alone in the woods, Laurie Wolff narrated.

"I wouldn't give you water that's been . . . tainted." Jeremiah strutted toward me; his imposing figure cast a large shadow. "Once I call the rangers, it'll take 'em a while to get here. We're gonna have a long time to wait together. It'll go a lot faster if you stop being so jumpy. But, look, I understand. Three girls alone in the woods with some big stranger."

I couldn't decide if the grin he wore now was considerate or alarming.

"Here," he said, "let me put your minds at ease." He grabbed my water with a calloused hand and slugged half of it back. Then he did the same with Stefanie's. Zoe still stood across the room by a desk. He held out his hand for hers. "Come on. Hand it over now."

"So how long have you been out here?" Zoe asked, passing it to him and watching as he gulped down two-thirds of her glass. His long swig felt punishing.

"A long, long time." Jeremiah swiped the back of his hand across his lips. "Not many people come out this far. Not many people at all." He offered back her glass, but when she tried to take it, he didn't release. The water sloshed and the man smiled, baring every one of his teeth like an animal about to strike. The hairs on the nape of my neck stood to attention. Finally, he let go.

"Thanks," Zoe said, matching his smile, baring her teeth. I recognized that twinkle in her eye. She was enjoying this. She couldn't really think he was the Bones Hollow Hunter, not if she was ruffling his feathers with such glee.

But then, Zoe had always been a fan of pushing people's buttons, especially the alpha males'. She'd once convinced me and Stef to play pool at a tiny dive bar in Wyoming. Stefanie and I had never played before, and Zoe knew the rules but was no expert. We were terrible, of course, and this was the only pool table around for miles. So, a growing line of men waited for us to finish.

At first, our audience thought we were cute. A few men sidled up to us, purring hints and suggestions into our ears. "Hold the cue like this, sweetie." "Stroke it like that."

But, after twenty minutes of nonstop giggling, and with the game no closer to ending, their suggestions became less flirtatious and more aggressive. "Hit it here! For fuck's sake, *here*!"

Then, after half an hour, Zoe finally decided to put the men out of their misery. She cleared the table in one go, boom, boom, boom. Apparently, she knew more than just the rules of the game. She was actually really fucking good, having played every weekend with her dad when she was a teen. She just thought it'd be funny to wind up the locals.

Some of them were so angry the bartender had to intervene. "Get the fuck out and never come back," he'd said, "or I can't promise what'll happen to you."

That night in the parking lot, a man threatened to stab me

with a pool cue. Zoe and Stefanie flipped the man off and got into the car, still laughing. I feigned laughter, too, but my friends couldn't see that I was shaking in the back seat.

I prayed that Zoe didn't let her games go so far this time.

We drank the water. The liquid tasted stale, like the dusty cabin air.

"How you like that, sunshine?" he asked, eyes unwavering from Zoe. "Best water you ever tasted, isn't that right?"

Zoe held his gaze, steadfast. "Delicious, thank you." She set her glass down on a bookshelf. "So, tell me, Jeremiah, how long have you been in this line of work? You have such rustic design taste. It's so primal, *manly.*"

Stefanie and I exchanged a look, though her expression did not convey the same message as mine. My eyes screamed with anxiety: *Why the fuck is Zoe doing this—she's going to push him too far!* But Stefanie's gaze glowed with pride and wonder: *Isn't Zoe such a badass?*

And in my brain, all I could hear was Laurie Wolff: *They found pieces of the three young women's bodies scattered along the trail like pine cones. Unlike all the Hunter's other targets, who had been unfortunate victims of happenstance, these girls had died because of their own reckless stupidity.*

Jeremiah smiled, tongue tracing his teeth. "Oh, I've always been building things. And tearing them apart. I've got the taste for it, I guess you could say." Then he strode over to a desk by the hall. The bottom drawer opened with an unsettling creak. He withdrew an old radio, so heavy he used both hands. When it hit the desktop, a cloud of dust plumed around it. "Now, tell me, how do you like the look of this, darlin'? Does it suit your tastes, or would you like to throw a little more of that sass my way? Because I'm starting to think that maybe you don't like the things in my home, and maybe you'd be more comfortable if you just went along on your way."

I squeezed the deerskin between my nails, waiting, praying Zoe wouldn't say something else to provoke him. Though maybe this was our chance. To leave now while we still could. Before another man threatened me with violence because of a silly game Zoe played.

"I'm just busting your balls, man," she said, doing that thing she often did with macho men, speaking on their level. "You'd be a lifesaver if you called the rangers."

"Literally," Stef added.

Jeremiah grinned. "Well, that's what I thought, now."

He switched the radio on and I waited with bated breath.

Static crackled in and out. Then he spoke into the receiver. "This is Jeremiah. Rick, do you copy? Over." He was on a first-name basis with the rangers. A promising sign, I hoped; it meant he'd been telling the truth and the rangers *did* know he lived here.

The lingering static was torture.

"Copy, Jeremiah," a man replied a minute later. "Ranger Rick here. Over."

Stef and I squeezed each other's hands with joy. An elephantine weight lifted from my chest. Obviously a serial killer wouldn't radio the rangers for us. Not that I ever *actually* believed it was him, but at least this proved it. This man couldn't possibly be the Bones Hollow Hunter.

"I've got three stray girls up here at the cabin, gotten themselves a little turned around. Dora, Cora, and Nora Meyers." He grinned at Zoe. "We'll be needing some medical assistance."

There was a long pause. "Copy that." Another long pause. "Are any immobile?"

"Mmmhmm, one's busted up her ankle real good."

"Roger. Well, get comfy. I'll be there in a few hours. Over and out."

I quickly checked the time on my phone again. One-thirty. We'd be on our way to the rangers' station before nightfall. My relief was overwhelming now, effusive. Help was on its way! "Thank you," I said as he replaced the radio in its drawer. "Thank you so much. Really."

Zoe moved back to the couch and elbowed me in the ribs as she sat down. She always thought I said thank you too much. "The only words you use more than 'sorry,'" she'd tell me. "Be cool," she mouthed now.

"Looks like we've got ourselves some time to kill," Jeremiah said, and for a minute he sounded like the cat who caught the canary, but then he turned that charming grin my way. "Now that you know my water's safe, what do you say we have ourselves a real drink?"

All charm aside, getting drunk with this man seemed like the stupidest thing anyone could do in the history of all stupid things. Especially given how dehydrated and probably malnourished we already were. We'd get smashed in no time. Well, I would. Stef would be a giggly mess. And Zoe would only grow mouthier. It was a recipe for disaster.

"Do you have any coffee?" I asked.

"Well, sure thing. But I hope you girls like it strong. There's no cream or sugar here."

"The stronger the better," Zoe said.

He moved silently back to the kitchen. The moment he was out of sight, Zoe elbowed me again, this time with praise. "Great thinking!" she whispered, hopping to her feet. "Come on, Stef, let's check the back room."

"Why?" I hissed. "He just called the rangers for us! It's not *him.*"

"Oh, please," Zoe said, "that doesn't mean he isn't our guy." She helped Stef up.

"What are you doing? Look at her," I exclaimed. "She can't even walk!"

Stef glowered. "I'm *fine.*"

Zoe couldn't contain her excitement. "Imagine Laurie Wolff narrating our story, but for real: *The brave girls combed the murderer's house, unmasking a dormant serial killer and finally bringing justice to all his victims.* Or, even better, I could finally start that podcast I've been talking about for years."

That's not what I imagined Laurie Wolff saying as they rushed down Jeremiah's darkened hall toward the back room.

Jade Edelman was left alone with a strange man in an isolated cabin in the wilderness.

Jade's two best friends weren't brave—they were assholes.

five

We have a special guest for you on today's episode, my sweet Little Savages. Detective Leeroy Bennett of the Bones Hollow Hunter investigation.

"Tell us, Detective, in your opinion, why does the Bones Hollow Hunter allegedly remain at large?"

"I suppose you're referring to the Lars Brunner situation. Well, I've got one word for you and your listeners: bureaucracy. There's no reason to sugarcoat it. After Wendy Whitmore in 2018, the pressure was coming down hard to make an arrest. Enter Lars Brunner. A weird, long-haired guy with a history of mental illness and a nervous twitch who didn't wash much, lived out of a van, and lied about his alibi. Certain suits from up above made it clear that he was our guy. And after his conveniently timed death, of course the investigation couldn't be officially closed. But

we were told to consider it unofficially so, and to move on and focus on other cases."

"But you never believed Lars Brunner was the Bones Hollow Hunter?"

"No, ma'am. Lars Brunner never presented as someone with the organizational skills or methodical planning necessary to commit these heinous crimes."

"Then let me rephrase my original question. Why had the Bones Hollow Hunter evaded capture until Lars Brunner took the fall? The killer had been operating for seven years at that point."

"As I'm sure you already know, there was a lack of forensic evidence at the scenes, but what you may not know is that they had been shot with arrows posthumously. There were plenty of wounds, but not a lick of blood on the ground. So, we all agreed that the victims had been murdered elsewhere and then positioned on the trail. But the question was where were they killed and how long were they held there beforehand? That's where me and my team couldn't come to terms.

"The leading theory was that the Hunter was another hiker who walked the trail every summer, or at least someone posing as one to get close to his victims. That's why Lars fit the bill. Another traveler could really get to know his victim, walking alongside her for a day or two before luring her to the middle of the forest, killing her, and then staging her body when he'd finished with it. But the bodies showed signs of starvation and deprivation. To me, that meant they'd been held somewhere for a considerable length of time. There was obviously more to this than just the killing. But mine wasn't a popular theory. Hikers often showed signs of malnourishment, is what my chief said. But, not like this they didn't. Not in my book anyway."

"If the arrow wasn't the cause of death, what was?"

"They aren't details I'd care to discuss. Out of respect for the families, you understand. What I can tell you is that these poor women did not die quickly. They suffered; that's all you need to know."

They suffered. I tried to push the podcast from my mind, but those words resonated in my head like a struck bell. Not because this man was the serial killer from a podcast we were listening to; I wasn't that irrational. But because it was a chilling reminder. Of what a man could do. And had done, here in this same wilderness.

Jeremiah appeared a few minutes later, three orange clay mugs balanced in one hand. He stared at the empty room, then stared at me.

"They went to the bathroom," I said, meek and small. Lying always made me nervous. "They'll be back in a minute."

"Is that right?" He smiled, one eyebrow cocked. "So, you drew the short end of the stick then, huh?"

"I . . . don't know what you mean." I couldn't make eye contact.

"Left all alone here with me." Jeremiah sat down beside me on the couch, so close our thighs touched. "Do they do you like that often?"

Subtly, I tried to ease away so that there was a space between our thighs, but I still felt the heat of him. He smelled like tobacco and fresh-churned earth. "Do what?"

"Leave you behind."

Though I could not meet them, I sensed his pale green eyes probing my face. My skin felt paper-thin, like he could see right through me.

He handed me a mug and set the other two on an end table, on coasters made of tiny bones pasted together. "Go on now, darlin'," he said, with an encouraging nod. "We call this black tar."

I glanced inside. The contents appeared to live up to the name. I'd never seen coffee this dense. It was like holding a cup of mud. I stared down with hesitation.

"You wanted coffee," he reminded me with a smirk.

I nodded. "Yes. Thank you." I was too nervous to drink. "I'll wait a minute for it to cool."

"No need, sunshine. It's a cold brew."

"Great." I tilted the mug. The contents were so thick they barely shifted. "Excellent. Can't wait."

I didn't like Jeremiah's question. It left me feeling unsettled. He'd taken one look at me and my friends and pinpointed me as the odd one out, the one who got left behind. It wasn't even true, but somehow the question needled its way into my stomach, worming like a parasite through my belly. As I fidgeted with my coffee mug, my mind went back to our last night in Florence. Zoe and Stef had left me alone atop the Piazzale Michelangelo so they could go hook up with these guys they'd just met at the bar. I'd stood there alone for twenty minutes in the pitch black, whisper-shouting their names because one minute they'd been right behind me, taking in the scenery, and the next minute the four of them had vanished.

I should have kept calm and realized they would never just outright leave me behind. But instead, I'd panicked, wondering if I should go to the police—not for them but for me, because now I was completely lost at four A.M. Just when I'd started walking down to the main road, debating whether it was riskier to hitchhike or walk to the police station, unsure of how I'd even find it—my friends rematerialized with sheepish grins.

I hadn't expected an apology. I'd been the stupid one, getting panicked over nothing. Besides, saying sorry had never been one of Zoe's strong suits. She spent our train ride to Rome mooning over what great kissers Italian men were—very on brand. But Stefanie had made it her mission to lavish me with gifts and sincere apologies.

I shouldn't have let Jeremiah's question get under my skin. He didn't know anything about our friendship. From the looks of this place, he didn't even have any friends.

Still, I started thinking of how my friends could make it up to me. Extra gelato and mojitos weren't going to cut it this time. But maybe I could leverage this current transgression of theirs to my advantage. After all, I'd finally have grounds to insist on at least one demand. No more podcast for the rest of this trip.

I stared down at the black tar coffee. I tried to think of it like one of the Jäger shots Stef and I loved to close a night out with. Go on; knock it back.

Finally, I forced a tiny sip. It was like drinking coffee grounds; I practically had to chew. But it wasn't the coffee that made my lips burn. I coughed. Whiskey?

"Hit you with a little something extra," Jeremiah said with a wink. "Moonshine. My own special recipe."

The strange man in the cabin had spiked Jade Edelman's drink with alcohol . . . and who knows what else? So much for not accepting drinks from strange men. Excellent. So glad to be here on my own right now. Thanks a lot, Zoe.

A dozen scars pockmarked the cowboy's hands, most of them small. Maybe they were from woodworking. Building furniture surely resulted in a few nicks. But I couldn't shake the thought that they were claw marks from creatures he'd killed. I suddenly imagined his large hand wrapped around a rabbit's throat. Tiny buck teeth burrowing into the webbing of his thumb. Then I flashed to his fingers squeezing my throat. We sat so close he wouldn't even have to reach.

"Yeah, it's nice," I said. "Strong."

Jeremiah stared at me like no man ever had before. Like he could eat me up in one big gulp, without even bothering to chew. I squirmed under his gaze.

My phone was tucked under my thigh. I glanced down at the screen. How could it only be ten to two? It felt like I'd been sitting here alone with him for an eternity.

"So, how long you girls been on the trail for?"

I wished he'd stop calling us "girls." Like we were children playing in the forest. We'd trained for months to go on this trip, walking for miles with practice packs to build up our endurance. Sure, not as much as some other hikers maybe did. But this was still a serious endeavor for us.

My answer was interrupted by a sharp floorboard creak from a room down the hall. Jeremiah's head swiveled in that direction.

Shit.

My hand flew to his knee without thought. I immediately regretted it when I saw the eager smile he turned back my way. This man probably hadn't felt a woman's touch in months, maybe years. Here I'd just handed him every wrong idea on a silver platter like a fucking idiot. God, I made such a terrible decoy.

"We've only been out here for three days," I said, stammering a little, slowly retracting my hand. "How about you? I mean, living here, not on the trail."

"Oh, I don't live here all year," he said, looking at my hands, now twisting in my lap. "Can't with all the flooding in the winter and spring."

"What do you do with all this stuff then?"

"Same thing I do when it's time to ship the items I sell. Pack it with me in trips and haul it back to the mainland. The furniture gets wood rot eventually." He kicked at the base of the bookshelf by the couch, showing me some sign of decay that my eye wasn't trained enough to see. "So I break it down, build some more. I don't have many items in life that I value much. Few things I do have go up in the attic during the floods; they're safe there." He wanted me to be impressed by his minimalist lifestyle; I could tell by the pride in his voice. Maybe under less stressful circumstances I would've been. He glanced down at his knee again, like he wished my hand was still there.

"Wow." I fidgeted, miles outside my comfort zone, at a loss for what to say but knowing that I had to keep him occupied. Did I feed his ego with compliments, or would that just send more of the wrong signals?

Wood scraped in the back room. Any minute now he'd realize what my friends were up to. Maybe if I buttered him up, he'd be less likely to take his anger out on me.

"That's so cool. I really admire your"—my voice was borderline shrill—"style of living."

He nodded at my mug. "You're not drinking."

Jade knew better than to drink any more of the man's coffee. But I couldn't think of an excuse to decline that wouldn't offend him. Reluctantly, I took a sip. It tasted even worse than before.

"Go on, you tell me something now; fair's fair," Jeremiah said. "How did you girls meet?"

Grimacing, I tongued at the moonshine-soaked coffee grounds clinging to my gums. "In middle school," I said, without thinking. Shit! Zoe had told him we were cousins. This was why I shouldn't have been left behind. I was a terrible liar; they knew that!

Jeremiah smiled ear to ear. "Do you mind if I smoke?" He leaned against me, the weight of his thigh pressed hard into mine, as he lifted one side of his body enough to pull a leather pouch from his back pocket. Of course he rolled his own; a real cowboy.

"No," I said, and he withdrew a small paper from the pouch and sprinkled tobacco into it with wide, dirt-stained fingertips. "It's your house."

Except this wasn't technically his house. And I did mind. But I'd inhale a roomful of smoke if it kept him distracted.

Jeremiah licked his fingers and it was strangely sexual. Like how my ex moved his tongue across his fingers before moving his fingers across me. Except Jeremiah wiped his fingers on his jeans and then rubbed them together for traction. He rolled the cigarette between his fingers, back and forth, shaping the tobacco carefully. He slid his tongue across the edge, binding it, staring at me all the while. "Do you want one?"

"No, that's okay. Thank you. I don't smoke." I tried my best to sound sweet, like I was graciously turning down the last chocolate in a box.

He lit the cigarette with a tarnished silver Zippo. Inhaled deep. Exhaled through his nose, a dragon with sparks in his eyes. I muffled my cough. Jeremiah leaned back, one arm resting on the deerskin couch. "You girls are awfully brave." Serpentine smoke curled around his lips. "A lot of people gone missing in these parts."

"A lot of women," I corrected.

"That's right." He inhaled. "So, is there a boyfriend waiting for you back home?" I cringed at the question. "I'll be honest, I don't think I'd let my missus go off round a place like this all alone."

"We're not alone. There are three of us."

He blew smoke toward my face. "But there's only one of you right now."

God, oh god . . . "Just for the moment." I cleared my throat, trying not to cough. "They'll be back any second." Then I thought I would be clever to add, "And they'd come running if I needed them." I remembered Stef's ankle too late but refused to amend my statement.

I checked the time. Five to two. What the hell was taking them so long?

Jeremiah thumbed his scar. "And is your friend always like that?"

"Which one?" I already knew.

"One with the pink hair. Is she normally such a spitfire or is it just my charming personality that brings it out?"

Floorboards squeaked from a back room. Were they *trying* to get caught?

"She can get a little ornery sometimes," I said, tensing as Jeremiah cocked his head toward the hallway. "I think she's just tired. We all are." I scrambled to keep his attention. "So, how far is the access road?"

He blew smoke toward the ceiling this time. "What access road?"

"Zo—Cora said that there was a road south of here."

"Well, I'm afraid that Miss Cora was mistaken. We're miles and miles from any road out here, sunshine."

I burrowed my nails into the deerskin, grinding my teeth. Of course there was no road. Just like there was no waterfall. I should never have trusted Zoe to navigate. I fucking told her we needed a GPS!

"Typical," I muttered.

He tilted his head to one side, waiting, an amused smirk tickling the edge of his scar.

"It's all just a big game to her—an *experience,*" I explained. "She always thinks she knows what to do and that she's never wrong. Even if she gets us lost in the fucking wilderness."

"Then, if you don't mind my askin', darlin', why do you listen to her?"

"Because she's usually right! It's infuriating. You never know when to call her out. She's the smartest, most incredible person; she lights up a room when she walks in. And sometimes when she calls me her best friend, I actually pinch myself at how lucky I am because she's so thoughtful, always there to pick me up when I'm down . . . And then at the same time, she's also the most exasperatingly arrogant, egotistical, selfish bitch!" I covered my mouth. I hadn't meant to let any of that spill out. "Shit, I don't know why I said that. It's not true. She's literally my favorite person in the whole world. It's just been a really stressful few days."

Jeremiah smiled sympathetically. "Yeah, I've got me someone like that in my life, too." He leaned forward and flicked cigarette ash onto his boot heel, watched it form a tiny gray mound. "You know, Dostoevsky writes about how a person can have both good and evil inside of them at the same time. Maybe it's not either-or with your friend, but both. Your friend is both the best person you know and the worst, all at once. I would know a thing or two about that."

The man was surprisingly deep for a recluse living in the woods.

"Um . . ." I blinked, not knowing what to say. "I mean, I don't think I said she was evil, but . . . I think I get your point." I rubbed my moist palms along my thighs. I wished my friends would hurry the hell up. "Do you like living out here?"

"Only place in the world I belong." He dragged a thumb across his scar, eyeing me. "Tell me, sugar, where do *you* belong?"

Jeremiah looked at me with a genuine keenness I wasn't used to. I could tell he wasn't interested in knowing that I'd been born in Michigan, or that the three of us lived in Chicago now; how we'd moved there together after high school. He wasn't after anything so superficial. Sweat gathered on the nape of my neck, beading along my brow. My friends were busy snooping through this man's private belongings and here he was trying to have some deep heart-to-heart. Meanwhile, it was only a matter of time before he realized what was up and I'd be the one to suffer the consequences. I couldn't stop staring at the enormity of his hands.

"Oh, I don't know really." Why weren't they back yet! "We like to travel a lot, so I guess nowhere really feels like home. And also, everywhere. Wherever my friends are, that's home for me. You know?"

"I like that." Jeremiah leaned back again so that his arms wrapped around the back of the couch, biceps on full display, underarm hair bushy and long, legs splayed confidently. "I like that a lot." He finger-combed his hair. "The three little angels who belonged everywhere, and nowhere. Fallen on my doorstep. I like getting to talk with you in private; you seem like the interesting one."

I squirmed, not sure whether to be flattered or disturbed.

"But your friends sure are taking a long time. Do you think they're all right? Maybe I ought to check—"

"They're fine, don't worry." My voice lilted upward, unnaturally loud. "Stef's probably just taking a long time because of her ankle."

Jeremiah reached forward suddenly. My body went rigid as he touched a fingertip to my cheek. "An eyelash." He showed me a single dark hair on his nicotine-stained finger. "Make a wish."

He stood up before I could respond. My eyes darted down the hall.

"Where are you going?" I asked, trying to hide my desperation.

"Ooee, you are jumpy, girl. And I get it. I understand why you're so on edge. Man is woman's natural predator."

Hearing him say it out loud made my stomach turn. Was that what a nice guy would say—or what a wolf would think he should say to put my mind at ease? Every muscle in my body clenched at the thought.

He knelt by a bookshelf across the room, searching for something. "But don't you worry now, I've got the medicine for you right here . . . somewhere. Trust me, this is just what you need." He flicked his dead cigarette onto the floor and snapped his fingers. "Here it is. I knew it was round here somewhere."

Jeremiah plunked an old tape player down onto the coffee table. He dusted off the top with one wide sweep of his hand. A plume of gray particles floated through the air, twisting with the smoke that still lingered. I cleared my throat.

"I know just what you need, baby girl." He pressed a button. "Music."

Then, to my utter horror and dismay, Jeremiah began to dance.

Jade could not decide who in this cabin she hated more: this man or the friends who had left her with him.

"Music always helps me relax." Jeremiah sidestepped toward

me, snapping his fingers, head tilted low and sideways like there was a cowboy hat on top. He started to sing along to Buffalo Springfield's "For What It's Worth."

My, Granny, what good moves you have.

I fidgeted, clueless as to how to respond. I wrung my hands. Then I sat on them, then placed them in my lap. Would it look too fake if I smiled? Should I bop my head along to the music? I didn't want to encourage him. But I didn't want to be rude, either. I had to keep him distracted.

I cleared my throat. "I like this song."

He spun around, still snapping his fingers.

"Not seen an old tape player like that in a long time."

Even Red Riding Hood had never endured such indignity.

Jeremiah sidestepped closer. "Come on, girl, get on up and dance with me." He beckoned me with an outstretched hand. "Come shake those hips."

Dear god, no. To hell with this.

"Maybe you're right, I should go check on my friends," I said, about to rise.

Jeremiah was suddenly on the couch again, so close this time his thigh was flat against mine. I could taste the smoke on his skin. "Dance with me." His Southern drawl was no longer charming.

"I don't really think I feel like it right now."

Noises creaked stridently down the hall.

His voice got low, rumbling from his chest, an animal growl. "Dance with me and I'll keep pretending those nosy little bitches ain't rifling through my personal things."

My hands trembled. Zoe's backpack was on the other side of Jeremiah's leg. I'd never get to Ripley in time if he attacked me now. I opened my mouth, but found I suddenly had no voice. No voice to say no. No voice to cry out.

"Relax!" Jeremiah slapped my knee, a loud guffaw bursting from his lips. "I'm just messin' with you, darlin'."

I glared, my clenched jaw quivering, before squeezing out a smile. "Funny."

"I wouldn't ask you to dance after what you've been through. I bet your calves are so knotted you can barely walk, let alone dance." He gazed at them now. I wished I wasn't wearing shorts. "I give a real mean massage, you know."

Finally, the welcome sound of footsteps shuffling toward us from down the hall.

"Sorry that took us so long," Zoe said nonchalantly, as if there was nothing out of the ordinary going on here. She flashed me a subtle smile. "Stef had a nasty fall."

"Are . . . you okay?" I asked hesitantly, a bad actress reading from her script.

Stef nodded, her limp ever so slightly more exaggerated.

"Didn't you hear us?" Zoe asked, as she helped our friend toward the couch. "We were shouting for help." She pointed her chin at the old tape player like an accusatory finger. "The music must have drowned us out. Hey, would you mind making some space?" She gestured for Jeremiah to move off the couch with a flip of her pink hair streak.

"Be my guest." He stood and stepped aside, every bit the Southern gentleman again. Had I heard him right before, when his voice had flashed to an animal growl? This was why I hadn't wanted alcohol. It dulled my senses.

Zoe eased Stef onto the sofa and then plopped down beside her. "Buffalo Springfield. Nice. My dad loves this song." Then

Zoe snapped her fingers as if only just having remembered. "Oh shit, I'm so sorry. We broke one of your pieces when Stef fell. I think it may have been some sort of bowl? I tried looking for some glue to put it back together, but I couldn't find anything. Whatever it was, we're more than happy to pay for it."

Were we? I never minded covering a couple of beers or even a train ticket when Zoe needed, because despite however much she claimed to save, she always seemed short of money. But I did very much mind covering for her bullshit. Especially since I bet that she'd purposefully smashed his bowl just for her alibi.

Zoe spotted the two clay mugs on the end table. "Is that the coffee? Great. I'm parched."

As Zoe reached for the mug, I felt like throwing mine at her.

six

"Bloody Mary," we'd said. Eleven years old in Stef's parents' bathroom with pink-tiled walls. We giggled, clinging to one another. "Bloody Mary."

If we said the name three times, a woman was meant to appear who would kill us all. Stef and I screamed, covering our eyes, unable to say it again. The anticipation and the fear of seeing a conjured face was far too great. I burrowed my cheek into Zoe's shoulder.

"I'm not scared of this bitch," Zoe said, defiant and brave. Then she shouted, a battle cry, "Bloody Mary!"

Nothing came for us and I was convinced it was because of Zoe. She'd been too fierce. Bloody Mary had taken one look at her through the mirror and changed her mind.

It was in that same bathroom that we made our pact when

we were thirteen. We each scrawled a wish onto a piece of paper with purple gel pen. Then we stuffed a rolled-up towel beneath the door and burned our wishes over a tropical-scented candle in the sink. Our first manifestation.

"Everything we write on this paper is a promise we're making to ourselves and to each other," Stefanie had said. "Therefore, it has to come true."

Zoe wrote: We will see the world.

Stef wrote: We will be badass bitches till we die.

I wrote: We will be friends forever.

I never told them that if I ever got a tattoo, it would be of these vows. They felt like a sacred edict that would bond us together forever. It's what I used to cite when boyfriends questioned me about why we were still so close after so many years. "The pact," I'd say, as if they were dumb.

But in a moment like this, I felt like the dumb one. I'd never break our pact. But perhaps it shouldn't mean that I follow this irresponsible madwoman anywhere and everywhere she wanted to go.

"So, Miss . . ." Jeremiah looked to me with a question mark. "Laura, was it?"

"That's *Dora,*" Zoe said with a shit-eating grin. "This is Nora." She tapped Stef's knee. "I'm Cora."

Jeremiah's left eyebrow lifted. "Right. So, Miss Dora was telling me you girls like to travel. What does your family make of all that?"

"Are you trying to gauge how many people will miss us if we disappear?" Zoe wagged a finger at him. "The answer is a lot. We're very close with our family."

"C'mon, now, that's not how I meant it," Jeremiah said, an amused smirk curled into his cheek.

"Thankfully the Meyers family understands that women aren't vulnerable little flowers, so they're all very supportive of our endeavors to see the world."

Jeremiah rubbed his scar. "If you say so." But when he said it, he said it to me.

Buffalo Springfield had long since finished and now it was Jefferson Airplane's "White Rabbit" crackling through the tape player. Zoe and Stef sipped their coffees, grimacing.

"God, that's strong." Stef giggled. She said nothing about alcohol. I wondered if theirs was spiked, too, or if I was just special. The *interesting one,* as he'd said, whatever that meant. I still hadn't recovered from the way his voice had turned into that animal growl, even if jokingly.

As if reading my mind, Jeremiah caught my eye and winked, making me squirm. I wasn't used to this level of attention. Not when Zoe and Stef were with me. Men almost never looked twice at me when they were nearby. There were a few rare exceptions, guys who appreciated my curves or thick mop of curly hair, and I usually ended up dating them almost on the strength of that alone. But most of the time, if we were out dancing or at a bar, men got caught on Stef's long legs or snagged by Zoe's piercing hazel eyes before they ever reached me.

I had this recurring dream of the three of us stuck in a bus edging over the side of a cliff. It was something that had actually happened in Costa Rica. We were in a bus trying to pass a motorcycle on the shoulder. Except we were driving down a muddy mountain road and the shoulder was a cliff's edge with a hundred-foot drop into the jungle below. The whole bus teetered. Wheels lifted off the ground. Everyone moved to one side. Some people started praying. My heartbeat throbbed in my throat, and I clung to Zoe's hands so tight my nails gouged four crescent moons into her palms. Then the bus cut off the motorcycle, nearly sending the rider careening over the edge, and righted itself on the road just in time. The locals had crossed themselves and gone back to reading their papers. I had cried.

But in my dreams, the bus plunged over the edge. Just before it did, time slowed. Thickened like pudding. A handsome man with indistinct features, whose face was never clear in the lucid light of day, busted through a window. Punched through with a single fist. He searched for someone to pull from the wreckage, knowing he had time to save just one. His eyes fell to Stefanie, but he kept looking. His eyes went to Zoe, and he passed her by. Then his gaze glued to me. He reached down, hand outstretched, and saved me just as the bus fell away, rolling down the cliffside.

It was a pathetic dream. A literal pick-me dream. I hated myself for having it. I'd never confess it to anyone, least of all Stefanie or Zoe, who already chided me for my fragile self-esteem. But, in a way, I enjoyed having these dreams, too. I always woke feeling refreshed. Because they were the only time that a man ever overlooked my beautiful friends and fixated on me.

Except for apparently now. In this fantastically screwed-up, toxic situation.

Jeremiah started to speak, but Zoe cut him off, singing along to a line of "White Rabbit." Then she dropped the clay mug of coffee. Black tar spread across the wooden floor. "Shit! I'm so sorry." She brushed the gritty juice from her legs. "I'm such a klutz."

Jeremiah cocked his head, all charming and smooth. "No bother, darlin'."

"Do you have something I could clean this up with?"

"I'll get you a towel."

As he walked slowly to the kitchen, Zoe called after him,

"Oh, and be a peach and grab me another cup of coffee, will you please?"

Jeremiah grunted. I couldn't tell if it was with humor or disdain.

Once he was out of the room, she turned to me. "Great thinking with the music! Those floors were creaky as hell; we needed the cover."

"We could still hear you," I said bitterly.

Stef giggled. "I nearly shit my pants when you dragged that trunk from under his bed. It was so loud!"

"No shit. And the music wasn't my idea. Captain Cowboy here wanted to show off his dance moves."

Zoe winced. "He danced?"

"Yes," I hissed. "It was awful."

"Aw," Stef said, "I wish I'd have seen that. Was he a good dancer?"

I slapped her arm, hard. "I'll tell you what. Next time, *you* stay behind and be the judge. I'm sure he'd happily put on another performance." I slapped her arm again, just for good measure. "I told you guys not to leave me alone with him. I was so uncomfortable! He's been coming on to me, and maybe he's a nice guy who's just lonely and a bit weird, but even so, it was so fucking awkward and—"

Stef silenced me with a picture on her phone. An old wooden jewelry box inside what appeared to be a large trunk pulled out from underneath a bed.

"Why am I looking at this? Why were you even taking pictures?"

"Evidence," Zoe said, like *I* was the idiot.

I tossed her tone right back at her. "It's just a box."

Stef swiped to the next photo. Inside the box, there was

an assortment of women's jewelry, a nest of silver chains and tangled bracelets. She flicked her thumb to show me individual pieces photographed in the palm of her hand: a golden leaf ring, a single pearl earring, a jade pendant necklace.

"So what? This isn't evidence of anything, except maybe his ex-girlfriends. And what gives you the right to go poking through his things? For all we know you've been rifling through precious family heirlooms. What if those are his great-great-grandmother's?"

"Give me a break," Zoe scoffed. "None of these are matching. Why so many single earrings?" She pointed at a picture of a fake mother-of-pearl horse pendant. "And no great-great-grandmother left behind this plastic shit as an heirloom."

"You don't know that. Who knows what this guy's family is like? I'm telling you, he doesn't seem like a killer. He seems kind of, I don't know, intense but . . . earnest? Maybe even sweet? It's hard to get a good read; my nerves are shot to hell right now."

"Sounds like you have a little crush." Stef smirked. When I shot her a look, she held up her hands. "Hey! I don't blame you. I already said he's hot."

I scowled. "He's *super* weird, no question. But that doesn't mean he kills people."

"He seems weird because he's a serial killer," Zoe said.

"Oh yeah, a guy is interested in me before you, so obviously he's a psychopath."

Zoe pinched the bridge of her nose. "Jesus, Jade, I'm being serious here."

I opened my mouth to speak again and fell short when I realized that she actually was. She *really* thought Jeremiah was the Bones Hollow Hunter. I hesitated for a moment, the stone-cold confidence on her face unsettling. I recalled his growl from before, the way his voice had changed. But then wouldn't I get annoyed, too, if the girls I helped were snooping through my house?

I thought back to how uneasy I'd felt standing on his doorstep, the shivers that had raced up my spine when I'd spotted the bow on the wall. Except, all of these were just feelings. Feelings from a paranoid girl who had been on the trail too long, listening to scary podcast stories. Feelings weren't proof, and neither was some random jewelry they found under his bed.

Zoe was so desperate for him to be the killer, always so hungry for adventure and for *that great story,* that she didn't care about the truth. This was all just a game for her, a way to finally start her own podcast. Well, I refused to play along.

"He seems weird," I shot back, "because he's living in the woods by himself, making ornaments out of animal skulls. Just because you're obsessed with all this Bones Hollow bullshit doesn't make him *the guy,* okay? Like the police wouldn't have found him living out here before now if he was—it's ridiculous! So, can you please just give it a rest and stay with me until the ranger comes? You've got your pictures; you can give them to the police when we're back and they can match them against evidence logs or whatever they do, and then you'll see how stupid you've been. But look," I glanced at my phone, "it's two-fifteen now. Let's just keep our heads down until we get out of here. I am genuinely begging you."

"Sorry, Jade, but there's still an upstairs." Stefanie's tone was apologetic, but I recognized that look on her face. It was the same sheepish yet annoyingly innocent expression she got whenever she and Zoe had agreed to something she knew I wouldn't approve of. "We really should check it."

"We're stuck here for another few hours, right? We've got

to look around more." Zoe squeezed my knee, trying to convince me with those big, beseeching hazel eyes. "What if we find Florence's compass? Or, even better, what if she's actually here somewhere?"

"No way," I said. "Can't you see how fucked up you're being? This guy is helping us. And unless your ankle has miraculously healed, Stef, his help is something we need. What happens when he gets pissed and throws us out? Or worse? We can't snoop through his stuff taking pictures just because of this weird obsession of yours. It's not okay."

"That's why you should wait here," Zoe said.

"Like hell I should. I'm not getting left alone with him again. Stef can stay, she can't even walk anyway."

"Would you quit with that! I can make my own decisions, thank you."

I snorted. Like Stef ever made her own decisions.

"And you don't even think he's the killer," Stef added. "You won't know what to look for."

"Even better. At least *someone* can be impartial."

Stef started to stand, but I was faster. I darted down the darkened hall, heart racing. Zoe was right behind me, her whisper hot on my ear. "Let me go first."

"Not a chance." I was taking charge, for a change. I stuck out an elbow so she couldn't squeeze by.

"The stairs are just there. Shh, quiet."

"Oh, like you were quiet before?" I hissed, easing my foot onto the first wooden step. "No problem."

"Hey! We tried, okay?" She stepped behind me, pressed into my back, her moist breath tangling in the hairs on the nape of my neck like a kiss. "It's not easy."

"No, not okay. Not okay at all." I stepped again. The wood sighed.

"See?"

I wanted to reach back and slap her.

I regretted now not having taken my boots off, but I'd needed to hurry. Clearly Zoe was right; keeping quiet in this house, when we hadn't learned every loose board like Jeremiah, wasn't so easy. But that wasn't my point. It wasn't that they should have been quieter, it's that they shouldn't have been snooping in the first place. Even more to my point, they shouldn't have left me behind.

Everywhere I placed my foot was wrong. I made noise with each step. The creaks and groans varied in length and volume, like an orchestra. The inside of the stair was a bass cello. The outside a violin. The middle, the full brass section. Fat beads of sweat collected on the bridge of my nose, dripping down like raindrops from a window awning, as I carefully selected which instrument to play. I was grateful it was Stef sitting on that couch right now and not me. I could hear Janis Joplin playing faintly from the living room.

I hoped he was dancing for her. I hoped it was awkward as hell.

We were meant to be on a fun hiking adventure. We were supposed to come away with thrilling stories about blisters and animal encounters. Playing serial killer detective hadn't been on my bingo card for this journey. I resented each and every step I took.

Finally, we reached the top. The upstairs was one large attic room. A vast wooden space stretched before us, a new orchestra of creaks and squeaks ready to burst into song. Half the floorboards looked rotted through. Holes and uprooted nails pock-marked the floor. There was virtually nothing up here at all. Just some wayward tools scattered across the floor and a couple of dusty wooden chests against the far wall.

"Okay, we checked. No Florence," I said. "Let's go back."

Zoe swiped her pink streak from her eyes. "Nice try."

"This doesn't look safe." I pointed to a blackened watermark with my toe. "We could fall through."

"This is why you should've stayed behind."

"Like Stef would've made it up those stairs."

"She would've complained about it less."

"You're right, actually. Because unlike her, I didn't come up here just to enable you. I've come up here to stop you."

"Well, you're doing a great job so far. This way." Zoe pointed to the left, pushing ahead of me.

I thought about yanking her ponytail.

She stepped carefully along the outskirts of the room. "Let's check those chests over there." She didn't speak in a whisper, but at least she kept her voice as soft as her footsteps. "If there are any newspapers inside, check the dates. Killers love to keep papers. Even if they don't have articles about the Hunter, they might still somehow coincide with his victims." She inched along, arms spread flat to the wall like she walked the edge of a cliff. "Look for dates like May 23, 2011. June 6, 2012." She stopped to snap a few pictures on her phone.

"What if it turns out he's completely innocent? Don't you think it'll be mortifying that you've done this—ransacked his things, taken photos . . . What happens when the rangers come and you look like a total asshole?"

Zoe aimed her phone at me and smirked. "When have you ever known me to be mortified?"

"That's not the badge of honor you think it is." She took a picture of me flipping her off. "This doesn't feel legal. Photographing people's things without permission. I'm sure that's got to be against some law. I love you to pieces, but I'm not going to prison for you, Zo."

"Look," she kept moving along the wall, "don't beat yourself up. Have you ever been able to stop me?"

I made a face. She didn't see it.

"Exactly. So, if you can't beat me, join me. And hurry up about it. We shouldn't leave Stef alone for too long."

"Oh, so you care about *her* well-being."

"She can't run as fast right now," Zoe said matter-of-factly.

Teeth clenched, I stepped lightly in her footsteps, carefully picking my way through the dry patches of flooring. With each step, the wood squealed. I flipped open the lid to the first chest before she could. Inside were books. "Happy?" I asked, unimpressed.

This was so pointless. Why were we up here? I thumbed through some of the titles. Dostoevsky, Tolstoy, Sartre, Machiavelli. It was an impressive collection. "How did he get all these out here? I didn't even have space in my bag for a notebook."

"They're probably from his victims," Zoe said, snapping pictures of them now.

"How many hikers do you know that carry copies of *War and Peace*?" I said, flopping it back down into the chest. "You're too biased to see this clearly. You interpret everything you see as a clue to fit the narrative that's already in your mind. You're a shit detective, Zo; I'm sorry."

She mimicked his voice now, with one eyebrow cocked. "If you say so."

Zoe crouched by the second wooden chest and the floor

groaned beneath her like an old man. I thought I heard the distinct crackle of splintering wood. Any step could be the one to send our feet flying through. Any sound could be the one to send Jeremiah racing upstairs to catch us.

But then I remembered a salient point. "Wait, he knew that you and Stef were snooping; he told me so. Why would he let you search the house if he had something to hide?"

"Because he thinks we won't be getting away?"

I shivered.

Zoe fingered a metal padlock on the chest, glee in her eyes. "Looky looky, what do we have here?"

"We can't," I said, trying to be clever. "It's locked."

"Exactly. Must be something worth hiding." Zoe looked from left to right, then spotted a claw hammer by one of the front-facing windows across the room. "One second."

"No, don't!" I said just as she stepped to the center of the room.

The soft wood crumbled beneath her boot and the floor swallowed half her calf. Splinters clawed at her shin, digging into her flesh, and she covered her mouth to muffle her cry. "Shit," she seethed through clenched, rattling teeth. "Shit, shit, shit." Her calf was stuck on a wide rusty nail jutting out and up from the broken floorboard. Her leg was fixed to it like another plank of wood. She tried to pry herself free, but stopped, biting her fist.

"Stay there," I whispered. "I'm coming."

I held my breath before taking my first step. It was like walking out onto a sheet of ice. The first board screeched but held steady. I moved closer cautiously, inch by inch, until I could reach her. The nail was buried deep in the meat of her calf. I examined it for a moment before carefully returning to the chest for a book. I handed her a copy of *Steppenwolf.* "Bite down," I said.

Grabbing hold of Zoe's leg, I pulled until it moved a fraction of an inch. Zoe growled through the book's pages. I waited for her to catch her breath and then I tried again, yanking hard. Her leg moved a little bit more. *Steppenwolf* quivered between Zoe's teeth. Finally, I ripped her leg from the rusted nail. Dark red blood gushed down, pooling in her woolen sock.

Zoe spat the dusty book onto the floor. "Fuck!" She swiped away a tear. Then she looked back to the claw hammer still on the shelf across the room.

"Leave it," I said, astonished.

"I can't." Lying on her belly, she moved her elbow as if to army crawl across the center of the room.

"I'd call you a crazy bitch," I said, "but you'd take it as a compliment."

"You get me so well." Teeth still gritted with pain, she flashed me a cheeky grin. "That's why I love you."

I sighed, hard, rolling my eyes. "Stay here."

I tested my first step with the tip of my toe, giving only a quarter of my weight. This wood felt firm. I moved onto it. I tested the next step again and did the same, inching across the center of the room with painstaking care.

By the time I reached the claw hammer, I pressed it to my chest, a hard-won treasure. I might need it soon. There was absolutely no way Jeremiah hadn't heard us downstairs. What would he be saying to Stef now about the nosy bitches in his attic? How long before he stopped allowing us this charade and stormed up here to see for himself?

"Yes!" Zoe whisper-cheered when the hammer was in my grip. "Well done!"

I tiptoed my way back, trying to retrace my exact path. By the time I reached the trunk, Zoe had already ripped off the edge of her black shirt and tied it around her leg. She snatched the hammer from me and used the claw to pry open the padlock. The metal groaned, and so did she, louder than she should, before it finally snapped apart.

"Hell yeah!" Zoe beamed, triumphant. She lifted the lid open wide.

"It's just clothes," I said, disappointed, frustrated, furious. "All of that and it's just clothes. This is what I've been telling you, this is a waste of time. Now let's go."

"Wait." Zoe burrowed through them, lifting out a navy blouse, then a green sweater. "These aren't just any clothes. They're women's clothes."

"So? That doesn't mean anything."

"All the victims were naked. Look!" Zoe dug deep and pulled out a yellow raincoat. "This is what Harper Reed was last seen wearing."

"*This* is what we call confirmation bias. It's a yellow rain jacket. The most innocuous piece of clothing ever. Everyone owns one."

"I don't. Can't you see?" She showed me a fistful of multicolored fabrics. "None of these things match. They don't belong to the same woman." Zoe whipped out her camera, placing each clothing article on the floor to photograph properly.

"Like I said before, he could have ex-girlfriends or wives. They could belong to other travelers who have passed through here. He told me he isn't here year-round. And you said this cabin used to get used more. These clothes could belong to anyone! They don't prove anything."

"You're not seeing it because you don't want to," Zoe said, taking another picture. "But I bet Laurie Wolff will think differently. Or Detective Leeroy. Or maybe I should just go straight to the news stations. I don't know. I haven't decided yet." She stopped photographing for a second. "Do you think I should talk to Laurie before or after I start my podcast? I don't want to insult the queen, but also she's kind of gonna be my competition."

"Oh my god, stop!" I snatched the shirts off the ground and shoved them back into the trunk. I slammed the lid shut. "That's enough. You got what you need. We're going."

Zoe and I twisted across the outskirts of the treacherous ground, listening to the music mumble through the floor. Beneath the band playing, their voices murmured. Then Stef's laugh came through clear as a bell. She was so much better equipped to stay behind than me. Or even Zoe. Stef could get along with anyone. Especially men. Of course she was fine; it probably wasn't awkward at all for her.

I took a step, and the floorboard emitted a high-pitched whine beneath my feet. The music downstairs stopped abruptly like a slap to the face. Zoe and I froze mid-step, a pang of anxiety fluttering in my chest. Silence stabbed at my ears.

"What was that?" we heard Jeremiah say, loud footsteps marching toward the hall. "Are your friends upstairs?"

Oh god, oh my god . . . he was coming! What would Jeremiah say when he caught us? What excuse could we possibly have for being up here?

Jade Edelman had listened to enough true crime podcasts to know what an angry man was capable of. She thought now of every violent crime she'd ever heard narrated to her through her friend's car stereo. Crimes of passion. Crimes of rage.

Strangulation.

Dismemberment.

A tooth wrenched from the mouth and an arrow pierced through the heart.

I clutched my friend's arm tight enough to bruise.

Stefanie's yelp was sharp, cutting through the ceiling straight into my heart. My lungs clenched. Had he hit her? What was happening?

But then she released an exaggerated moan. "Ow! Shit, that hurts. Can you help me up?" She must have fallen or pretended to trip. There was an achingly long pause before we heard his footsteps recede.

"I'm so clumsy," she said with a giggle, and I could picture the way she held his biceps, staring up into his green eyes. "I'm sorry, I was just trying to turn the music back on. I love that song." Then she added, "They'll be back in a second. And I could really use a cigarette. Would you mind? Quick, 'cause if they see you rolling for me, they'll be total nags."

A second later, the music returned. Breath reentered my lungs, the tide rolling back to shore. Zoe sighed, too, the tension in her arm easing. I wanted to pinch her. It was her fault we were up here to begin with. Instead, I let her biceps go.

"We'll need to question him," Zoe whispered into my hair as we reached the top of the stairs.

She chose now to tell me this, here on the stairs, because she knew I couldn't argue. I turned to express my frustration. "What?" I mouthed, and put my weight on the center of the stair, to the full brass section's delight. I cringed, holding my breath.

Zoe waited until I stepped again, mirroring my path, and said in a voice so hushed I could hardly hear, "Stef and I talked it out already. We'll tie him up."

Unbelievable. While I'd been getting serenaded on a deerskin couch, my friends had been plotting to tie this man up for questioning. Obviously, they didn't care about going to prison.

"With what?" It took effort to whisper this hard. Sweat matted the hair at my temples, pouring down my neck.

"You packed floss, didn't you?"

"You've got to be kidding."

"It's super strong. I saw a vid—"

"Shut up," I hissed. "Just shut up. I don't want to hear anymore." I stepped and the floor screamed louder than ever, sounding like the dying rabbit my family cat had once caught. We froze, my heartbeat pounding in my throat.

As we finally reached the bottom step, I turned back and saw it. Droplets of blood dappled the stairwell in our wake. Zoe had left a trail. Jeremiah would only need to walk down the hall now to find undeniable proof that we'd been meddling upstairs. I pointed, eyes panicked.

"It's fine," Zoe mouthed. "Keep him in the living room."

With *floss*?

"And what are we going to say we've been doing all this time?" The words leaked through my gritted teeth. "The bathroom, *again*?"

Zoe shrugged. "I'll think of something. Don't worry about it."

"Oh yeah, sure. Just don't worry. No problem."

But my anxiety was suffocating. Because I knew Zoe *would* think of something, and that I had more chance of magically conjuring a car for our escape than I did of dissuading her. Her tenacity knew no bounds once she'd made up her mind. Like when Stefanie had gotten a job as a waitress in high school, and every day she would complain to us about the manager, who wouldn't stop hitting on her. Yet, Stef *insisted* that no one do anything about it because the money was too good.

As if that would stop Zoe.

It became her pet project—her singular obsession. And once she set her sights on something, there was no getting in her way.

Zoe found out everything there was to know about this manager. Where he'd gone to college, where he lived, where he walked his dog. She'd even found his mother's address. Then, once she'd compiled her dossier, she and I went to the restaurant one night when Stef wasn't working. We waited hours, eating nachos and playing thumb war, until the manager had finished his shift. Then Zoe followed him out to his car.

I'd watched it all from the safety of the restaurant's back door. But I heard her clear as a bell, a true-blue hero—just like she'd always dreamed of being. She'd slapped a manila folder against his chest and told him, very calmly, that if he didn't stop harassing his staff, she'd send the contents of that folder to everyone he knew, including his boss, and most especially, his mother. Inside was a flyer she'd printed with the title: *PREDATOR: I LIKE UNDERAGE PUSSY,* and a big picture of his face.

He'd turned six shades of red and sped off. Stef told us that he'd quit the next day.

Zoe's unwavering resolve had always been something I'd admired, that I could only dream of possessing. It was what I loved about her. But, at times like these, that same quality felt like a curse.

My stomach twisted into a tightly coiled spring as we walked back into the living room. Stef was seated on the couch. Jeremiah was beside her, leaning back, legs splayed, smoking another cigarette. Stef was smoking one, too. "Oh my god, guys!" she said, seeing us. "Jerry here was just telling me about a time that he hunted a bear."

Jerry. Stef was so much better at this.

Not that playing interested in dumb men was something I cared to be good at. But it'd always been a particular skill of hers.

"You ran off before I could give you that coffee," Jeremiah said with a raised eyebrow. "Got it here for you." He nodded to the end table. "Or maybe you somehow quenched your thirst in my attic?"

I gulped, a searing dryness in my throat, but Zoe didn't even flinch.

"You're funny. Sorry we took so long." She gestured to my crotch. "It was a lady emergency. Total blowout. All hands on deck."

Great. Another lie for me to maintain. No worries at all.

Jeremiah scooted aside to make space for us. "Maybe I shouldn't sit," I said, trying awkwardly to keep the ruse going. "I don't want to mess up your nice couch."

"Oh, don't worry about that, darlin'," Jeremiah said. "Blood never put me off." His smile could strip the skin off a snake. I shuddered. "This couch has seen its fair share." He tipped his head back when he laughed.

Zoe and Stefanie chuckled along, but I could not. As I joined them on the couch, my mind flashed to the deer carcass dripping blood outside. I suddenly felt dirty sitting here.

What time was it? I patted down the cushion for my phone. I was sure I'd left it here. Or had I replaced it in the side pocket of my backpack?

"So, how many girls have you had in here?" Zoe asked. "Is this the most you've ever had at one time?"

I rolled my eyes. Zoe thought of herself as some sort of artful instigator, but in reality, she was just extremely annoying.

"Most certainly." Jeremiah leaned toward her, one elbow on his knee.

Zoe was trying to prove me wrong about the clothes and jewelry belonging to his exes. But all she was going to prove was that he was a horny guy who thought he was about to have a foursome.

"Have you had many girlfriends?" Zoe asked.

"There was a Mrs. once . . . but she's gone now."

I knew it. The clothes and jewelry could easily belong to his ex-wife.

Stef understood the assignment without being told; the mission was to disprove my theory. "Go on, Jerry, what's your body count?"

Jeremiah winked. "A gentleman never tells."

This line of questioning wasn't going to get us anywhere but in trouble. I shot Zoe a vicious look, begging for her silence.

Instead, she smiled as she turned to me. "Hey, Dora, did you pack any floss?"

seven

"No, Cora, I don't think I did," I said.

Stef nudged me with her knee. "No, you did. Remember?"

"Nope," I said. "Definitely none in my bag."

"I saw you use some," Stef said.

"I finished it."

"What's all this commotion about?" Jeremiah cut in. "I've got some floss. Though I suppose you probably know that by now, as much time as you've spent in my lavatory."

Guilt stabbed my stomach. All this man had done was take us in, and how had we repaid him? By going through every inch of his property—something he could rightly kick us out for, and yet here he was making light of it. "That's fine," I said. "We don't need any."

"Actually, I do." Zoe turned to me, annoyed. "Trust me," she mouthed.

Fat chance.

Wrong about the waterfall. Wrong about the access road. And it was exactly because Zoe was so damned sure of herself that I was sure she was wrong about finding a serial killer, too. Now, after rifling through his things, she thought she could tie up a very-likely-innocent man for interrogation. Not even thinking about all the things that could go wrong! What if he overpowered us before we bound him? What if the floss broke? What if the ranger arrived and found we'd been holding this man—a man he knew—hostage?

"Consequence" was a foreign word to Zoe. Normally, I admired that about her, but not this time. I needed to take control of this situation.

"Hey, Jeremiah, do you have any cards?" I asked, looking left to right on the couch for my phone. It felt like we'd been upstairs for an hour, but it'd probably only been ten to fifteen minutes. I needed to know how much of this nightmare we had left to endure before the ranger arrived. Not knowing was its own form of torture. "Maybe we should play a game. To kill the time."

Zoe pointed the barrel of a finger gun at me. "Great idea!"

Her enthusiasm wasn't a good sign. Maybe I'd just played right into her hand.

"I think I got some cards in the bedroom." He hitched up his belt when he stood. "Don't you girls go anywhere now."

I rolled my eyes as he left, grateful for Bob Dylan's voice crooning through the tape player, covering my own. "I'm such an idiot," I said. "He probably thinks we're going to all play strip poker now. Hey, Stef, have you seen my phone? I was sure I left it here."

"Maybe we *should* play poker," Stef whispered. "Guys do a

lot of talking when they think they're about to have sex. In my experience."

"I'm going to pretend you didn't just suggest that." I wanted to pull out my hair. "Why is it such a crazy idea that we just chill the fuck out and wait for the ranger? We didn't find anything upstairs."

"Bullshit." Zoe had already whipped out her phone to show Stef the pictures. "See?"

Stef gasped. "Harper's yellow rain jacket!"

"It's just a raincoat," I said. "A million people have ones just like it."

"But have a million people wearing one gone missing not far from this cabin?" Zoe asked.

"No, but—"

Stef had already begun talking over me. "Should I record him when he comes back?"

"Probably more than a few hikers carry one," I finished, though neither Stefanie nor Zoe was listening. Then to Stef, I replied, "Obviously not. But can you check the time?"

Zoe ignored me. "It eats up the battery. We should conserve, just in case."

"You guys are delusional if you think we've just *stumbled* onto the Bones Hollow Hunter when no one else has been able to find him for over a decade. I mean, what are the odds of that? Zero!"

The floorboards hadn't made a peep and Jeremiah was back. "Here we go," he said, waggling a faded box of cards. "What's your game?"

"Texas," Zoe said.

He smiled. "My kinda girl." With one hand, he grabbed the coffee table and dragged it closer to the couch. The skull ornaments rattled. "Can't say I have much money on me, though. And I'd certainly hate to rob you ladies blind."

Oh my god. He really *did* think we were going to play strip poker.

I knew what Zoe was going to say before she said it.

This was not happening. I was in a fever dream. A nightmare. I was going to wake up any minute now covered in sweat and mosquitoes.

"We can bet with other things," Zoe said.

Stef flashed a coquettish smile.

Who even *were* these two women next to me? They weren't my friends. Friends wouldn't do this to me. Friends wouldn't put me in this position.

But then who was I kidding? Of course *these* friends would. These were the same two who had orchestrated my first kiss by inviting my crush to a party and then getting us all to play spin the bottle. When I spun, Zoe all but elbowed the bottle so that it fell on Brad. It was mortifying. Naturally, they acted like they'd done me a favor and maybe they had, because I'd probably never have had my first kiss without some intervention. But one thing was clear. *These* friends never cared one little bit about my comfort zone. They saw it as a personal challenge. A glass ceiling that, according to them, I needed to shatter.

"How's about that real drink now?" Zoe suggested. "I think this calls for it."

"Is that right?" Jeremiah's pale green eyes twinkled, eager. "I got just the thing. She knows what I'm talkin' about." He pointed at me, grinning ear to ear. Then he skipped off to the kitchen.

His steps were in time to the mixtape playing. Mick Jagger sang as Jeremiah disappeared into the other room.

"Oh yeah, I forgot to mention he spiked my coffee," I told them bitterly. "You're crazy if you think a single item of clothing is being removed from my body. I will take my backpack, the compass, and the map, and I will march right out that door. Don't think I won't." The last thing I wanted was to march aimlessly through the forest, so I hoped they wouldn't call my bluff.

"Don't worry." Zoe put a hand on my knee. "No one is getting naked. Except for maybe Stef, because she's hot for him."

Stef rolled her eyes, smiling. "Whatever."

"I'm not comfortable with this," I said, unamused. "Just look at the facts. The only thing we *know* is that he's taken us in and he's offered us help. Everything else is just suspicion. We can't ransack his house and tie him up and question him because you're projecting this whole big scenario. That's insane. More than that, it's wrong."

"Maybe we should tell her," Stef mumbled.

What the hell did that mean—tell me what?

Zoe cut her off with a look. "If it makes you more comfortable, we can forget the cards. But then it's back to the floss. Whichever you prefer, Jade, it's your choice. But, make no mistake, we're questioning this bastard. This is a once-in-a-lifetime opportunity."

"C'mon," Stef urged me. "We've come this far. You can't back out on us now; we came here for an adventure! This is fun!"

"We're going to be telling this story until the day we die," Zoe said.

That's the line she always used. Before she convinced me to do things like jump off a bridge with only a bungee cord attached to my ankle. Or to accept an invitation to some private villa from a man on a bicycle whom we'd only just met. To be fair, those were great stories. Normally, she was right. But this time was different. Zoe wasn't just asking me to abandon my inhibitions for an evening. She was asking me to commit a crime.

"Think about it," Stefanie added. "We could be famous."

"Better," Zoe said. "We could be heroes."

My stomach twisted, sour. They were just two little girls playing detective for fame and valor. If we were twelve still, it'd be cute. But we were grown women now and it was anything but. Jeremiah wasn't some pawn they could play with; he was a real person. And if they were right, it was even worse. They'd have us toying with an actual psychopathic murderer.

"Let's pretend you're right, just for kicks," I said. "I don't think provoking a serial killer is a smart move. And if you're wrong—which you almost definitely are—and you antagonize and threaten some weirdo living in the woods, what then?"

As I spoke, Zoe opened the side pouch of her backpack. She withdrew Ripley, holding the knife in her hand for a beat before placing it in her pocket.

"What you're doing is dangerous, Zo. This isn't a game."

"Of course it is," she said, lifting her eyebrows in Jeremiah's direction as he returned from the kitchen, bottle in one hand and four glasses pinched in the other. "It's a card game."

Jeremiah set his bounty down on the table and poured us each three fingerfuls of a clear liquor from an unlabeled glass bottle.

"My own personal recipe," he announced, full of pride. "Best moonshine there is." He lifted his glass to ours. "Cheers."

"Skol," Stef and Zoe said in unison. The four of us clinked our glasses together.

We waited until he knocked his back. Zoe was the first of us to shoot hers, straight down with barely a grimace. Then came Stef, who winced like she'd drunk a cup of mouthwash. I took a deep breath and tossed mine down the back of my throat. It burned so hot I gagged.

Jeremiah clapped me on the back. "It'll put hair on your chest, all right."

I coughed, already feeling the liquor. As predicted, on an empty stomach it'd gone straight to my head. My smile felt looser. "Yeehaw."

Everyone laughed. Zoe's hazel eyes glowed with pride when they met mine. I resented how my heart fluttered at the sight. Despite all her flaws, still at my core, I craved Zoe's approval.

"Never mind poker," Zoe said now. "I've got a better idea." She reached for the card pack and began to shuffle, tossing them with the ease of a casino dealer. Then she handed one face down to each of us. "High card gets a dare."

I felt stupid. My cheeks bloomed with shame. This had been Zoe's plan all along. Of course she'd never planned on playing strip poker. Zoe was reckless in many ways—too many—but she would never pressure me into something like that. There was a mile of daylight between getting me to kiss my crush in middle school and getting me to play strip poker with this weirdo. I shouldn't have doubted her.

"A dare from who?" Jeremiah pulled the desk chair over to the corner of the coffee table and sat down on it backward, so that his legs were splayed around the sides, package on full display.

"The dealer, of course." Zoe smirked.

"What if you get the high card?"

"Then you can give me a dare, champ. Aces are high. Let's have a look."

Each of us flipped our cards. I had a seven of spades. Stefanie the queen of clubs. Zoe had the two of diamonds. And Jeremiah had the king.

"Ladies and gentleman," Zoe said, a radio news announcer, "we have a winner."

Jeremiah rubbed his scar, his eyes keen. "What's it gonna be, then?"

"I dare you to tell me . . . does the name Harper Reed ring a bell to you?"

"Can't say that it does." Disappointment furrowed between his brows. "Is that it?"

"Yes." Zoe dealt us each another card.

Jeremiah's pale green eyes hadn't so much as flickered when she'd mentioned that name. Not a hint of recognition. Not a wince of guilt, or even anger. Jeremiah had no clue who Harper Reed was. I knew this was pointless.

We flipped our cards. Again, Jeremiah's was the highest. "Must be my lucky day."

"I dare you to tell me, does the name Florence Marsh sound familiar?"

Jeremiah frowned, annoyed. "No."

This game clearly wasn't what he'd thought it'd be. How soon before his impatience blossomed into a temper? I flashed to that angry man in the parking lot threatening to stab me with a pool cue.

Zoe dealt again. This time Jeremiah got the ace of spades.

He rubbed his scar with a wicked smirk. The charm was fading from his eyes, that twinkling glitter of amusement replaced now by a bristling impatience. "I think you better let me cut that deck this time, little lady."

"Be my guest," Zoe said. "But first, your dare."

"If you're just gonna ask me about another damn name, I can go ahead and save you some time," Jeremiah said. "The answer is no. I didn't exactly come live out here for the company, you hear?"

This was wrong. Jeremiah was so obviously not the Bones Hollow Hunter. He was just a man being harassed by the three girls he'd offered to help. He'd probably never offer to help anyone again because of us.

"Let me cut that deck now," he repeated, sterner this time. It was a demand not a request.

Zoe handed him the cards. He split them into two piles and then moved the bottom half to the top. Zoe dealt us each another card. Once again, Jeremiah drew the highest.

His laugh was without amusement, bitter and full of scorn. He wagged his finger. "I don't know how you're doing it, sunshine, but I know you're playing me."

"Are you always this suspicious?" Zoe asked.

His smile vanished. "Women like you have only ever proven me to be right." He tapped his finger on the table. "That was your dare. Hit me again now."

Another high card for Jeremiah.

His cheeks reddened, steam rising to the top. "Tell me how you're doing that."

"Doing what?"

"Don't play coy with me, little girl. You're in my house. You tell me right now."

I'd known this was going to happen. She was going to piss him off and it'd all go south. Goddamn it, Zoe, why couldn't you just listen to me one time! Jeremiah was right to suspect her of foul play. She'd gone through a huge magician phase as a child, obsessed with learning every card trick she could. While Zoe had outgrown this passion, she still whipped out her tricks at parties and bars. She could sleight of hand Jeremiah to death. And I knew that was exactly what she planned to do.

Any minute now, Jeremiah would snap. He looked more than ready, a boil about to burst.

"Hey now," I cut in, clearing my throat, so anxious I could cry but trying to maintain the illusion of calm. "How's about another drink, huh?"

Jeremiah grimaced, eyes stone cold. Every hint of his Southern charm was gone now. He stared at the ground for a long minute, like he was trying to weigh his response. Then finally, with a stiff head nod he gave me permission to distribute more moonshine. I poured us each another shot.

"More," he said, voice a growl.

I poured him another fingerful.

"Not just me."

My hand shook slightly as I added more to the rest of our glasses.

"Drink." His pale green eyes, no longer aimed at the ground but straight at me, looked mean.

We each knocked it back. It was somehow even more wretched the second time. Jeremiah watched us before drinking his, then sipped it down like a cool cup of water.

"I don't like fancy tricks, you hear?" He wiped his lips with the back of his hand. "None of that funny business, now. I'm not about that."

"No funny business here," Zoe said. "Do you want to shuffle?"

"No!" It came out like a wolf snapping his jaws. "No more cards. I'm done playing."

I flinched at the bark of his voice. Stef tensed, but her eyes shimmered with excitement. One look at Zoe told me everything I needed to know. Jeremiah might have been done playing, but she was not.

eight

"There's another detail that supports my theory," Detective Leeroy Bennett told the podcast. *"Another reason I suspect they were held in a separate location. Autopsies showed that the victims were all menstruating at their time of death. There's no way that's a coincidence. So then how did the Bones Hollow Hunter target women on their period?"*

When we'd first listened to this episode, I'd envisioned a hunter in the forest, nose tilted to the air, catching a whiff of blood. A shark picking up the scent of a single droplet of blood in over a million droplets of ocean water. A predator stalking his prey.

But Zoe had a different theory. She pictured a friendly fellow backpacker, someone who lured you close. "Not Lars, obviously; he looked too crazy. Someone charismatic, charming." Hers was a far more sinister hypothesis, one that I couldn't bring myself to fully imagine. Not because it was difficult to believe. But because it was the sort of killer Zoe would have convinced me to trust. She was always cozying up to strangers on our travels, and because of her, so were we.

"The simple answer," the detective said, *"is that he didn't. Which proves that he must have held these women at a separate location—tormenting them in the most unimaginable ways, judging by their wounds—long enough for them to go through their cycle. And when her monthly bleed came, that's when he took her life."*

This segment of the podcast replayed on the tape deck of torture in my brain as I squirmed on the deerskin couch now. I wondered about the lie we'd just told, the imagined blood between my legs. I couldn't meet Jeremiah's gaze, which still blazed with fury. He breathed a little too heavy now, jaws clenched, a blue-green vein in his temple throbbing. He looked like he was straining to hold something inside of himself back.

Silence lingered in the room like an affliction. The mixtape somehow did nothing to ease the pain, but only amplified it tenfold. Our human silence felt so stark in contrast to the faded, almost jaunty sound of Simon & Garfunkel's "Mrs. Robinson."

"You know what, you're right," Zoe said. "You've got me. It was just a card trick. I'm sorry."

Holy shit, did Zoe just say she was sorry?

I felt my chest lighten. Maybe I'd been wrong. Maybe she'd finally come to her senses. Maybe she'd finally decided to stop. Maybe it could all still be okay! Warmed by the liquor, a smile spread across my cheeks.

Jeremiah sucked his fang-like tooth. "Show me how you did it."

"No can do, my man." She shook her head. "It's against the magician's code."

"Then what the fuck you tellin' me for?" He stood back from his seat, so aggressive the chair toppled to its side. I clenched my thighs together to hide the tremble in my legs.

"So that you know you're right."

"You can't tell a man what he already knows. This is bullshit." Jeremiah snatched the bottle like he might just club her with it. My breath caught in my throat. I only exhaled once he tipped the liquor to his lips. Then, to my surprise, he extended the bottle to me. "I get what you were saying about her earlier. This one's a real snake in the grass."

Zoe's and Stefanie's heads both snapped to me. My cheeks grew hot. "Um . . . that's not what I said."

"So, what *did* you say, Dora?" Zoe's smile was stiff.

"I know the three of you ain't kin, she told me that much." Jeremiah sounded a little too proud. He shook the bottle at me, liquor sloshing inside, but I didn't take it. I longed for a shell that I could recoil into. "Said y'all met in school, isn't that right?"

"That's only because our mothers were estranged, so we'd never met until then," Zoe said, always so quick on her feet, too quick. "We didn't even know we were related for that whole first year. Once we found out, it was huge news. A national network even wanted to do a reality TV show about us. But it was my mom who turned it down. Dora's and Nora's parents still haven't forgiven her; to be honest, it's caused a bit of a rift."

I snatched the bottle from Jeremiah. The clear liquor poured down my throat too fast and I spluttered, but immediately took another gulp all the same. My empty stomach sizzled as it hit, my throat burning. I should've known better than to think Zoe had come to her senses. She was a daredevil riding a barrel over a waterfall and she'd take us both down with her.

"You guys know I'm a terrible liar," I said, passing Stef the bottle. "Why keep this up?"

Zoe kicked my boot. "I think you've had enough to drink, *cuz.*"

"What?" I said, feeling loose in both tongue and spirit. "I'm sick of your shit today. We wouldn't even be in this mess if it weren't for you."

"Hey, come on, that's not fair," Stefanie said, forever the peacemaker. I'd always thought she was the sweetheart of our group; I'd never realized until now how annoying it could be. "She didn't make me twist my ankle. This isn't her fault."

"But she's the one who said there was a waterfall. She's the one who said there was an access road. Jeremiah told me; there's no road nearby. She's been wrong about everything, Stef."

"Because you could've done so much better navigating this trip." Zoe raised her eyebrows.

"Actually, yeah, I could have. I'd have used a GPS for a start."

She rolled her eyes. "That's not real navigating."

"It's your desperate need to be a self-taught expert on every subject that's the problem. There's nothing wrong with using a GPS."

"Ha, is that so?" Zoe sucked her tooth now. She looked just like Jeremiah. "You want the truth? If you'd really wanted the GPS, you would have brought one. No one stopped you from buying it. The *truth* is, you love when I take the lead. That way you don't have to accept responsibility for a single decision in your life. Whatever goes good or bad, it's all laid at my feet. You have no agency. And quite frankly, it's exhausting always being your scapegoat."

"Okay," Stef intervened, arms stretched between us, "let's all just take a breath."

Jeremiah grabbed the bottle from her. "Nah, now, sugar, these two need to duke it out. Leave them to their business." He spun on his heels, singing along to Simon & Garfunkel's merry chorus.

I kept my eyes trained on Zoe. "Okay, so that's what you think of *me*. If *I'm* such a blind follower, then what do you call Stefanie?"

"Hey!" Stef whirled on me. "What the hell? Don't bring me into this."

"Why not? You always have your head so far up her ass it's sometimes hard to tell the two of you apart." I didn't know where this was coming from, but it felt good.

"That's not fair," Stef said, wounded. "Really uncalled for, Jade."

Jeremiah's laugh sounded eerily like a wolf howl. "Jade." He pointed to me. "Stefanie." He pointed to her. He switched his eyes to Zoe. "So then who am I missin'?"

She jutted out her chin. "Your mother, by the looks of this place."

"That tongue of yours is too sharp for your own good." Jeremiah's hungry smile stretched from ear to ear. He wagged his finger. "One day . . . it's gonna get you into trouble."

Zoe's hand went to her pocket, and I almost felt the metal weight of Ripley pressed into her palm as if it were my own. "Maybe," she said, cool as the waterfall we'd never reach. "One day. Far from now. But not today."

Jeremiah and Zoe stared into each other's eyes for far too long. Stef and I remained frozen. Every muscle in my body tensed. Sweat sprouted along my brow, trickling down the side of my face, but I was too anxious to swipe it away. Too anxious to breathe, let alone move a solitary finger.

Jeremiah broke the standoff suddenly. He twirled around to the music, smiling again. As if nothing had ever happened. His green eyes twinkled with unsettling glee. It was her that he looked at, but me he spoke to. "I don't know how someone as lovely as you can keep such poor company, Miss Jade. I think you'd do well to get yourself some better friends."

"I've been giving you such a hard time, Jerry," Zoe relented, softening now. "I'm sorry."

There it was again, an apology! But I knew better than to believe it was sincere this time.

"I've never done this for anybody. But I'll tell you my card trick, okay? Peace offering. Yeah?"

Jeremiah swayed his hips to the new song, "Bennie and the Jets." "Go on then."

Stef and I had never seen her explain a single card trick. Not to us, not to anyone. My mouth almost dropped when she reshuffled the deck and began to demonstrate. Stefanie and I exchanged a quick glance, equal parts shock and joy, before returning our eager eyes back to her.

"I palmed the high cards and then I did what they call a top change when you weren't looking." As she spoke, she shuffled and then showed us the ace of spades.

"I was always looking."

"Everyone thinks that. The number one trick up a magician's sleeve is misdirection." She dealt three cards and then showed us the ace was on top.

Jeremiah rubbed his scar. Then he looked right at me. "Oh, she's a snake in the grass, all right. Just like you said."

What was he trying to do? My friends' postures stiffened. "I really didn't say that," I told them. But they wouldn't look at me. Stef's lips remained pursed with suspicion; Zoe's teeth on edge.

"Anyway," Zoe said, placing the deck on the table, "no more card tricks. Let's start fresh. Drink?" She lifted the bottle but didn't pour anything until he'd nodded his permission. "You weren't kidding about this moonshine; best I've ever had." She didn't refill my glass, instead leaving the bottle on the table for me to pour my own.

A sour uneasiness swirled in my belly. My hand trembled as I sloshed the moonshine into my cup. I stared imploringly at Stef, praying for that sweet peacemaker side of her to come back out, but she wouldn't even glance my way. The tension building up between us was unbearable. Not just from our argument moments ago, but now from Jeremiah shit-stirring, too. It was fine when they talked about me behind my back, but God forbid I say a word about them not in their presence. They shouldn't have left me behind! Even as self-righteous as I felt, I wanted him to piss off back to the kitchen so that I could explain. So that we could resolve our conversation. I hated when we fought. I hated even more that *he* got the apology that should have been meant for me.

Zoe picked up his chair for him, urged him to sit back down. Once he had, she returned to the couch and poured him another shot. "My name's Zoe."

He rubbed his scar. "Zoe."

"Sorry for lying. But try to see it from our perspective. Lone guy, cabin in the woods. A girl can't be too careful, right?" Now that everyone's glass was full, she lifted hers as a toast. "To Jeremiah. For taking us in."

Relief settled into my shoulders, loosening my nerves. I felt cautiously optimistic now. Zoe's charm was working, seeping into his skin whether he liked it or not. We might still manage to avoid disaster yet.

My friend touched her glass to his. "Our knight in shining armor."

Careful, Zo . . .

I cut in, before she could go too far, "Really, we appreciate this so much. Thank you."

The four of us drank.

"What time is it?" I asked. "Shouldn't be much longer before the ranger gets here, don't you think?"

"Oh, you're not in such a rush to be free of me now, are you?" Jeremiah said, with a charismatic smile. "We were all just now finally starting to get along."

"Of course," I said. "That's not what I meant. I just meant, we'll get out of your hair soon. You sounded busy when we came in. Chopping something?"

"Just a little project downstairs. Nothing that can't wait."

I felt my friends' eyes light up before I saw them. The flash of intrigue in their minds.

He had a basement.

"We've got plenty of time left here together now, sunshine, don't you worry."

I closed my eyes, but I could still see Zoe's deadly smile imprinted on the inside of my eyelids like sunspots.

"Perfect," she said.

nine

"So, there's a basement?" Zoe asked.

I knew she wouldn't be able to help herself. It was impossible to dream, even for an instant, that she would let that comment float on by.

"That's impressive. Did you dig that yourself?"

"No, of course not," Jeremiah said, amused. "I didn't build any part of this cabin."

"Except for all this beautiful furniture, right? I don't know which I find more impressive," Zoe said, hungry-eyed, eager. "Your handiwork or your book collection. How on earth did you get all these books out here? I couldn't even find space in my bag for a notebook."

She stole my line.

"Who says everything in this cabin is mine?" Jeremiah picked a tooth with his index finger and then inspected it. "I don't stay here year-round. I come and go."

I told her! Zoe was wrong again. I restrained myself from giving her a self-righteous look. No matter how much she deserved one. The man didn't live here year-round. Which meant that nobody knew how many people came and went in his absence. The box of jewelry could have been left by anyone. The trunk of clothes might be nothing more than miscellaneous items forgotten by travelers over the years.

Though that didn't explain the padlock, this felt like a moot point. Because the padlock could have been left by anyone, too.

"What about that, Jerry?" Stefanie gestured to the unstrung bow hung on the wall. "Is that beauty yours?" I hated when she tried to emulate Zoe. It was like watching her squeeze into a dress that didn't quite fit.

A sly smirk lifted one of Jeremiah's cheeks. "It belongs to the cabin."

"So, I guess that means you have a real life you go back to from here?" Zoe asked. "I find that hard to picture somehow. You strike me as a live-off-the-land kind of guy. You must be miserable back in the real world."

Jeremiah looked pensive. "This here, *this* is the real world. It's back there that's fake."

"I get that." She nodded. "I'm happiest when I'm traveling. I feel like it's when I'm my truest self."

She was being earnest now. It was one of the reasons we all loved traveling. It'd always been one of our core bonding points. Now all I could think was: If what I'd seen today was Zoe's truest self, maybe me and my best friend had less in common than I'd thought.

"How long have you been hunting?" Zoe asked.

"Since I was six."

"Six!" Stef exclaimed. "Seems awfully young."

Jeremiah shrugged. "Not in our family. Only time my old man ever talked to me was when I had a gun in my hands. Hunting trips were how he bonded. If you could call it that."

"Traditional male connection at its best," Zoe said.

"Sounds kind of fucked up," Stefanie remarked. "No offense."

"Wasn't the worst of it." He rubbed his scar slowly now, dragging his thumb down it like a teardrop. "My old man was what you might call a troubled soul . . . Not half as bad as my mama." Jeremiah made eye contact with me now. Why me? Heat flooded my cheeks. "But I don't like to talk about them."

"So, do you have siblings?" Zoe asked. "Or were you an only child?"

Jeremiah's jaw clenched. "You ask a lot of questions, darlin'."

"It's the booze," she said with a rosy smile. "It's gone right to my head. Empty stomach."

Just as I had predicted.

"Do you have anything to eat? I'd hate to put you out any more than we already have. You said the ranger is gonna be a while yet, and if you don't want me chewing your ear off . . . food would help."

Jeremiah stared at her for a moment, like he was sizing her up. His lip quivered. Then he stood abruptly. When he spoke, it was with all the charm of a salesman. "You girls better not be vegetarians. Don't go breakin' my heart."

"Definitely not," she assured him. "We love meat. Especially Stef." She elbowed our friend in the ribs.

"Is that right, now?" Jeremiah smirked. "Well, I've got some jerky just for you. My own special catch."

Chunks of flesh had been removed from the bodies, I heard

Laurie Wolff say. Except she'd never said that in the podcast. That was something my sick brain had come up with just now. Planted there, no doubt, by this ridiculous notion that Jeremiah was the Bones Hollow Hunter. Because we, of all people, just so happened to randomly stumble upon him in our hour of need in the middle of the wilderness. Yeah, right.

Still, my hunger had morphed into a rancid, sour queasiness. I couldn't help but ask, "What kind of meat?"

Jeremiah started to roll another cigarette. His third in what seemed to be about an hour and a half, though it was hard to tell exactly how much time had passed. The sunlight outside still only trickled through the boarded-up windows in tiny golden strands. I wondered if I'd even be able to tell the difference inside when it went dark. I hoped not to find out.

"Let me guess," Zoe said. "Something impressive. A bear?"

He lit his cigarette before answering, pulling deep. Smoke rose from his nostrils like steam from a geyser. "She's in my kitchen. Wanna see?"

"She?" Stefanie asked, her voice small.

"Oh yeah," Jeremiah said. "I only eat females. They just taste so much better."

My throat suddenly felt so dry I could choke. *Florence Marsh, Florence Marsh, Florence Marsh* played on a paranoid loop in my brain.

Jeremiah let the silence linger for far too long. When he finally spoke, it was to Zoe, his voice sweet as a toothache, that Southern drawl sickly smooth like molasses on a hot summer's day. "Why don't you come with me and see, sweetheart? Your friends can wait here."

Even if Zoe didn't suspect this man of being a serial killer, she knew better than to follow him into the kitchen to see this mysterious kill. Obviously, she would say no. Any sensible person would say no.

My sweet Little Savages, it is with great sadness that we report Zoe was not, in fact, a sensible person.

"Sure," Zoe said.

"I'll come, too," Stefanie added, a little too quickly.

Goddamn it, I couldn't let them go alone. The three of us were in this together.

"Great." I sighed, reluctant, on edge, a pound of stress and fear weighing down my chest. "I guess we'll all go."

As I followed my friends into the kitchen, my heart beat double time. Laurie Wolff's smug, husky voice whispered on repeat, *Florence Marsh, Florence Marsh, Florence Marsh.*

ten

Zoe and Stef pushed through the kitchen door first. Jeremiah trailed behind us and I could almost feel his smile. We strode into the galley kitchen and the first thing I noticed were the flies. Buzzing everywhere, so loud my ears hummed. A dark mass of them collected against a dirt-shrouded window above the sink. They swarmed against the glass, desperate to escape. Like they knew something I didn't.

The long wooden counter to the left was cluttered with animal parts. Skins, pelts, claws, teeth, spinal columns dangling beneath the mounted cupboards like wind chimes. Scattered between it all was a small hotplate and an assortment of knives. Straight knives, curved knives, tiny boning knives . . . The butcher's cleaver by the deep metal sink had not yet been cleaned and flies buzzed on its red-smeared surface. I shivered.

Zoe saw the body first and gasped.

The animal carcass was so enormous that everything else in the room faded into a hazy background. All I could see were those razor-sharp claws scraping the ground. They dripped from colossal paws that dangled over the sides of the kitchen table. The table was swallowed by the body's enormity, everything dwarfed by its presence. Even the two chairs looked like tiny toys.

"A cougar," I breathed. Of course it was. Did I really expect to find Florence Marsh spread across his kitchen table? Still, the relief I should have felt never came. There was a tightness in my chest, a tension that wouldn't release.

"That's right," Jeremiah told me, standing so close behind that I could feel his breath in my hair. "Caught her just a few hours before you angels waltzed in here."

I stared, motionless. This was probably the same cougar whose tracks we'd followed. *This* was the image that had haunted my dreams while on the trail, that had plagued my thoughts throughout our hike. Now look at her.

This once fearsome beast sagged over the round table like a Salvador Dalí painting, drooping, a melted husk. She'd been stripped of her regal, terrifying aura, reduced to nothing more than a lump on some man's table. Waiting to be skinned and dismembered and separated into parts on his kitchen counter, then sold off to strangers on the internet. An overwhelming sadness hit my stomach as I stared into her dead black eyes.

"Holy shit." Zoe walked forward slowly, like it might spring off the table.

Jeremiah's shoulder brushed mine now, no longer behind me but directly by my side. He looked pleased by the awe on Zoe's face. This was the reaction he'd wanted. Zoe turned to him before reaching out to touch the cougar's fur. Her fingers spread across the big cat's shoulder.

"Wow." Her eyes were wide with wonder.

Stefanie limped to the table, giggling, still drunk. She stroked the cougar's side. "It's so soft," she whimpered, bottom lip pouting. "Poor kitty."

I remained farther back, frozen. Jeremiah was at my side, between me and the kitchen sink where the flies buzzed and cluttered. He knocked arms with me now, almost grabbing my hand but not quite. When he spoke, he leaned in close, and his whisper rustled to me like leaves across a gravel road. "What do you think, Miss Jade? Not a bad catch for Captain Cowboy, huh?"

My heart clenched. Shit. He'd heard us talking before.

Which meant he'd almost certainly heard us talking every time he'd left the room.

I felt the tension in his body as if it was my own. Again, I flashed to the pool cue threatening me in the parking lot. This time in my mind, the man had snapped it in two already, both ends sharpened like a stake. My eyes fixated on the butcher's knife gleaming on the kitchen counter. The sticky blood, gooey and thick, dripping from its edge.

Beads of sweat sprouted from my head to my toe, trickling down my thighs. I was too scared to shift away from him, like he was a rattlesnake that would strike at any movement. His one arm remained touching mine, and with his other, he gestured at the slain beast draped over his table. "Take your pick," he said to Zoe, as if he was perfectly content and nothing was wrong. "Whatever piece you like. I'll carve it out for you myself. A claw, a tooth—hell, even an eye. Whatever you want. It's on the house. A little souvenir to remember me by. If you felt like waiting a few hours, I could clean off some of the bones. But that'll take some workin'."

For one delicious moment, Zoe was speechless. Not so quick on her feet for a change.

The once regal queen of the forest stared with glassy dead eyes. Her tongue lolled out of an open mouth, impotent fangs on display.

"You said that you liked my work." Jeremiah looked at her when he spoke, but his smile seemed meant for me. He tapped my palm with his index finger, lightly, taunting me. Every muscle in my body shivered with tension. "Thought you'd appreciate one hot off the press. Or would you rather just taste her meat? I got some jerky drying now. Won't be ready yet, but I could roast it over a fire if you wanted a bite."

"That's so cool, Jerry," Zoe said, eyes drifting all around the room now. She scanned the shelves of the tall kitchen hutch in the corner, riddled with animal parts and pelts. No drying jerky in sight. But that's not what she was searching for. "Thank you. Um, you know." She stared a beat too long at the dusty brown rope rug in the corner. "Let me put some thought into this." If she took one look at my face, she'd have realized something was wrong. But she was too busy looking for a cellar door, too busy running her fingers through a dead cougar's fur.

"How about the tooth?" Jeremiah suggested. "A classic souvenir."

Of all the things for him to suggest . . .

Zoe's fingers stopped stroking. Her eyebrow twitched. She glanced at Stef, just briefly. I knew what those two were thinking before she was stupid enough to say anything. "You know the Bones Hollow Hunter took the teeth."

She tried to sound nonchalant, but it didn't matter how relaxed her tone was. Jeremiah was onto her game. Bitterness oozed from his rigid body, so strong I could taste it.

Look up, look up! Look up, you fucking idiot. Look at my face! If she would just make eye contact with me!

But Zoe was a dog with a bone. "You've been out here a long time, off and on. C'mon, you must have seen a few things . . . have a few theories."

"Yeah, Jerry," Stef said, still drunk and giggly, "give us the inside scoop."

She pulled out her camera to take a picture of the dead cougar. Zoe crouched, pressing her face to the big cat's, posing with her tongue out. Then the two of them examined the photograph before Zoe decided that she wanted another, this time, tongue in. Stef let loose her straight black hair from its ponytail to take a turn posing. Her normally photogenic features—high cheekbones, pouty lips—looked monstrous somehow, pressed to the dead cougar's fur.

I watched them, my teeth clenched, chattering with both rage and fear. Jeremiah's skin burned against mine. The heat traveled up my arm, up my neck, down my throat, scorching my insides until I felt like I could scream. I was a frog in the boiling pot. We all were. How could my friends not see? He stood next to me, smiling ear to ear, eyes sharp and hungry. Every one of his teeth glistened.

The better to eat you with, my dear.

"Now, why you gotta do that?" Jeremiah's impossibly square jaw quivered with tension, his smile fixed. "Why you gotta bring up something so nasty?"

Finally, Zoe clocked Jeremiah's face, the severity of his tight grin. She tried to brush it off. "Just making conversation," she said. "Didn't mean anything by it." But as she spoke, her eyes flitted to the rope rug in the corner of the room. Big enough to cover a trapdoor to the cellar? "Say, I think I need another drink. Would you mind grabbing the bottle for us, Jerry?"

Jeremiah's ravenous smile twitched. "Why do I get the feeling that you just want me to leave this room?" He cut her off before she could speak. The charm left his voice more with every syllable, like it was being drained from a cup. "You've already searched near every damn inch of this place. And I think I've been more than tolerant, wouldn't you say?"

When none of us answered, Jeremiah shouted it. "Wouldn't you say!"

I flinched as his arm knocked harder into mine. I wanted to move away, but I couldn't. I held my breath to stop myself from crying.

"Yes." Zoe's voice sounded shockingly meek. I'd never heard her sound so small. She tried her trademark put-you-at-ease smile; it didn't fit right. "We haven't—"

Jeremiah cut her off again, but this time with the whip of his glare. "Don't insult me, little girl," he said finally. "I told you how I feel about fancy tricks. You promised me no more. So why don't you go ahead and be straight with me now." The charm had returned suddenly, as if it'd never even gone. "Tell me what you want, sweet pea."

"Okay, fine." Zoe squared her shoulders, dropping her smile. "Let's cut the bullshit. Stef, record this."

Stefanie's hands quivered in their eagerness to be useful, her eyes hungry to join in the fray. She held up her phone like some sort of shield that could protect her. Bold, brave. Easy when she stood across the room from him. Jeremiah's elbow felt like a blade pressed to me, a looming threat.

"Where were you in May 2011?" Zoe asked.

"Can't remember." Jeremiah smiled.

"Were you at the cabin in June 2012?"

"I don't recall." He swiped his tongue across the top of his teeth slowly, lip curled into a snarl. "Sounds an awful lot like you're suspecting me of something. Thought I told you I don't take kindly to accusations."

Zoe moved away from the cougar, stepping around the side of the table, toward him. Toward us. She made eye contact with me now for the first time, just fleeting. Yes! Finally! She clocked the panic on my face and stuffed one hand into her pocket. I tried to draw comfort from the steel knife I knew her fingers touched.

"A man found at this cabin was questioned in relation to Rae Fischer's murder in 2017," she said. "Do you know anything about that?"

Wait, what? That had never been in the podcast. But before I had time to process what she'd said, Jeremiah grabbed my wrist hard, like he'd slapped me with a metal shackle.

"What you got in that pocket, sweetheart?" He spoke to Zoe like she was a toddler. A little girl with a toy to show her daddy. "Are you gonna pull a knife on me?"

"Not if I don't have to," she replied coolly.

"Why would you have to? Here I was thinking I've been nothing but nice to you ladies, the picture of hospitality." Jeremiah tightened his grip on me. "You're the ones who've been sniffing through my cabin like dirty little rats, scrounging for cheese. Spitting in the face of my good nature." He ran a tongue over his fang-like teeth. "I'm not always such a patient man. Any other day and I might not have dealt with you thieves so cordially."

"Thieves?" I said, desperate. If Zoe wasn't going to defuse

this situation, then I had to try. "I'm sorry, sir"—Zoe scoffed at this—"for how we've behaved. You're totally right. You've been nothing but nice and we've taken advantage and I'm sorry. But I promise you, we haven't stolen anything." I tried gently to tug my wrist away from his vise grip, but he was too strong. "We're sorry, okay?"

"Stop apologizing," Zoe snapped. "Especially not to this monster."

"These vile little creatures don't deserve you for a friend, Miss Jade," Jeremiah said. "I know for a fact that lanky bitch has something in her pocket."

Goddamn it, Stef, what did you take?

"Something that does not belong to her," he continued, "and I'll be having it back."

"It doesn't belong to you, either," Stefanie said, fearless behind her phone. "I'm taking these to the police so that the victims' families can identify them."

The jewelry. She'd taken the jewelry tin. Damn it, weren't the pictures enough?

Jade's friends had graduated from idiotic sleuths to moronic thieves hell-bent on self-destruction.

"Now you're going to tell us what we want to know," Zoe said, pulling her knife out for him to see, flicking the blade open.

Great. Now she was adding assault with a deadly weapon to our list of crimes.

Jeremiah leaned in close to my ear. "Your snaky little friend here just threatened me with a knife. Can you believe that?" He squeezed my wrist so tight I thought it might snap. I yelped.

"She'll put the knife away, okay? Zoe, just put it down," I pleaded, no longer grateful for Ripley's presence. "Please, just let go of my wrist. You're hurting me."

Zoe moved forward a step. “No more lies.”

“You’re calling *me* a liar?” Jeremiah spat the words. His voice low and mean, like a predator’s growl. He picked up the bloody cleaver from the counter. I shrieked. “Quiet!” he barked, still holding me tight. “All you women done since you walked through that door is lie.”

He pointed the cleaver at Zoe like an arrow. “You want truth, now? That’s what you came here for?”

“Yes,” Zoe said. Her voice was firm, but fear leaked through her hazel eyes.

“The truth,” he laughed the word, “is you don’t know how lucky you are.” My whole body trembled as he spoke, my eyes fixed on the blood dripping from the butcher’s knife. *Splat* onto the wood floor. “You’re lucky it’s me that was here and not someone else that answered that door. Lucky,” he jerked me over to the sink counter, “that it’s me teachin’ you girls a lesson today, because believe me it could be so much worse.” He slammed my palm down flat onto the countertop, fingers spread wide. I was his puppet. Trapped inside my own skull, I had no control. “The *truth* is you don’t know how good you got it today. Because, lucky for you, I have a sense of control.”

He whacked the cleaver down onto the counter and the three of us screamed in unison. I squeezed my eyes shut, waiting for the pain. I looked to find the cleaver had connected with the wood and not my hand. The blade had come just an inch shy of my skin. Tears gushed down my cheeks.

“Leave her alone!” Zoe charged forward, blade aimed at his belly.

“Don’t you take one more step!” He uprooted the blade from the wood and waved it at her, hacking at the air. “Get back!”

Zoe inched backward, knife still quivering in her fist at waist height.

"That's it, sunshine. Just like that. Good girl." Jeremiah smiled ear to ear, his expression wild. "Not so tough now, isn't that right? I been telling you, someone's gonna get hurt with all these games you like to play."

Jeremiah didn't break eye contact with her. His stare bore into Zoe's face as he smacked the bloody cleaver back down onto the wooden counter again. This time, he chopped it onto my fingertip. The dirty blade hacked through my bone. The top knuckle of my left ring finger popped off like a carrot top.

I screamed before the pain came. For a few seconds, it didn't hit me. Then it exploded, flaming through my finger, scorching my whole hand. Gushing hot just like the blood from my severed fingertip.

I could hardly hear anything but the sound of my own guttural terror, but I thought I heard him say one word. "Oops."

Blood surged, pouring down my hand, running down my arm. Jeremiah snatched a grubby blue dish towel draped over the faucet. With his teeth, he ripped a strip off and wrapped it around the bloodied nub, tying it off around the second knuckle. "There we go, nice and tight, baby girl; you'll be all right. Don't you worry now."

He did it all so fast, I was still screaming, my cries ripping my throat raw. Stef was sobbing, howling in wide-eyed horror, hands to her cheeks. Zoe stood dead silent only a foot away, mouth open, face gray, frozen in shock. Blood flooded through the blue dish towel, darkening it, then reddening. Bone-throbbing agony stabbed through my hand, pulsing up my arm, radiating through me like the gasping, choking, screeching that rattled my body.

"Quiet now," he said, but I couldn't stop wailing. "Quiet!" His voice thundered over my screams, silencing me, Stef, too. "That's better. Now, you probably won't believe that I didn't mean to do that."

Tears and sweat and confusion swirled, melding together. Was he laughing? I couldn't think straight, let alone listen to his words. I couldn't breathe. I couldn't breathe!

"That didn't have to happen. There didn't need to be any bloodshed." He looked to Zoe, rage twisting his mouth. "I was trying . . . This is *your* fault! If you hadn't come at me, I'd never have— I didn't want to!" Jeremiah spat at her shoe.

"Keep recording," Zoe barked.

Then she rushed him, knife stretched out in front of her, slashing at the air as she charged. Jeremiah threw me aside like I was weightless. My head cracked on the counter. I collapsed to the floor. My eyelids fluttered and then shut to the sounds of Zoe's screams.

eleven

"Wake up!" Stefanie patted my cheeks, again and again, shaking my shoulders. "Please, Jade, wake up!"

I opened my eyes. I was in my mother's upstairs bathroom and Zoe was holding back my hair as I puked into the bowl. Stef patted my face with a cool washcloth. Wait, no.

"Wake up, wake up! Oh my god, are you okay! Can you hear me? Jade! Jade!"

My vision focused. Dark, musty log cabin walls came into view. A single naked bulb dangling from an overhead wire. The edge of a wooden countertop, dripping blood. Stef's and Zoe's worried faces hovering over mine. I touched my right hand to a throbbing pain on the side of my skull and blinked at the red-stained fingers I pulled away.

"Jade, oh my god! You're alive!" Stef said.

I eased myself onto my elbows. Jeremiah was gone. Panic swept through me like a gale wind. "Where is he?" I said, terror rising in my chest.

"He left," Stef said.

Pain returned to my finger like a cannonball. It walloped into me, pulsing down through my hand, into my wrist. The blue dish towel was no longer blue. It was bright red, utterly soaked.

"Holy shit," I said, as if only just now remembering. Trauma raged through me, my whole body quaking. "Oh my god, *my finger,* my fucking finger! Look what he did to me!" I'd probably never be able to wear a wedding ring. Or learn to play guitar like I'd always promised myself I would. My hand would be disabled forever. Tears flooded my face like the blood down my arm.

"It's okay," Stef said, though her bottom lip quivered like a little girl's. Her face was ashen, her beautiful chocolate-brown eyes clouded with terror. Days-old mascara stained her cheeks from where she'd wiped her tears away. "I got the tip for you. It's in my pocket. A hospital can totally reattach it. I saw it on a reality ER show once."

My stomach swirled. Hot bile spurted out of my mouth and I puked onto the wooden floor beneath the sink.

Zoe held back my hair, like she had countless times before when I'd been wrapped around a toilet bowl. "It's going to be okay," she said, her voice shuddering with uncertainty. Her dainty nose was split open at the top. Dried and wet blood painted her face and chest.

"What did he do to you? What do you mean 'he left'?" I finally asked, swiping the vomit from my lips with the back of my arm. "Why? Where is he?"

"He left," Stefanie said. "Zoe ran at him with the knife and he punched her in the face, and then turned and left."

Purple bruises crowded Zoe's eyes. I touched my right hand to her cheek but she pulled away. She'd always hated how perfect and elegant her nose was; she'd probably like it more now that it would scar.

"Let's get you patched up, huh?" Zoe's fingers trembled as she pulled the sweaty, matted curls back from my face. "Stef, hand me that dish towel from the counter." She wiped strands of vomit I must've missed from the corner of my lips with the frayed edge of her black shirt, already torn off at the waist. "I think we should wrap this better."

Then she pulled the hair tie from her loose blond ponytail. Pale golden locks kissed her shoulders. The pink streak, now stained red, fell against her bloodied face. Stefanie passed her the blue dish towel—the same one Jeremiah had torn a strip from with his teeth. Maybe flecks of his saliva still graced its edges. I didn't want the cloth anywhere near me, but I had little choice. Zoe folded the towel into as small a square as she could, then pressed it down hard onto my wound. I howled, white-hot pain blazing. With her other hand, Zoe quickly twisted the hair tie tight around my second knuckle like a tourniquet, fastening the new wrap firm to the old, drenched one.

I fell into her embrace, breathing through the agony. Stefanie hugged me from behind.

"Great job," Zoe said. "You're doing good."

"So good, babe," Stef echoed.

"Nothing is good!" A sob burst from me like a scream. Guttural, raw. I wailed into Zoe's shoulder. She cradled my head, rocking me. "He . . . he . . ." I couldn't even say the words again. I closed my eyes and buried my face into her, red blotches painting my vision. I cried until my throat burned.

"I know," Zoe repeated over and over, as she petted my hair and Stef rubbed circles on my back. "I know. But it's going to be okay. We're going to get out of here. And he is going to *pay.*"

After a minute, Zoe gently cupped both my puffy, tear-blotched cheeks and pried my face from her. Her hazel eyes shined bright like stars, staring deep into mine. All trace of trembling and uncertainty had vanished from her now. Zoe had recovered her resolve, her sense of leadership. When she spoke again, her voice was strong, rallying. "Look, he's gone for now. But I doubt he's left the cabin, and I have no doubt at all that he's going to come back. And probably with that bow. We need to act fast. We should barricade the kitchen door so he can't get back in. It'll buy us time."

"Time for what?" I demanded. "We have nowhere to go! We're trapped!"

"Don't worry. Everything's going to be fine." Zoe's mantra. Our fearless leader. "We're going to get out of here. Don't worry."

Desperate for reassurance, I let her words comfort me, like I had so many times before. Zoe might have gotten us into this mess, but she was the only one I could trust to get us out. She was our rock.

I sucked in another deep breath, feeling mildly calmer now. I swiped snot away with the back of my arm, sniffling. "The more you tell me not to worry, the more worried I am." I tried a weak smile.

A smirk flickered on the corner of her lips as she brushed a tear from my cheek with her knuckle. "I know."

"How about that for the door?" Stefanie pointed to the tall hutch against the wall. She hobbled to the furniture's side and tried hefting it with her shoulder. But she couldn't get purchase without putting weight on her ankle. She yelped, attempting it anyway. "God, it's heavy as a bitch. I'm gonna need some help."

Zoe was quick to her feet, right by her side. Dizzy, head throbbing, fingertip searing, I scrambled upright. Together, we struggled to pull the tall wooden hutch away from the wall. The bone ashtrays and skull bowls skittered from its shelves. Fire, fresh and angry, blazed through my hand. I roared in agony, but I fought through the pain. My friends needed me to.

It took all our combined strength to shuffle the hutch around the kitchen table where the cougar still drooped with dead eyes and lolling tongue. Heads down, sweating and grunting and growling with exertion, the three of us plowed into the hutch until it was finally wedged all the way against the kitchen door.

Drenched with sweat, trying to catch a breath, I collapsed against the wooden frame. "Okay," I exhaled the word. "What now? How are we going to get out?"

"There's a window." Stef pointed to the mass of flies on the glass pane above the sink. It was just big enough to imagine wriggling through.

To do that, we'd have to climb atop the counter. The same bloody counter where, tangled among the other animal parts, my severed fingertip had just been. My stomach roiled at the thought and I tried to push the memory away. The sight of the cleaver soaring down. I buried the image deep inside of myself. I had to focus. Escape was our only goal now; the only thought I had room for in my brain.

"I've got a plan, okay?" Zoe said.

I felt my soul lift. Of course she did. Zoe always had a plan—even when she didn't, she somehow pulled one together.

But any consolation I'd derived from this evaporated with Zoe's next words. "We just need to find the basement."

"What? Why?" I scrambled to my feet. "Please don't tell me you're still thinking about your stupid fucking podcast. I am *done* playing Nancy Drew."

Zoe brushed the bloodied pink hair streak back from her eyes. "Listen, I think I saw some cellar doors when we were in the backyard. Which means there's another exit down there. If there is, then the basement is our best way out."

"That's too many *ifs*. Look around you! Where even is the basement? We have our chance to leave now out this window. We have to take it." I looked to Stefanie, pleading. "*Please!* Talk some sense into her!"

Stef looked back and forth between the two of us, uncertain. "I don't know, Zo, maybe she has a point. . . ."

"Oh, because stuffing your broken ankle through that tiny window seems like the better option?" Zoe marched to the corner of the room behind the dead cougar on the table. She flipped over the rope rug and let out a triumphant battle cry. A hero standing atop her prize, victorious, she stared straight at me. "Well, looky here. If it isn't a hatch door."

"I don't care," I said. "It's too risky. I'm not going down there."

A fist pounded the kitchen door, startling us. The hutch rattled.

"Little pigs, little pigs, let me in!" Jeremiah sang in a voice that would plague our nightmares if we lived long enough to have any.

Zoe flung open the hatch. Its hinges creaked. "I'm going down," she said, hurried but stern. There was a wild, frenzied hunger in her eyes. "You can come with me or stay here with him."

"Hope you didn't miss me too much," Jeremiah said, heavy breath lapping at the door. "Thought I'd give you sweet peas some time to *recuperate.* I promise, I just want to talk with y'all. To say sorry. Why don't you go on and let me in now." Then his voice got husky and low. "There's nowhere to run."

"You don't even know for sure if there's a door down there," I whispered. "He could break into the kitchen and trap us. Let's go out the window."

While you still can, Laurie Wolff purred.

Jeremiah pounded the door so hard I shrieked. "Are you girls talking about me? Does that tall bitch still think I'm handsome?"

"Fuck you!" Stef shouted, though she sounded less bold now.

"The ranger is going to be here soon!" I called through the barricade. "Then you'll be sorry, asshole."

Jeremiah snickered, ghoulish. "Is that right?"

"Would you give up on the fucking ranger already!" Zoe seethed. "When are you going to get it through your head? No one is coming to save us."

"Then who was that we heard on the radio?" I demanded.

"Let me in!" the Big Bad Wolf howled.

"Listen, Stef has the jewelry box, right?" I walked to Zoe. I clutched her hand, pleading. "You've got all your photos. She's got that asshole attacking me on video. Let's just take this to the police and see what they make of it. But let's go out the window. Now."

Tick tock goes the clock, Laurie Wolff sang to me. *Your time is running out.*

Zoe put one hand on top of mine. "Trust me. This is going to work. We're going to go into that basement and find our way out of here. We only have so long before he gets into the kitchen."

She turned back to the hatch door. “Now is our chance. Come on.”

Zoe took the first step down into the darkness. She shined her phone’s flashlight into the entrance, which seemed to me the mouth of an abyss. A cavern that would swallow her whole. Not for the first time, I couldn’t decide if my friend was incredibly brave or impeccably stupid.

Stefanie looked to me, sympathetic, but resolved. “She’s right.” She hobbled toward the hatch door, where Zoe was ready to help her down. “If there’s a way out down here, then it’s the better option. We have to take it.” She sucked in a deep breath, ready to dive in. “Zoe’s never let us down before.”

But I couldn’t help but feel like she was trying to convince herself of this more than me.

“Ooeee!” Jeremiah punched the door. It sounded like a gunshot. “You’d best open up; I’m not gonna wait here all day!”

I looked to the dirt-caked window, to the flies that clustered and struggled to be free. They sent me a message: The window was our best escape. My friends might have lost their minds, taking a risk on a basement door that might not even be there, but it wasn’t too late for me. I could break the glass and escape before Jeremiah made it outside.

Except then where would I go? No map. No compass. Not enough food or water. I’d wander for how long before reaching the Bones Hollow Trail? Even then I would be days away from our car, or shelter, or supplies. And even if I did somehow make it to our car, Zoe had the keys. What were my options?

These were the questions I rattled off in my brain as I followed Stef and Zoe down into the basement. My justification. Good, hard logic. I had no other choice than to follow. But I knew the truth, deep down. These were not the reasons that I let them lead me down into the inky blackness. No matter what, no matter how illogical or suicidal, I would follow my friends. I couldn't leave them behind.

"I'll be seeing you soon, sweethearts," he called. "I'll be seeing you real soon."

twelve

Graduation day surprise. That's what Zoe had announced before she'd driven us to the state park instead of to our high-school graduation. There, she presented us with a joint like it was a holy artifact. She and Stef already smoked occasionally, at parties mostly, but I'd never partaken. Today felt like the perfect day. My initiation into the adult world.

With my head feeling light and airy, Zoe led us into a cave. The tunnels there wove deep into the earth. The perfect location for teenagers to hang out and drink on weekends. Broken bottles and cigarette butts littered the ground of the largest cavern. With only a lighter to guide us, Zoe bravely led us down one of the smaller shafts. We ventured forward slowly, crouching beneath the rocky ceiling, clutching on to one another. A tangible energy surged through our linked hands, from Zoe to Stef, from Stef to me. We were one entity, an unbreakable chain.

Eventually, our crouch turned to a crawl. On all fours, we journeyed deeper into the cave until we crawled on our bellies through the rocky earth.

"Worms," I snickered. "We're like the worms."

I giggled first. But it was Stef's infectious laughter that set us all off. We were an unstoppable force, cackling hysterically into the dark tunnel's silence. The reverberation of our joy echoed back to us and made us laugh harder.

We burrowed deeper. The passageway grew narrower still, so that the rocky walls squeezed my elbows. The blackness was so thick I couldn't see Stef's ankle in front of me. Zoe held the lighter but none of its illumination reached back to me. The cave swallowed it up like a demon. The ceiling shrank closer. Panic set in and spots of color flickered in my vision. I imagined myself wriggling into the mouth of a hungry beast. I was worming my way to death. I was being eaten. I would die here.

Zoe heard my frantic breathing. "I've got you," she'd called back to me. "Follow the sound of my voice." Then she broke out in song. When I realized she was singing "I Will Survive," my panicked breath softened. My gasping turned to a faint chuckle, then to outright laughter. Then Stef started singing along, too.

The tension eased from my chest with every inch forward we crawled, the off-key warble of their chorus somehow the most soothing sound imaginable. I didn't know how Zoe knew that this shaft had an exit, but I trusted that she did. I started singing, too. The tunnel slowly grew wider, the mouth finally opened. Then from around a corner, daylight poured in, kissing my cheeks. I wept then, but with utter joy. I'd been released from the jaws of death. Zoe had led us through the darkness to the other side.

This cellar smelled the same. Dank, earthy, hollow. There was no light down here except for the small white orb projected by Zoe's phone. I smelled the cedarwood walls before I could see them. Moisture leaked through, a cool layer of mold and moss coating the ground, the air, sitting atop my tongue. The damp dirt floor clung at my boots.

The cellar stretched the length of the cabin. I didn't know anything about engineering, but a dozen spiderweb-strangled wooden support beams didn't feel like enough to hold the structure above us. I crouched instinctively, as if shielding the back of my neck could protect me should the cabin collapse. I couldn't hear Jeremiah's footsteps, but I listened keenly, wondering how much of our movements he could hear.

Cobwebs stroked my face, clinging to my hair even after I'd tried swiping them away. A large wooden desk was in the right corner. It held nothing out of the ordinary at first glance, just a handful of carpentry tools. Various pieces of wood that had been sawn and sanded into all sorts of shapes were strewn across the floor. Table legs. Chair backs. Doors. Nothing down here looked abnormal at all.

This was his woodworking shop. Just like he'd said. I imagined him taking stock after the floods each year, scrapping the damage, rebuilding anew. His rustic, self-sufficient lifestyle would be admirable—the kind of eco-friendly existence the three of us often talked about aspiring to—just a shame he was such an asshole, living our dream.

"Take pictures of everything," Zoe ordered.

"What?" A cyclone of anger and terror and confusion swirled

inside of me. "You said we were getting out of here! Let's find the doors."

"We will. But we may as well gather as much evidence as we can while we still have the chance."

"Evidence!" I scoffed. "There is no evidence! There's nothing down here, just like there was nothing in the fucking attic. Enough of this ridiculous fantasy!"

"I think we should tell her," Stef said. "Please. We need to."

"She'll just freak out more."

I felt like I was the last sane person on the planet. My head might explode at any moment. "Tell me what!"

"The forum I told you about." Zoe said it almost offhand, with a sullen eye roll, like some sort of teenager unwilling to meet her mother's scornful gaze. "It was never for the Bones Hollow Trail. It's a citizen detectives' community, devoted to finding the Hunter. Someone unearthed a police report from the case and shared it. A man who called himself Waylon Mitchell was found staying here in the cabin seven years ago, just after the seventh victim, Rae Fischer, was found. He had no form of ID confirming his identity. He was briefly questioned, they never searched the property, and then nothing else came of it. And then *a year later,* Lars Brunner came into the picture when he reported finding Wendy Whitmore's body, and that was just case closed? A whole year went by, and they never properly looked into the one man living in the area. Don't you think that's more than a little suspicious?"

"Are you kidding me?" I couldn't believe this. *That* was her smoking gun? "A man not called Jeremiah was once questioned here and you think that's proof of something? *That's* the reason you're so sure it's him? *That's* why you would rather risk staying to take pictures when there's a finger-chopping maniac upstairs!"

"He obviously gave a fake name. It was Jeremiah they questioned."

"Let's just say it *was* him. It would have been pretty weird if he hadn't been questioned by police at least once. He's been staying off and on in the only cabin remotely near where the victims were found. How do you know the police didn't look into him properly? They obviously didn't deem him a suspect after questioning him. So, if anything, that just proves he's innocent!"

"But that's just it," Zoe insisted. "People online say the cops never followed up to verify his identity—the guy didn't even have ID! And there's no good reason that they wouldn't have searched the cabin; it's public property, police didn't need a warrant. Their whole investigation was obviously a shitshow. This cabin and the man living here should have been investigated properly."

"And these online nerds know all this because they're police officers? They have access to the case files?"

"Some of them, yeah. They're retired. They still have connections in the department. Who knows, if the police hadn't fixated on Lars Brunner, then maybe they would have eventually circled back and actually looked into the cabin thoroughly. But they never did. Most people think that the Hunter let Lars take the fall—others even think that he's the one that hanged him. But the fact of the matter remains that someone was living here at the time of the murders, and they never investigated him properly. Which means, there's strong reason to believe that *he*," Zoe pointed to the ceiling, "is our guy. Especially after what we found, Jade. And the way he attacked you. Come on. Open your eyes."

"Open *my* eyes? You've got such tunnel vision for the Hunter you can't even see straight. Maybe you're right. But you've got yourself so convinced that you won't even *entertain* the idea that you might not be—because God forbid the almighty Zoe is wrong once in her fucking life!—and that's *why* I have to be the one to question you! Just," I took a deep breath, trying to emulate the rational calm that I wanted her to have, "think about this sensibly for a minute. You cannot be so unshakingly certain that this man is a serial killer. The only thing I'm *certain* of is that he's a crazy whack job living in the woods who *you've* pushed too far. As far as he's concerned, we're thieves who attacked him first. You threatened him with a knife for fuck's sake."

"So he chopped off your finger? Yeah, because that's a totally rational thing to do." Zoe pulled at her pale blond hair. "Please, Stef, talk some sense into her because I can't. . . ."

I turned to Stefanie. "I'm not saying he's not a total nutcase. Obviously, he is. But can't you see how stupid you're both being? Serial killer or not, that guy is dangerous and you're down here wasting time playing detective when all of your *evidence* is completely circumstantial. He doesn't even live here all the time. Not only are the things in this house not necessarily his, but it might not even have been *him* that was questioned. The fact that you won't even consider that as a possibility makes me think you're way the fuck off base here, guys."

Even in the dim light, I could see Zoe's pitying expression, like I was a bird with my head in the sand. "Jade."

"Don't give me that look," I said. "I hate when you give me that look. It makes me want to slap you."

"*He's* the one who told us he doesn't live here all the time," Stef said, like she was trying to break it to me gently. Like *I* was the fucking idiot. "Obviously we can't trust anything he says."

Zoe stepped closer to me and touched my shoulder. "I know you're mad at how out of control this has all gotten, and you probably have the right to be."

Probably?

"But we're almost in the clear now. We're going to find our way out in just a minute. But while we're down here, we may as well find the proof that'll put this monster away for life. Just think about it: *We'll* be the ones who caught the Bones Hollow Hunter!"

"How can you still care about that right now?"

"How can you not?" She pulled her hand away and shined her phone light around the cellar. All I could see was woodwork and tools and cobwebs. "Look, if we escape now, whatever evidence might be down here will probably be destroyed by the time the police come back. This is the only opportunity we're ever going to get." Zoe didn't wait for me to respond. She resumed her search, walking along the far wall, scouring objects, taking pictures.

"Come on, Jade." Stef took out her phone. "We can't stop now. Not when we're so close."

The sudden, repetitive flash of Stefanie's camera blinded me. I walked into a dangling chain and pulled at it, turning on a single bulb. The shadows it cast gave me chills.

Stef and Zoe scanned the room for clues, photographing as they went. They moved with ease, as if this new room had gifted them with amnesia about the real danger we faced upstairs. The madman they'd enraged. The lunatic who had maimed me . . . *poof,* forgotten from their minds. Were these even the same girls I'd followed through that cave?

Was I?

Stef tripped on something and yelped. Her ankle was only

going to get worse if she didn't stop. Apparently, this wild goose chase was more important than her health and safety. Zoe was immediately by her side, supporting her. But what use was helping Stef walk when everything else she was doing put her life in jeopardy?

"Enough pictures already. You've got what you wanted. There's nothing here," I said. "We need to find that exit."

I started walking toward the far end of the cellar. Here, the sound of the mixtape still playing upstairs in the living room trickled through. The single bulb's light didn't stretch this far. This corner of the cellar was shrouded in darkness. My phone was still upstairs; unlike Stef and Zoe who had theirs permanently on hand, I'd wanted to unplug for this journey. How tragic that aim seemed now. I must have put it back in my backpack, I decided.

Jade knew deep down that her phone was not in her backpack. It was far more likely that the finger-chopping lunatic had stolen it, for whatever purpose she didn't want to know. Denial was her favorite tonic.

For a smart girl, Jade could be incredibly stupid.

I swallowed the jagged lump in my throat. "I need some light. Over here."

Zoe helped Stefanie limp closer and they waved their phones like magic wands from side to side, narrow searchlights crisscrossing back and forth. I spotted three rotting wooden steps leading up to large double doors. Relief shuddered through me. There really was a way out!

"There," I said, eagerly pointing to the exit. But my friends' lights had fixated on something a few feet to my left. I turned to see.

There, against the wall, was a dusty foam sleeping pad. The

kind we had packed, but old and frayed; its formerly gray color was stained with bodily fluids. Patches of rotten yellow. Circles and splashes of a dark, rusted red. Zoe's eyes glimmered, rapturous. All I could see was the image of a girl tied here, weeping. Flashes of ankles bound to wrists, of a body hog-tied. The searing memory of his cleaver hacking through bone made my stomach somersault.

Zoe and Stefanie snapped pictures furiously. They stopped only to high-five. I clapped a hand over my mouth, dizzy with disgust and revulsion. Not just for the mattress, but for my friends. All they cared about was their evidence.

"This . . . doesn't mean anything," I insisted, but my heart wasn't in it anymore. My voice sounded far away. "It's just an old mattress in the basement."

Zoe and Stef gave me the same look, like they were one person.

Blind rage surged through me, throbbing like my severed fingertip. "The doors are right there and all you care about is getting proof for your damn podcast!" I fired these words at Zoe like bullets from a gun. "Haven't you done enough?"

"Done enough of what?" Zoe's genuine confusion only stoked the flames of my fury.

"You watched a man chop off my finger!" I almost started sobbing again saying the words, but I held it back, choosing anger this time. "*Look at me!* This would never have happened if you hadn't put us in this position."

"Look, I'm sorry that happened, I am. It's really, truly, fucking horrifying. He's a monster—it's what I've been trying to tell you! But are you actually blaming *me* right now because *he* attacked you?"

"No! Yes! You provoked him." I stabbed my mangled finger in her direction. "If you'd just let it go and waited for the ranger like I'd said, he wouldn't have done this."

"Yeah, and if she hadn't been wearing such a slutty dress, he wouldn't have raped her. Wow, never thought I'd hear that coming from you, Jade. Especially given what he did to you."

"Don't put words in my mouth! You know that's not what I mean. And after what he *just did to me,* you should be on your knees begging me for forgiveness."

Zoe scoffed. "I'm sorry that happened. Truly. But it is unfucking-believable that you're blaming me for this."

"You guys!" Stefanie intervened. "Let's save this for once we're out of here, yeah? We have more important things to worry about right now."

Any rational person would have meant the unhinged man upstairs. Any sane adult would have meant escaping this nightmare. But no. My friends were neither sane nor rational. They had both turned to the mattress. My eyes reluctantly fell on the rust-red stains, and bloody images sprayed my mind like paint on a canvas, pictures of gruesome pain and torture. My finger burned. Bile rose in my stomach, hot acid building in my chest. The room spun violently around me.

"I don't care about your fucking podcast! I don't care about your evidence! The man upstairs is seriously deranged and that's all I need to know." I rushed to the double doors and pushed on them now. They rattled but would not open. "I don't care, I don't care, I don't care! I just want to get out of here! I have to get out! Let me out!"

The ceiling boards squeaked, little clouds of dust billowing with every one of Jeremiah's steps. He had already demonstrated how silently he could move across the cabin, never eliciting a single floorboard sound. He wanted us to hear him now. He wanted us to know he was on his way.

"He's coming!" I screamed.

"Shhh, be quiet," Stef pleaded, looking to the ceiling. "He can hear us."

"We have to get out of here!"

Zoe clapped a hand over my mouth. She stared up with bulging eyes at the floorboards creaking overhead. Tiny columns of dust rained down on us like ash after a bomb. He was right above us now.

"Here, kitty, kitty, kitty," Jeremiah called. "Here, kitty, kitty."

Bang! It sounded like a cannonball ripping through the ceiling. He stomped his boot again and I flinched, crying into Zoe's palm. She squeezed my lips tighter.

"It's okay," she mouthed.

"You girls like to play so much, let's play," he said. "Little game called hide-and-seek. Come out, come out, wherever you are. . . ."

His feet shuffled, jauntily hopping back and forth. Jeremiah was dancing again. His boot heels kicked the floor to the rhythm, showering us in dust. He was mumbling along, too, grunting the lyrics just low enough that I couldn't quite hear. . . . It sounded like he was singing along to James Brown's "Get Up, I Feel Like Being a Sex Machine." God, I hoped I was wrong.

Jeremiah stopped moving sharply. "I just want to talk to you, Jade, baby girl!" His voice thundered down over us. "I never meant to hurt you! It was an accident, I swear!"

"Breathe," Zoe whispered. "Just breathe."

I obeyed, sucking in a lungful through my nose and letting it shudder back out.

"That's it. Doing great. Keep breathing." Zoe looked around fervently. "Okay, the door is locked," she whispered, but it seemed she was speaking to herself, taking stock. "Maybe we can hack it open. He has a ton of tools down here."

Her eyes sparkled when they fell on something across the cellar, back by the stairs. I followed her gaze and felt my chest lighten. A boarded-up basement window, almost invisible from the lack of light it provided. It was amazing she'd seen it at all.

Jeremiah resumed dancing. He tapped out a merry little jig. "I like you, Miss Jade. I was just trying to make a point. You understand me, don't you?"

Jade was finally someone's Dream Girl. Too bad he was a psychopathic maniac. Stay tuned for our next episode of Be Careful What You Wish For.

I breathed in time with Zoe.

"Right. Okay." Zoe pointed to the window, confident again, reinvigorated. "That's our exit."

She removed her hand slowly from my lips. I sighed, but made no other sound, calmer now. The room had stopped spinning. Then she gestured for me to take Stef's other arm and together we hefted her back toward the middle of the cellar, by the workbench. Zoe disengaged from our tripod here, searching through the array of carpentry tools on the worktable until she found what she wanted. A crowbar and a hatchet. She handed me the crowbar.

"Here's the plan," she whispered. "I'm going to go back to the cellar doors and make a fuck ton of noise. He'll think that's where we're trying to get out. That way he won't hear you guys when you break open that window. Then we'll both give Stef a boost out first, and she can pull us up."

"What then?" I asked.

"If we get separated, meet behind the shed out back."

"Good thinking." Stef nodded.

"No, I meant, what then?" I demanded. "We're still lost in the middle of the fucking wilderness! It's gonna be dark before long. It must be at least three or four by now. He's going to chase us. He knows this forest better than we ever could."

"He might look strong, but he's older than us. We can still outrun him. I can get us back to the car," Zoe said. "Trust me. We'll be fine."

"What? Stef can't run! And how do you know a way back to the car from here?"

"Don't worry about that now. Let's just get out of this basement. Yeah?"

Jeremiah stomped harder. "Little rats in my basement . . . *I hear you. . . .* " Though it was on the far side of the cellar, the ceiling above them still shook. "You'd best come up here before I come down there!" His voice boomed throughout the cabin.

Zoe opened her arms and the three of us hugged, foreheads touching. We drew in a deep collective breath and exhaled. Then Zoe, hatchet in hand, raced to the other side of the cellar, singing at the top of her lungs. When we finally made out the lyrics, Stef and I spared a moment to look at each other and smile.

She was singing, "I Will Survive."

thirteen

Zoe hacked at the cellar doors, voice hoarse as she belted the Gloria Gaynor song. This and the methodical swing of her hatchet provided just enough sound to cover us. Stef took the crowbar first, prying at the thick wooden boards nailed across the basement window.

"Ready or not," Jeremiah bellowed above the noise, "here I come!"

Zoe crowed right back, "Come and get us, motherfucker!"

We didn't have much time. Soon he'd be at the outside cellar doors and no doubt he had the keys; he could be down here any minute. Stef winced, biting her lip with pain. She'd put too much weight on her ankle in order to gain purchase with her arms.

I held out my hand. "Give it here."

My arms quivered with the effort, muscles and fingers burning. Sweat dripped from my face. Finally, I removed the first of three boards. It clattered to the ground. A swath of heavenly daylight spilled in.

Zoe had forgotten the verses' lyrics and was chanting the chorus on repeat. I couldn't see her from here. But I could hear her swing, again and again. Her fervor galvanized me. Though my fingers throbbed, angry and inflamed, I carried on. At last, the second board fell to our feet.

"Yes!" Stef whispered, fist-pumping the air. "That's it! Keep going!"

Sweating, teeth grinding, I put all my strength into the last board. Dust and sunlight rained over us now as it fell aside. "Yes!" Stef squeezed my shoulders. But the work wasn't over. Looking away to shield my eyes, I thrust the crowbar into the window once, then twice. Glass shattered, clinking to the ground. I used the tip of the bar to clear the frame as best I could, Zoe's hoarse song still serenading in the background.

"Zoe!" I hissed. "Zoe! Come on!"

Upstairs, silence. No more footsteps. No more mixtape. The absence of his sound twisted my stomach into violent knots. But I couldn't lose my shit again. I had to keep it together. Zoe stopped singing and, hatchet still in hand, raced back to grab one of the many chairs by the worktable. We pushed this to the wall and, together, helped Stef to climb atop it.

She grimaced, the glass digging into her forearms as she wiggled through the opening. Bright afternoon sun greeted her, but for how much longer would it remain? God, I wished I knew what time it was. It was two-fifteen the last I'd checked, before Zoe and I went into the attic. Surely, it must have been at least four by now. I was on the chair next, ready to follow. But as Stef turned to reach a hand through to me, her head whipped to the right. She screamed and then she was gone, out of sight.

"Stef! Stef!" I cried, scrambling at the window, digging my nails into the dirt.

Zoe pushed me from behind as I clawed my way up. My head emerged from the window.

"Your little friend hopped away." Jeremiah's wolfish grin greeted me. He had been standing in front of the window just far enough back that I hadn't seen him from down in the basement. Now I was swallowed by his dark shadow. He crouched, face looming directly above mine. "Let me help you, sweetheart." He grabbed my hand. "Don't worry. She won't get far. Not with that ankle."

I screamed violently and flailed, a fish on a hook. "Zoe! Zoe! Help me!"

She pulled at my legs as hard as she could, but Jeremiah held strong, yanking right back. My chest slid across the broken glass, back and forth, tug of war. It sliced through my T-shirt, biting at my flesh. Jeremiah tugged hard until my torso was fully through the window.

"Let me look at this finger." Jeremiah squeezed at the second knuckle and I screamed with pain. "Ah, that's not too bad. Just the tip, like I thought. I was worried I might have taken a bit more!"

Zoe jerked me downward so that only my head poked through the window. Jeremiah held me by one arm. My entire limb burned, muscles and bone stretched too far. My arm felt it would pop from its socket any minute.

"You do forgive me, right?" he asked.

I couldn't make words through my tears. Zoe pulled again

hard, just as he let go. I fell on top of her, breaking the chair, hitting the ground with her arms still wrapped around me.

Jeremiah poked his head through the broken glass. "I'm willing to forgive you, Miss Jade. All that stuff you were talking about before, about your friend down there . . ."

Zoe glared at me.

"I didn't say anything!" I hissed.

"It really struck a chord with me. Because I know what it's like to keep the wrong company. To follow people you know you shouldn't."

Zoe dragged me away from the window. "We need to split up," she whispered.

"Learn from my mistakes," Jeremiah shouted down. "Don't blindly follow that girl into the darkness."

"You go out the kitchen window," she told me.

"No, we need to stick together."

"He'll catch us. We have to split up."

"What about you?" I asked.

"Don't worry about me, I'll find my way out." But there was a shimmer behind those hazel eyes I didn't trust.

"Why do I feel like there's something *else* you're not telling me?"

"Don't start," Zoe snapped. "Not now." She looked to the window, but Jeremiah's face had vanished. She stepped closer to it, searching. "Shit, he's gone. We have to move."

"And we'll get out of here because you can get us back to the car?"

"Yes, I told you. Now, come on, we don't have time for this." She pulled on my arm.

I dug in my heels. "No. I'm sorry. This is bullshit. You're

keeping something from me. How can you get us back when we have no clue where we are?"

"Is this really the best time to be strategizing together? You've let that psycho get into your head about me. Ignore him." Zoe jutted out her chin, annoyed. "I'll explain it all to you later."

"Explain it now."

"Will you stop being such a fucking child and move already!" Zoe seethed. "This is not a big deal. But *he* is. He's going to hurt you more, Jade. Hurt us. You saw that mattress! He keeps them down here."

"We don't know that." Even as I said the words, I couldn't make myself believe them. But I refused to believe Zoe, either. Hers was an unfathomable reality, worse than any nightmare we were already in. If she was right, then I wouldn't be able to cope.

"For fuck's sake, Jade, we need to move! He's coming for us!"

"And whose fault is that?"

Zoe slapped me, and not just with her words this time. Her flat palm struck my face. "I'm sorry," she said immediately, grabbing me by both shoulders. "But you need to get a fucking grip. Interrogate me later. But get your ass up to that fucking kitchen now or there won't *be* a later. Go!"

I shook my head, the shock from her palm jolting me. She was right. We had to move. I grabbed the crowbar and raced back to the kitchen stairs. Zoe darted off toward the far side of the cellar, disappearing into the darkness. Outside somewhere, Stef was hiding. I prayed she'd made it to the back of the shed unseen.

We were scattered. I couldn't quite put my finger on why—it was more than just the physical distance between us—but somehow our once unbreakable chain now felt broken.

fourteen

I crept out of the cellar carefully. I expected to find his dusty cowboy boots at eye level as I emerged, his wolfish grin waiting. But the kitchen was blissfully empty. The only eyes waiting for me were the cougar's. I moved past it with my crowbar clutched tight, just in case.

The upstairs was eerily quiet now that the mixtape was off. I couldn't help but feel that silently behind the kitchen door, Jeremiah swayed his hips, waiting for me to come and dance.

I glanced down at my bandaged, severed finger and shivered.

I moved with surgical care toward the kitchen window, placing each foot down softly, slowly, as though I was picking through broken glass. Caked with dirt, the windowpane was practically opaque. But not fully. I lifted the crowbar, ready to strike, when a large dark figure moved across the window outside. I dropped to the floor. Shit! Had he seen me?

No way, I tried to tell myself. The window was too dirty, and there was little light inside here. It was easier for me to see him in the daylight outdoors than it was for him to see me. I didn't know if this was true, but I told myself it was. It was the only way I could get back onto my knees. But I still couldn't make myself stand, so I crawled across the kitchen floor.

If what I told myself was true, then it meant I had an advantage. I knew where Jeremiah was: outside. Which meant that the house was empty. I could make it out the front door; this was my chance.

I rose to my feet once I'd reached the hutch, safely out of view from the window now. With all my strength, I barged my shoulder into one end. Solid cedar, the hutch weighed a ton. It had been difficult to move with the help of my friends, and on my own it was almost impossible. My boots slid on the hardwood floor as I heaved my body into the hutch's corner. Finally, it shifted. I kept pushing until it budged enough for me to struggle through the gap and slip out of the kitchen door.

The living room was empty, which was a sight that should have come as a welcome relief. But there was something sinister lurking in these shadows. A menacing calm lingered here, tickling the hairs on the nape of my neck. I shivered. Then I hurried to the front door. It was locked.

I rattled the doorknob, twisting and turning and shaking until the whole frame shuddered. But the door would not budge. There was only a keyhole, with no latch for me to turn on the inside; no way for me to unlock it. Was that normal? It didn't feel normal. Why would the cabin have a door that needed a key to be opened from the inside?

My mind flashed to the mattress downstairs. The dark yellow circles. The splotches of brownish blood. No, I wasn't going to think about that. Or Zoe's face when she saw it. Eyes not filled with horror, but leering captivation, even glee. How she seemed to care more about her future podcast than her friends' safety.

I had to stay focused. There must be another way out. But all the windows in the living room were boarded more thoroughly than the one downstairs. I wasn't confident I'd have time to pry them apart with my crowbar and the noise would draw Jeremiah. Upstairs! The windows hadn't been boarded up there. Maybe I could climb onto the roof and down a tree, or a drainpipe. I raced down the hall.

I darted by his desk and stopped when I remembered the radio inside. I didn't care what Zoe thought about the ranger. We'd *heard* him answer. He said he'd be here in a few hours. Surely, he was close by now, but I needed to know.

The vintage metal two-way radio base was twice as heavy as it looked. And it looked *heavy.* I plonked it onto the desk and turned it on. Static filled the air. My heart flapped frantically inside my chest, a bird in a cage. The last time I'd used a radio it was the walkie-talkie Stef had in her house, which she gave to Zoe and me during sleepovers.

"Over, over," Zoe would breathe into the receiver. "The parents have gone to bed. I repeat, the parents have gone to bed. This is not a drill."

I cleared my throat now. "Over, over." I felt stupid. Was this what people actually said? "This is Jade Edelman, at the cabin near the Bones Valley Trail. Or shit, Dora Meyers, or whatever. That was a fake name. Me and my friends, we need your help."

A minute passed in static silence.

"Mayday, mayday, we need help!"

Okay, that was for boats.

It was clear that Jade had no idea what she was doing.

This was stupid. I shouldn't be wasting any more time. My finger hovered over the red power switch.

Just one more try.

"Come in, Ranger Rick," I said, a little more confident, "my friends and I are at the cabin. We need help."

"Copy, miss," a crackling voice returned. "Help is on the way. You ladies just hang tight."

Yes! Zoe was wrong! The ranger *was* on his way. I breathed a sigh of relief so heavy, I had to sit down. I fell into the desk chair like I'd just dropped anchor. "Something else has happened," I stammered, refocusing myself on the mission at hand. "We've been attacked."

"Was it an animal?"

Yes, I wanted to say. He was.

"The man that lives here, or stays here sometimes. The one you spoke to before. He attacked us. We're not safe here."

The ranger's static pause was torture. "Are you sure, miss?"

"He assaulted me!" I told him. "He sliced off my finger!"

"Calm down now, miss; take a breath. We'll get this sorted out soon enough. Don't you worry."

"We can't stay here. We can't wait for you. It's not safe."

The ranger exhaled into the radio. The static and his breath sounded like rain. "All right," he said after a moment. "All right. If it'll make you more comfortable, why don't you follow that stream out back. Follow it east. That's the way I'm coming. I'll find you."

"How far away are you?" I asked.

The radio went full static.

"Hello? Are you there?" Damn it. I slammed my thumb onto the power switch.

Still, I felt reassured. Calling the ranger had been worth it. I'd confirmed that he was on his way and he knew we'd been attacked. Now if the worst happened and we went missing, he would know who to blame. If we were going to die, at least Jeremiah wouldn't get away with it.

Zoe's trail of blood still pockmarked the steps at the end of the hallway. I sprinted up the stairs with abandon now, the full orchestra of creaks and moans playing. I tiptoed around the edge of the room, moving fast. Then I pressed my face to the first dusty windowpane overlooking the backyard.

I couldn't see anyone, just a stream bubbling along. Rusted shards of metal and tools scattered among dead pine needles in an otherwise empty plot of grass. Stef and Zoe were probably already huddled safely behind the shed.

But Jeremiah was the one I needed to pinpoint. I couldn't decide which window to escape from unless I knew where he was. I moved swiftly around to the front windows to check. Still not a soul in sight.

The music downstairs trumpeted at full volume.

He was inside.

I smashed the front window with the edge of the crowbar, eyes flitting back and forth between my task and the top of the stairs. I expected him to charge me at any moment. The same Buffalo Springfield track he'd first danced to played again now, which told me Jeremiah had taken the time to rewind the tape. He had stood there, waiting for it to wind back to the start, just to play it again now.

The bastard was toying with me.

I'd never been the fearless one in our group. Zoe and Stef had talked me into some crazy adventures, but standing on mountain ledges and zip-lining over gulches was never anything I did without trepidation. I sprung out onto the cabin roof now without a moment's hesitation. I didn't think of the two-story fall onto hard earth; the fear of broken limbs never even crossed my mind. I burst out of the window like I was born to do it. Like I'd done it a thousand times.

Like I was Zoe.

fifteen

It was only once I was outside that I realized I hadn't stepped onto a roof. I'd scrambled at full speed onto the porch awning, which was steep, with wooden shingles so old they crumbled under my boot treads. I burst onto this canopy, gaining no purchase, and immediately rolled.

Shingles tore away in my hands as I grabbed at them, tumbling down. Just as my feet hit open air, I managed to grab the ledge. It was with my wounded left hand. I screamed, growling from the strain, and I strived to get ahold of the ledge with my right hand. I couldn't. Stabbing pain shot through me and I knew I wouldn't be able to hold on for long.

Now every worry I'd normally have had about shattered bones and lifelong disabilities finally raced through my brain. If I fell from this position, I'd snap my legs like twigs. I glanced down, expecting to find a twelve-foot gulf between my feet and the ground, but I was happily surprised to find that it was much less than that. Six feet, give or take. That wasn't so bad. Right?

The memory of something Zoe had once said haunted me now. "You're not super into those things," she'd told me when she and Stef had gone rock climbing at the gym without me. "Please don't be mad; we didn't think you'd mind. I mean, come on, you've got to admit, you're terrible at falling."

"How can someone be terrible at falling when they have a rope?" I'd demanded.

"Exactly."

Terrible at falling. God, I hoped she'd been wrong.

I sucked in a lungful of cool air now, exhaled, and let go of the ledge. I turned as I fell. Both heels plowed into the earth and I rolled forward clumsily, eating mud and pine needles as I face-planted into the ground. I took a moment lying here, waiting for the searing fire of a splintered bone or lacerated skin. But there was little more than a stinging in my hands and knees.

Ha, ha! Who's bad at falling now!

I wiped the mud from my face and, keeping low to the ground, raced around the back of the cabin toward the shed. I felt certain that Zoe and Stef were already there. Faster than me at everything, even escape. I looked forward to seeing their faces when I told them I'd just jumped out of the upstairs window. In my mind, Stef would be surprised, and Zoe would look impressed. Though, in reality, it would probably be the other way around.

I shouldn't still want to impress either of them. Not when I was on the run for my life because of their little detective games. Maybe I shouldn't even tell them what the ranger had said. Zoe would only argue and make me feel like an idiot for believing him. Maybe I should just go meet him first by myself. It'd be so much more gratifying to come riding back triumphantly by the ranger's side, the cavalry here to rescue them.

I looked to the stream, trying to orient myself. The front of the cabin had been facing us when we first arrived, heading south. Which meant that the stream bubbling behind must run east and west. See? I didn't need Zoe telling me what to do. I could figure this out on my own. I'd add this to my list of triumphs to brag about once I fetched the others from behind the shed. Then I'd *tell them* our next move. They could take a turn following me, for a change.

Crouching as low as I could, I inched around the side of the shed. It was bigger than it looked. Longer than it was wide. My heart stopped when I heard his voice.

"I know you're out here, sweetheart!" Jeremiah bellowed. It sounded like he was at the front side of the cabin. "I know you called the ranger."

I pressed my back to the shed, flat as I could.

"I hope you didn't say nothing that would tarnish my good reputation." Jeremiah's voice moved around the side of the cabin. "Hope you've not been telling tales."

I inched around to the back of the shed, and when I turned the corner, the ground bucked beneath my feet, launching my stomach up into my throat.

There was no one here. Nothing but a muddy patch of grass overshadowed by a mammoth fir tree. The stream rolled peacefully a couple yards away. On the other side of the water was a densely forested hill.

I steadied myself against the shed, blinking slowly. Tears nipped at the corners of my eyes. Had Stef and Zoe left me?

"The ranger will be here soon and you can be on your way,"

Jeremiah called out. "I really hope we can bury the hatchet and make some nice memories now with the time we have left."

No, my friends wouldn't leave me. Obviously, I'd learned today that they would do a lot of fucked-up things. But surely they would never abandon me here. Leaving me alone on a piazza at night to make out with some boys was one thing. But ditching me with a man they believed to be a serial killer was another.

Maybe Stef and Zo were inside the shed! That would be a much smarter place to hide. Stefanie had probably had no choice, with her busted ankle. The shed door would've been closer than limping around the back.

Jeremiah whistled a tune now. The jolly melody struck a sinister tone as it grew louder, closer. The happy whistle of an unburdened man, not a care in the world, nothing but a song in his heart. Body shaking, back pressed flat, I slid around the other side of the shed. I looked left to right before emerging around the front.

Jeremiah was still on the side of the cabin, by the cellar doors. Whistling with malevolent calm. The hairs on my arms stood on end.

As I reached for the door handle, I tried to imagine myself as a chameleon. My arm was camouflaged into the shed. He wouldn't see me. He wouldn't see me. He wouldn't see me. My fingers wrapped around the metal handle and I pulled.

It was stiff at first. Too stiff to open with just one hand. Or maybe it was locked. Either way, I couldn't risk trying again. Jeremiah whistled closer. I ducked back around the side, crouching down at the back of the shed.

"Miss Jade, darlin', there's no need to hide now," he said from somewhere close in the backyard.

My breath whimpered from my lips and I clapped my palm

over my mouth, felt it shudder through. The pine needles crunched beneath his boots. He was near enough now that I heard each step distinctly. His whistling stopped short in front of the shed. My heartbeat thundered against my ribs.

"You know it was your little friends got me so aggravated. I was just trying to teach them a lesson. I shouldn't have gotten so carried away. Let me make it up to you."

I couldn't bear to think what "making it up to me" would look like from a man like him. A man who lived alone in the woods skinning animals and taking trophies. Who thought an appropriate response to a young woman threatening him was to demonstrate his abundant control by wildly waving a cleaver around. A man who kept that stained mattress in the basement.

"Why don't you rejoin the party now?"

Jeremiah was so close I could smell him. He was just by the shed door. I bit my hand to keep from screaming. He was going to find me. He was going to find me and then god only knew what he was going to do.

I had to run.

But I couldn't. I couldn't move a muscle. I couldn't catch my breath. I couldn't breathe at all. I was having another panic attack. Any second he would find me and drag me back into that house and lock me inside. Zoe wasn't here to calm me this time. I was all alone.

"Your friends are already inside," Jeremiah said. "They're dancing. Can't you hear them?"

This was normally when Zoe would talk me down. Breathe, she'd tell me, just breathe. But it wasn't her voice I heard in my head now.

Jade just needed to breathe. Laurie Wolff's husky tenor was surprisingly soothing. *In. And out. In. And out.*

After a minute, the pine needle crunch departed, moving farther away now. His whistling resumed, fading into the distance. I withdrew my hand from my mouth, gasping for breath like I'd been held underwater. And I had been. But this time it wasn't Zoe that had gotten me through.

It was me.

• • •

When we were twenty-one, we went to a corn-maze labyrinth Halloween party. I was dressed as Alice in Wonderland. Zoe was the Queen of Hearts. Stefanie was the White Rabbit. It was my year to come up with the theme. It'd been Stef's idea to make the costumes slutty. My blue corset squeezed my breasts till they looked like balloons about to pop.

I only felt more ridiculous as the night went on. The sharp cornstalks scraped my exposed flesh, painting a bright red rash across my chest. I looked like slutty Alice with syphilis. My block heels dug into the trodden moist earth and bits of grass and straw clung to me more with each step; I felt bovine. My friends and I had already assessed the viable dating candidates; there were at least five or six good-looking guys mingling around the farm that night. It was obvious that none of them were going to look twice at me.

"Don't be stupid, babe," Stef had said. "You look hot. Insecurity is just a state of mind."

Easy for her to say with her long legs and perfectly proportioned nose.

"Banish the negativity! Let flowers of confidence grow." We'd pregamed together, and Stef had gone a little harder than the rest of us, by the looks of it.

"Insecurities are weeds." I'd tried to sound more tart than

bitter. "They're much easier to grow than flowers. They sprout from the tiniest patch of dirt, and no matter how many times you root them out, they keep growing back."

"Then that's what we're here for," Zoe had said. "To help you keep plucking them out one by one."

One minute my friends were with me, all of us drinking our cups of spiked cider, laughing at the haunted scarecrows, and screaming at the programmed jump scares. The next minute, they were gone. I didn't know how it'd happened. They must've turned right when I'd turned left. I backtracked, but somehow hit a wall. This wasn't right. I called out to them, but there were too many ambient sounds laced with the night song of cicadas and birds. Too many people here, scattered in this maze. The wind whispered through the dead corn, and when the stalks swayed it sounded like rain.

I thought I heard a laugh like Stef's. I followed it and bumped nose to nose with a girl dressed as Indiana Jones. She wore boots. Practical. I should've worn those. I regretted letting Stef talk me into these heels.

It took me half an hour to get out of the maze. By then I'd finished my shockingly strong cider and was drunk and frantic, a toxic combination. I found Stef and Zoe in the barn at the bar, laughing as if nothing was wrong.

"What the fuck?" I'd exclaimed, coming in hot.

"Oh my god, there you are!" Zoe threw her arms around my neck, happy-drunk in the way I was not. "We've been looking for you!"

"At the bar?"

"Well, we were spiraling." Zoe laughed way too much as she said this.

"Around and around and around in circles." Stefanie giggled; apparently this was some sort of inside joke. "Like a spiral, get it?"

I did. I just didn't see why it was funny.

Stef slapped a hand on my shoulder. "Until finally we were like—"

Zoe finished her sentence. "No more spirals! We said, this is ridiculous."

"That's one word for it," I sniffed, bitter, unamused. I tugged at the mud-stained white fishnets riding up my crotch.

"It made no sense to get more lost looking for you," Stef said, still snickering. "We knew you'd find us here."

"And it all worked out!" Zoe handed us each another shot.

It all worked out. Zoe's lifelong motto.

It all worked out. So, you can't be mad at me.

Well, this time, at this cabin, it fucking hadn't. Nothing had *worked out.*

Coming to a complete stop now for the first time in ages, it suddenly hit me how desperately I had to pee. My bladder pulsed, bursting. I hadn't peed since this afternoon. What time was it now? At least four-thirty or five, at a guess. But I couldn't risk it here. What if he came back and caught me, pink shorts wrapped around my ankles? I didn't watch horror movies, but I bet anything those heroines never had to worry about this.

The afternoon sun had begun its long, slow descent behind the trees. Though still light, daytime was giving way to early dusk. The air grew cooler, crisper. But still I waited behind the shed. Zoe and Stef were probably hiding somewhere else, lying low until they could safely make their way here. This was the spot where we'd agreed to meet. They would be here.

But the longer I waited, the less confident of this I grew.

Maybe they'd found a new spot to hide, somewhere they assumed I would think to look. Like they had at the corn maze.

Or maybe Jeremiah had been telling the truth and they were safe inside. I imagined him in the cabin right now, urging my friends to dance. The three of them had buried the hatchet with another shot of that disgusting moonshine and were partying with him now. It was a thought that was at once as comforting as it was infuriating. Yet it was still a better image than the others that festered deep in the folds of my brain. The ones I'd been trying so hard to push down.

Jeremiah speared the two girls with his arrow once through the leg, wounding them, Laurie Wolff narrated the brutal images racing through my mind. I squeezed my eyes shut to silence her voice, but the podcast wouldn't stop playing Laurie's newest episode.

These girls were no different than the cougar draped over his kitchen table or the deer strung up on his front porch.

Except I couldn't just hear her voice. I could envision all the hungry listeners, devouring her every word. Her Little Savages, feasting on our pain.

I couldn't take it anymore. I couldn't sit here imagining, waiting, for one more second. The awful realization of what I had to do churned inside of me; my body trembled. But I had to learn the truth. Stef and Zoe weren't coming and I had to find my friends. No matter the cost.

I slid my shorts around my ankles and relieved myself behind the shed. There was nothing waiting for me here but Laurie Wolff's awful voice and the loathsome podcast we had become a part of. It was time to go.

sixteen

I darted toward the side of the cabin quick and low as a cat, a cougar even. The movement warmed my arms and legs and now that I'd begun to move, I couldn't stop. I'd survive for only as long as I kept my limbs moving. Otherwise, this damp cold would take hold and I would freeze.

I checked the cellar doors. Immediately, I saw why they wouldn't open for us from the inside. A thick metal chain graced the doors like a necklace. But Zoe had done good work with the hatchet. She'd hacked herself a hole big enough to squeeze through. I plucked a thread from the fractured wood. Beige, like her hideous cargo shorts.

Zoe had gotten out.

I was happy. Then immediately pissed, because where was she—and then worry took hold, because where *was* she?

And what about Stef? She'd crawled out the window, seen Jeremiah, and tried her best to run. He hadn't given chase, choosing to play tug-of-war with me instead. Which meant she could have made it to the trees. She might still be hiding there.

Should I go look for her in the forest? What was I supposed to do?

Maybe Zoe had been right all along. Perhaps Jade secretly loved her friend making all the decisions so that she never had to make any for herself. Maybe Jade really did have no agency in her own life.

Fuck you, Laurie. And fuck Zoe, too.

I could make my own decisions. I'd show them. I'd show myself.

I had to think about this logically. Before I went blindly searching the trees, I needed to rule out the cabin. I put my hand on the gap in the cellar door to push my way through. A pointed shard of fractured wood sliced my palm. I winced, examining the wound only briefly. It wasn't too deep. I plucked out a visible splinter. This sort of gash would've been a gold star winner a couple nights ago; but now, if we were all seated around the stovetop comparing wounds like they were notches on a belt, this one might not even be worth mentioning.

A broken ankle, broken nose, severed finger . . . Stef, Zoe, and I would have quite the collection of new battle scars to compare next time we saw one another.

If there was a next time.

I couldn't think like that, though.

If I ever *forgave them*—that was better. A much more palatable thought. Much better to think they were alive to be angry with than any alternative. Anger was preferable. I fanned the flames inside myself as I peered through the gap into the dark cellar.

"Zoe," I hissed. "Stef!"

I could still make out the music playing upstairs. Cheap Trick's "I Want You to Want Me" trickled through the floorboards. More time had passed than I'd thought. I didn't remember this song playing before. Or perhaps he'd changed the tape. A chilling image of indifference, switching a mixtape to keep the mood.

Should I squeeze inside? The image of the stained mattress pummeled my brain. I couldn't stomach thinking about it, let alone seeing it. Not now. It was information to be processed later, somewhere very far from here. It wasn't possible for me to look at this situation objectively right now. Not after I'd listened to that podcast so much the smug narrator lived rent free in my head.

Jade Edelman was wasting time.

"Zoe, Stef!" I whispered again through the splintered gap in the door. "Where are you?"

I stopped to listen for movement in the house. No stomping feet. No dancing shoes. If Zoe and Stef were up there, they were quiet . . . and very still. If they were up there, that didn't bode well.

They clearly weren't here in the cellar. Laurie Wolff was right. I couldn't drag my feet any longer. But going inside felt like a fool's mission, suicidal. I needed to get a better look from the outside.

A gentle rain started, falling softly against my face. I turned and the toe of my boot pressed on something hard, buried in the damp earth. There, among the fallen shards of wood, gleamed something metal and shiny. Ripley.

Zoe had dropped Ripley.

She must have dropped the knife as she'd squeezed through

the gap. And yet my heart throbbed hard in my throat as I picked Ripley up and inspected the open blade. It looked clean, but then I wasn't so sure. Maybe the edge had a red hue. . . . Images of a struggle forced themselves on me. What if Jeremiah had caught her as she'd tried to escape?

There was blood on the blade. Jade could see it clearly now.

I rubbed my palms against my thighs, trying to clean them. I felt sick and dirty, like I stood neck-deep in murder.

This was just my imagination running wild. Zoe was all right. Of course she was. She was Zoe.

Except everybody's luck runs out eventually, Laurie interjected, her voice low and menacing.

I folded Ripley and put it in my pocket. Then I heard an unmistakable sound. Footsteps. Coming from the front of the cabin. I raced around the side and pressed my back hard against the wall. Could it be Stef? Zoe? Should I call out? I held my breath, lungs burning.

Silence. Long, torturous silence. So piercing it hurt.

"Is that you, little mouse?" Jeremiah's voice hit me so loud I jumped. "Squeak, squeak, little mouse."

I tried to shift farther down the wall of the cabin. The dead leaves and pine needles beneath my feet sang like a canary.

"Are you there?" Jeremiah's voice crept closer. His breath whispered to me through the rain. "I can hear you."

I should run. But which way? Back around the other side of the cabin, or out into the woods? How fast could he catch me? I felt paralyzed by indecision.

Jeremiah stood by the cellar doors now. I could hear him, soft and close. "I know it's you, Miss Jade."

He couldn't know that. Not unless he already knew where Stef and Zoe were. My stomach churned as I pictured them inside, bound and gagged on the deerskin couch. I gulped, throat sandpaper dry.

"Wanna know how I know, baby girl?" He sniffed so loud I flinched. "It's your smell. You smell sweet as a peach on a hot summer's day. *Ripe.*"

I shuddered, fear prickling every hair on my body. I needed to go, run, do *something*! But my feet remained infuriatingly planted on the wet ground.

"I'm gonna be a gentleman and stay put, sweetheart, give you to the count of three to speak up. All I wanna do is talk. But if you don't say something, then I'm comin' round this corner. And I don't think you'll like that."

Tremors rippled through my bones, teeth chattering.

"One," he crooned.

What the hell was I doing just standing here? If I wasn't going to run, then what was my plan? To wait in silence until he pounced? I couldn't trust that the second I opened my lips he wouldn't spring around the corner. But at least if I spoke there was a chance he might not. I sucked in a deep breath, yet still no words came.

"Two . . ."

Come on, Jade, do something!

The "three" started to form on the tip of his tongue. It was now or never.

Finally, I forced the words out. "Where are my friends?"

"Well, be still my heart, she speaks!"

I tried to steady the quake in my voice, to sound strong. "Just tell me where they are."

"What's in it for me?" The words growled from his chest, low and deep.

"All we want is to go home. We won't tell anyone what's happened here, I promise." I was grateful Zoe wasn't here to listen to this. She'd tell me to quit groveling. "You can just let us go and we'll forget we were ever here."

"What makes you think I care about that?"

My stomach clenched so tight I could hardly breathe. "Obviously my friends think you're the Bones Hollow Hunter. If you don't let them go, then I'll have to go to the police and report you for assault . . . and false imprisonment! I'll show them all the pictures we have. The box of jewelry. The padlocked trunk of women's clothes. Your bow. That stained mattress in the basement." I twitched just thinking about it. "It won't look good for you."

"I already told you none of that is mine. That soiled cot's been in this cabin longer than me. I've never touched it."

"We'll just let the police be the judge of that. So, you choose. You seem like a man that values his privacy. If you don't want a whole troop of investigators tearing this place apart, then just give me back my friends."

"You're not very good at making threats, are you now, little lady? Come on." He laughed, a wicked chuckle rattling in his throat. "Put your back into it and maybe I'll reconsider."

I swallowed a ball of tears, choking them down, but he could still hear them when I spoke. "Jeremiah, *please.*"

My mask of strength and calm was slipping. My friends were gone and I was alone. Everything in my body told me that I needed to run, to save myself while I still could. This deranged lunatic had bloodlust on his mind; I could feel the heat of it radiating from around the corner of the cabin. This small section of wall that separated him from me. But I couldn't leave Stef and Zoe behind, not if he had them.

"I've got a better idea, baby girl." Jeremiah breathed in deep again, a wolf smelling his prey. "You're different from them other two. They're conniving, like all the other women I've ever known . . . but I like you better than them, so I won't chase you down." He punched his fist into the wood and I shrieked. "But you know I could."

I felt for Ripley in my pocket. My hand trembled around it, too nervous to take hold. This knife was useless for someone like me. I'd never be able to fend off a huge guy like Jeremiah. I was a sitting duck lingering here, waiting for him to wring my neck.

"Instead," his voice dropped to almost a whisper, so sinister my blood ran cold, "how's about we have a little race?" Jeremiah paused for an agonizing moment. "Which of us can track a wounded animal faster, d'you think? With that busted ankle, Miss Stefanie should be real easy to find. I'll nab her in a heartbeat. I don't know how long it'll take you. . . ."

So, Stefanie wasn't with him. My whole body shuddered with relief, followed by immediate horror as the reality of his words fully sunk in. She was wounded somewhere out there in the forest, hiding. She was an injured animal and this man tracked animals for a living. But before I could speak, to plead my case, he hammered the wooden cabin one more time, jolting me to my senses.

"I'll give you a ten-second head start. On your mark . . . Get set . . . Go!"

seventeen

I sprang forward, my boots sliding on dead leaves and mud. The rain had lightened to a mist. The sun had begun its long descent, the soft light grayed by the clouds. Moist coolness hung heavy in the air and the taste of the distant sea was salty on my tongue.

I raced toward the last place I'd seen Stefanie. The basement window. She'd taken off toward the right, so I searched the grass and the brown pine needles for any trace of a trail. What a joke. Like I was some kind of hunter. Like I'd ever have a chance of tracking my friend down.

A bent leaf caught my eye. I looked closer and found a boot print in the soft earth. I searched about a Stef-leg's distance from this and found another mild indentation. Holy shit, maybe I *could* track her.

I lost sight of the trail as soon as it reached the forest's edge.

I checked frantically over my shoulder now. No sign of him. But I had no doubt he was watching. Pale green predator eyes peeking out from somewhere in the moss-drenched woods. I was grateful for the late summer sunset, but beneath the tree canopy the light dimmed, making the treads hard to track. The ground was too lush with moss and ferns to keep sight of such subtle markings. But I'd been right in my earlier assumption: Stef had run for cover and she was hiding somewhere in these woods.

Jeremiah might be a hunter who knew this forest. But *I* knew my friend.

I listened to the soft birdsong. If she was hiding within sight of this place, she would call out to me. I waited for a beat before venturing farther.

Stef was a climber. She, not Zoe, had been the one who had convinced me that I could brave the rock wall in San Vito lo Capo. "Just don't look down, and trust the rope," is what she had said. "Let your inner badass out."

I scanned the treetops above me. If Stefanie could climb, then this was where she'd be. But with her busted ankle, this seemed impossible. I moved steadily, checking behind every trunk and fern. I searched every visible treetop. Terrified of getting lost, I kept close to the tree line, always with the stream in sight.

If Stefanie was out here hiding, then maybe Zoe was, too. I half expected her to gallop up behind me, my white knight ready to swoop in. I even expected to walk headfirst into Jeremiah's chest. To have my skyward gaze interrupted by his smug smile. But it was like I was the only person in this entire forest. Maybe even the only person alive. The solitude was terrifying. The longer I marched over hollow trunks and around large boulders, the more I longed to see my friends' faces. My heartbeat raced. Please, Stef, show yourself!

"Stefanie!" I called out now. "It's me!"

Only the birds replied. I tried to cling to the thread of hope still glimmering inside of me. Maybe Zoe had already found Stef and they were huddled together behind some boulder, waiting for me to come.

Zoe was with her, I told myself again and again. Zoe was with her and she was safe.

I remembered all the times they hid from me behind trees only to jump out and shout, "Boo!" I almost wept with the desire for that now. I'd give anything for them to leap out, to make my heart lunge up into my throat. I'd cry and slap their shoulders and hug them so tight they couldn't breathe. This could all be part of the story we'd tell one day. Zoe could have her way—it could all work out and I wouldn't be mad. I promised this to the void, as if promising it would bring it to fruition. Like a wish made on blown-out candles.

"Stef!" I cried again, desperate, yearning. "Stefanie! Zoe! It's me, come out!"

The sound that came back to me was not the one I longed for. A blistering scream from somewhere deeper in the forest. I stopped, chilled to the bone.

It could have been an animal.

"Stef?" I called again, softer now.

Again, the scream replied. This time it didn't stop. The spine-chilling screams continued, an unending reel. They were screams of utter horror. As hollow and primal as it sounded, I still recognized the voice.

It belonged to Stef.

"Stefanie!" I screeched, running toward the sound. "Stef!"

Where was Zoe? Couldn't she hear us? We needed her!

I wrenched my ankle between two rocks and smashed my

knee hard into the ground. "Stef," I wept, pulling myself up. "I'm coming!"

I followed the sound deeper into the trees, no longer caring to keep the stream in sight. No longer caring if I got lost. Then the screaming stopped. The blood-chilling silence that followed was interrupted only by the oblivious birdsong above. I felt torn between directions. Did I go into the heart of the forest, following the origin of the sound? Did I go back to the cabin? Maybe Jeremiah would simply take her back to his living room, sit her down on the deerskin couch, and announce himself winner of this ridiculous little contest.

That's all this was, after all. A game. A sick, twisted recreation for a bored, lonely man. We would find him with an almighty I-showed-you-dumb-girls, self-satisfied expression. And that would be the end. Another story for us to tell. Another it-all-worked-out notch for Zoe's belt. That's all.

Thinking this didn't make it feel true.

I tried saying it aloud. "This is just a game." It felt even less true somehow.

"Stefanie is fine," I continued as I walked, and the mud licked at my heels. "He just scared her, that's all. He's a crazy asshole, not a serial killer."

I pictured him slinging her body over his shoulder, carrying her back to the cabin. Like a dead deer. The cabin seemed the most likely place to take her, so I made up my mind. I turned around and raced back the way I'd come, praying I wouldn't get lost.

I knew that he was dangerous, but unlike my friends I still clung to the facts. I couldn't be certain that Jeremiah was the boogeyman of the Bones Hollow Trail. Logically, it was totally improbable that three girls could stumble upon this Uncatchable Serial Killer so easily. Even so, I heard Laurie Wolff's words in my head as I ran. I couldn't turn off her voice.

He carried her to his secluded cabin. Set her down on his deerskin couch. He tied her wrists and ankles. Stripped Stefanie down to her bra and underwear.

I watched it all unfold in my mind. A car accident I couldn't look away from. A true crime podcast I couldn't shut off. The innocent voyeur. Isn't that what we'd been until now—the voracious listeners, her Little Savages—being entertained by horrible crimes?

When he brought her into the basement, Stefanie's arms and legs had been slashed to ribbons. He tossed her mutilated body onto an old mattress, stained with the blood and fear of all the women who had come before. He hog-tied her feet and hands behind her back then took out his hunting knife again. He peeled back her lips. She struggled and writhed, but he held her down. The killer forced his blade into her gums and pried out a tooth. Her top left canine.

Then he held her mouth open wide and dropped the tooth in. Pressed his wide palm over her mouth and nose until she swallowed.

I stopped running and painted the moss and leaves with vomit. I didn't have time to catch my breath. I didn't have a moment to lose. I ran so hard my legs burned and then I ran harder still.

• • •

John Denver trumpeted through the broken windows. My boot heels were heavy with mud, and clumps of pine needles clung to me with every step, weighing me down. I felt clumsy, like an old machine clunking toward the cabin. My wet hair clung to my cheeks. The picture of heroism.

I'd planned on going through the cellar door, but then I passed by the dirt-caked kitchen window. The glass was shattered. Had Zoe found her way back in? Why would she have come through this way and not the basement?

Digging my tiptoes into the mud, I peered inside at the pile of broken shards in the sink. My throat tightened. There was so much blood. Had there been this much before? My blood had painted the area, splattering the floor, the window frame, the sink, spraying the animal bones red.

Looking from left to right, I noticed that the room was empty, save for the dead feline on the kitchen table. The flies that had once clustered here had been liberated, but still a few lingered around the cougar. The ones too dumb to fly free. I stared at them, flitting in and out of the dead predator's ear. It felt disturbingly like looking into a mirror.

Broken glass clawed at my palms as I pulled myself through the window, but somehow it barely fazed me. I moved with certainty, realizing now that I hadn't even thought of my mutilated finger in ages. Maybe it wouldn't hold me back so much, after all. Or maybe I was just stronger than I'd ever realized.

I squeezed through the gap between the hutch and the kitchen door and slipped into the living room. I didn't wait to see who was inside. I didn't hide in the kitchen, afraid. There was no more time for cowardly hesitancy. My heart hammered beneath my ribs and a bitter metal taste glazed the back of my throat.

Stepping inside the living room was like stepping inside a nightmare, one narrated by Laurie Wolff. I kept as low to the ground as possible, sweat rolling down my cheeks, praying I wouldn't be seen. Stefanie was on the couch. Even from behind, I could tell by her posture that she was lucid, awake. Stef never hunched; she sat like a ballerina. But there was no elegance to her body here. Her shoulders were so rigid they trembled. Jeremiah leered over her, smiling, sadistic. His silver belt buckle was practically eye level. In his hand was a four-inch hunting knife.

I thrust my right hand into my pocket and felt Ripley's slick steel on my fingertips. Drew in a deep, cooling breath. I ducked low, inching forward as quietly as possible.

"You see this groove right here?" Jeremiah waved the knife in front of her, and the blade reflected Stefanie's terrified face back to me. "This is called a fuller. Now, some people call it the blood channel. They think it allows the blood to flow out of a wound. But that's just a misconception." He crouched down so he could show her more closely, like he was displaying a pretty ornament and not an instrument of death. A smirk lifted the corner of his scar. "Flesh contracts when it's been cut. It closes off around the blade." His pale green eyes sparkled with sinister joy. "You wouldn't lose any blood until I ripped it back out."

She whimpered. "Please . . . we're sorry, okay? We just want to go home."

I scampered across the dusty floor and pressed my back flat to a large wooden support beam, peeking out from around its edge.

"You can't leave yet," Jeremiah said sweetly. "The fun ain't even started!" He touched the knife to her cheek. I held my breath and watched as he slipped the blade behind her head and cut the hair tie from her ponytail. Long raven locks fell around her face. "Now, that's better. Pretty as a picture." He tweaked her nose.

I crawled out from behind the beam and stayed hidden, ducked behind the back of the couch. My lungs ached as I steadied my breath, trying to stay calm. I looked underneath the couch at Stefanie's feet. Her ankles were tied together with twine. Maybe if I lay flat, I could reach under and cut her free. . . .

"Well, hey there, good-lookin'!" Every limb quivering with horror, I lifted my eyes upward, inch by inch. Jeremiah towered over me, staring down with a vicious smile. I hadn't even heard him walk around to the back of the couch. "Just in time for the party."

I stood slowly.

Stef whipped her head around to look. "Jade!"

I wanted to run to her, but Jeremiah pointed his blade at me and my hand throbbed instinctively, remembering. "Not so fast now, sweetheart," he warned.

"You won," I said. "Fair and square. You won the race." I stepped backward slowly, both my hands outstretched like he had a gun. When he didn't object, I inched around to the front of the couch as I spoke. "You proved your point. We should have accepted your help. Okay? Please, Jeremiah, all we want is to leave now. You won. Just let us go."

He followed me around to the front of the couch, rubbing a thumb down his scar. He pointed the knife at my eye, his voice stern, charmless. "I ain't won nothin' yet. Sit down."

My bottom lip trembled so I pinned it down hard with my tooth. The sharp taste of iron kissed my tongue. "I don't want to."

"I didn't ask what you want. Sit down."

"No." A tear rolled down my cheek. I hated myself for crying. "The ranger will be here soon."

"Then why you crying?"

"I'm not." I swiped the back of my hand across my face.

Stef sniffled into her shoulder, unable to wipe her tears away. She was bound at the wrists, too. "Please," she repeated. "We're sorry. We just want to go home."

"Shut up, bitch." Jeremiah said it without malice. As if "bitch" was a perfectly normal name, like Sally or Susan. "No one's talking to you."

Where was Zoe? Where was she when we needed her? She'd gotten us into this mess and now she'd abandoned us. I'd been wrong before; I wasn't equipped. This wasn't my role.

"You know I didn't mean to harm you, Jade. You believe me, don't you, now?" The yearning in his eyes terrified me. The look of a vulnerable man who needed my reassurance, who needed it so badly he would take it by whatever means necessary.

I nodded, tears still streaming. "Yeah," I said. "Of course. I believe you."

"I've always been like this, y'know. I get overzealous, carried away. My old man was proud, said this kind of fury was just in my nature. That I had the wild in me." His low Southern drawl cracked, his voice rattling from somewhere deep in the back of his throat. "Mama thought otherwise. She said it was the devil." He swallowed whatever tears he might have been choking back. "Hell, who am I to say which of 'em was wrong, and which was right."

I stood still as a statue. I couldn't focus on his words. Only on the desperate, hungry look on his face. He needed something from me. I knew he'd hurt me if I didn't give it.

"You're a good listener, Miss Jade. I could see that about you from the moment I first laid eyes on you. These other two, they're the talkers, isn't that right? But I bet they don't ever listen to what you say half as good as you do them. Talking to you makes me miss her, y'know. My wife. You remind me of her."

I cringed, trying to hide the fear from my face. I needed to look the part, the good girl, the kind heart. It's what he wanted.

"I'm just so lonely, to tell you the god's honest truth. I've grown tired of this life. Out here. The isolation was intoxicating once, but now it feels like poison. Like it's maybe rotted my soul. I've forgotten how to act properly, in front of good company. I've not had anybody to talk to in so long. Or maybe it's just that Mama was right all along. Maybe I do have the beast in me."

A sob burst from Stef's lips. "Just let us leave, you crazy fucking psycho!"

Jeremiah backhanded her hard across the cheek. The sound resonated through me, needling my spine. Stefanie cried, wailing into her shoulder.

"You women are all the same." He stared at the back of his hand as if it was unclean. "I get my hopes up. Time and time again I think, this one, she'll be different. But then all any of you do is let me down. You all just want to leave."

I felt the heat rising in his chest, into his cheeks. A bomb about to detonate. I stepped closer to him now, toward the outstretched knife. Then I was speaking. The words poured out of me without any consideration or thought. "Well, you were right about me," I said. "When you said that I'm different from the others. It's scary, honestly . . . how well you see me. Because no one else ever really has. You, like, *really* see me. And I've been having a hard time processing that."

Jeremiah's pale green eyes probed me, searching. They sparkled with hope and doubt. He let me lower his knife with a trembling hand.

"I'm not ready to leave. I don't want to," I told him. "All I want, actually, is to dance with you."

I moved closer. Forcing a confidence into my eyes that didn't belong to me. I could taste his earthen tobacco scent. I swayed my hips. Jeremiah's gaze hung on my every movement. I took hold of his hands, guided them to my waist.

"You are so beautiful," he breathed, full of longing. Words that I'd always dreamed of hearing. To be the prettiest one in the room, despite my beautiful friends. My stomach roiled, rotten, but I kept my breath steady. "Come here." Jeremiah pushed his lips into my ear. They grazed my lobe, a kiss. "I ain't ever gonna let you go."

I rubbed one hand on the small of his back. With the other, I took Ripley from my pocket. I flicked the blade open.

"I'm gonna keep you forever," Jeremiah whispered.

I plunged the blade into his back. Deep, to the hilt. Warm blood licked my hand. Then I jerked the knife back out and it poured. Jeremiah thundered, a deafening roar, and I thrust it back in again. Then again. He clubbed his arm across my face, tossing me aside.

Then he was on me. Slobbering like a wild animal. "You bitch!" The word held every bit of malice now. "You fuckin' cunt!"

Stef screamed and flopped to the ground, inching closer, unable to help. "Leave her alone!"

Jeremiah raised his fist, ready to hammer my face. I stabbed the knife into his belly. Then I pulled it out and stuck it into his side. Then his throat. I jerked it back out and hot blood rained over me.

His body slumped on top of me. A brick building collapsed over my bones. I couldn't move. I couldn't breathe. I never knew a person could weigh this much. Shock shivered through me uncontrollably. I had to get out. Get him off me. I screamed, struggling beneath his immense weight.

It took all my strength to slide out from underneath him. Quivering still, I scrambled to Stefanie on my knees and cut the twine from her wrists and ankles. I stared at the bloody knife in my hand. Ripley, dripping red. Like the carcass still dripping on the porch. I hurled it across the room, wanting it as far away from me as possible. Like the knife itself had possessed me and was alone guilty for the crime just committed.

I could hardly force myself to look at him now. Jeremiah's body slumped in a crimson puddle, his cheek smeared across the floor, mouth slightly ajar. He looked like the cougar, a splayed corpse, dead and undignified. My teeth chattered, my body trembling head to toe. Stef wrapped her arms around me, speaking words I could not hear. I stared at Jeremiah. Did I do that? Was it really me?

He'd been about to hurt my friend. It was self-defense—he had a knife. But then so did I. My head spun in circles. I felt sick, depraved. Shame filled me, icy cold.

The flash was what caught my eye. I looked up to see Zoe standing in the kitchen doorway. She was alive! She was here!

My relief at her presence morphed into dread and then a flood of anger when the second flash went off.

Zoe was taking pictures.

eighteen

"That's my girl!" Zoe hooted. "You were amazing! An absolute legend. Say something for the camera."

I felt diseased. I couldn't move my pallid body from the floor and sat stunned, shivering. My stomach heaved but there was nothing left to throw up. I glared at Zoe, our coach, our fearless leader. She was unrecognizable.

Stefanie knelt down beside me and seized me by both shoulders. She squeezed my cheeks and kissed one. "My fucking hero!" She looked to Zoe. "Oh my god, did you see all of that?"

"All of it," Zoe said. "Jade, you were incredible."

Normally, those words coming from her would have made my heart sing. Now, they made me shiver. "So, you saw me fighting for my life, and you just stood there?"

"Saw you kicking ass, you mean," she said, as if that was meant to be a compliment. "I knew you had him."

"Oh, you knew? Because *I* didn't know. I thought I might die, but apparently you took one look at the situation and decided I had everything under control. So, it's all okay, then? It all worked out, right?"

"Take a breath," Stef said sweetly, like she was talking to a child. She pulled herself from the ground, brushing herself off.

"I almost died, and she took pictures!"

"C'mon, it was a smart move," Stefanie said. "Kind of genius, really."

"Genius?"

"Think about it," Zoe said to me. "We're going to be famous now. Heroes!"

"The Bones Hollow Hunter victims who turned the tables. I can see the headlines now. Maybe we'll even get a movie deal." Stefanie beamed from ear to ear.

Their smiles filled me with disgust. Just moments ago, they'd watched me stab a man to death. His body lay mere feet away, blood still pooling, and here my friends looked elated. Like this was the best thing that had ever happened to them.

"Give me that!" I scrambled toward Zoe, clawing at the ground and then springing up like some sort of animal. I grabbed for the phone. "Give it to me!"

"Whoa, hey!" Zoe replaced it in her pocket. "Calm down, okay?"

Stef tried to touch my shoulder. I shook her off. "Don't touch me," I spat. "Do you realize what just happened?"

"You did what you had to," Zoe said, softer now, soothing. "You saved Stefanie's life."

I laughed, bitter. I wouldn't be soothed by her. Not this time. "We don't know that! You have no hard proof!"

"We do," Stef said. "He was going to kill me, Jade. I know it."

"Well, I'm glad *you* know it. Because I don't. I don't know anything anymore. He could have just been fucking with us! All I know is, I'm the one with blood on my hands."

"You didn't do anything wrong," Zoe insisted.

I told him to trust me and then I shoved a blade into his back. Tears gushed down my face feeling it all, the warmth of his blood showering over me. I realized that I was soaked in it. A crimson droplet rolled off my fingertip and dripped onto the floor.

I'd killed a man. I couldn't wrap my brain around it. I couldn't accept it. Jesus Christ, I didn't even believe he was the Hunter—he could have been some lonely, deranged man having a mental health crisis. I might have just killed an innocent man and these two stood here celebrating.

"None of this should have happened," I cried. "We should never have even been here! Where the fuck even were you, Zoe? Where did you go?"

"I was hiding, obviously. Look, you're having a panic attack. You just need to take a breath."

"Bullshit! I don't believe you." The room was spinning. "You were probably off taking fucking pictures!" I gasped for air. Zoe tried to put a hand on my back, to soothe me as she always did, but I wouldn't let her. I slapped her away.

My brain felt hot, like a system overheating. I couldn't process what was happening. Two days ago, we were on our trip. Our hiking adventure months in the planning. Now I was in the cabin from one of Zoe's stupid online true crime groups, having just committed a murder. This couldn't be real.

Suddenly, it hit me. We didn't end up at this cabin by mistake.

We weren't listening to that fucking podcast just because it was Zoe's and Stefanie's new favorite. We had come here to look for the Bones Hollow Hunter. Zoe had this mapped out from the beginning. It's the only thing that made any sense.

"You planned this." I could hardly speak the words. They came out as a whisper, hoarse and raw, scratching at my throat like claws. "You planned all of this before we even left."

Zoe tried a flippant smile. It came across like a sneer. "You mean for you to kill Jeremiah?"

"Don't play fucking dumb with me," I snapped. "You know exactly what I'm talking about. There was never a waterfall, was there? That's why it wasn't on the fucking map, because it doesn't exist. And when Stef broke her ankle, we were never headed to an access road. You weren't just wrong, you *lied.* You weren't trying to get us somewhere safe. You were trying to take us here." I drilled into Zoe with my glare. "Be honest. When you saw that stupid boulder that looked like every other boulder under the sun—that was the landmark for this cabin, wasn't it?"

She threw up a single hand, dismissive. As though we were talking about a dress she borrowed without permission, and not a calculated manipulation. "Yeah. Okay. I might have had this in mind."

I shook my head, like I might wake up from this sleep. But no, this was reality. The entire trip until now, days of hiking, months of preparation—*that* had been the dream.

"This whole trip has been about the Bones Hollow Hunter. All those pep talks about how this hike would be life-changing, character-building, how we'd come out here and face nature—how we *needed* to do this hike—that was all just bullshit, wasn't it? A fucking sales pitch."

"Come on, Jade," Stef started to say.

I cut her off. "No. Don't defend her. She lied about all of it!"

"I think you're making a bigger deal out of this than it needs to be," Zoe said in her calming voice.

"So let me get this straight. You brought us to this cabin on purpose to catch the Bones Hollow Hunter—who might not even fucking be here! If this place's location was so well documented by internet detectives, then why has no one else made this fun trek?"

"It's not *for sure* the cabin in the police report." Zoe spoke through gritted teeth, reluctant. "It's just suspected because it's the only documented cabin even remotely near Bones Hollow Valley. It was used by rangers and hunters; that part was true. And obviously it's pretty hard to get to, so I guess no one else has tried."

Or been stupid enough to.

I would've clapped if it weren't for my severed finger. "So this premeditated shitshow has been nothing more than a wild goose chase from the start. Excellent. And you continued taking us here even after Stef got hurt. Bravo, Zoe, really, bravo."

"Where else were we going to go?"

"Not to a suspected serial killer's cabin!" I gnashed my teeth to keep from screaming. "Did you think this through at all?"

"There were obviously going to be supplies at the cabin, and we needed shelter!" Zoe spoke like this was the foregone conclusion anyone would have come to. "Would you rather we had wandered aimlessly through the forest and eventually starved to death? I knew we could handle whatever was here or else I wouldn't have brought us. And look, we have. *You* have! You're one tough-ass bitch. You should be proud."

Proud. Bile burned the back of my throat.

"I will admit that I didn't plan everything perfectly," Zoe said. "But we can fight about this later, okay? You're getting all worked up."

"Don't do that. Don't fucking patronize me! Did Stef know?" I whipped my gaze at her. "Who am I kidding? Of course you did. She tells you everything. But not me, right? I'm the spoilsport. The party pooper. The deadweight. *Don't tell Jade,* right? That's what you guys agreed?"

Stef looked wounded, guilty even. "It really wasn't like that. . . ."

"Oh yeah? What was it like? Tell me! How could you be okay coming here with your ankle—are you stupid or just suicidal?"

"I trust Zoe." Stef bristled. "She knew what she was doing. We were on a mission, and I wasn't going to fuck that up for us."

"You're just not thinking about this clearly." Zoe tried to make eye contact as she spoke, but I refused to look at her, couldn't bear to. "We wanted to catch a killer. Now it's even better. We've *stopped* him. Permanently. We're not just any part of the story—we're the end of it."

"That's why you came here," I hissed, spitting venom. "To be famous. To start your own podcast? That's why I had to kill a man. For your fucking glory."

"You don't need to make it sound so sinister." Zoe rolled her eyes, dismissive. "It's not like that. This is for the victims more than anything else. Think of Florence. We could give closure to her family."

"Where is she then, Zo?" I snapped. "Florence? Florence! I don't see her anywhere."

"We'll keep looking," Stef said. "There's got to be evidence of her somewhere."

"A man is dead." The words burned on my lips. "Don't you care?"

Zoe spoke evenly. “No, a killer is dead. I’m glad.”

Finally, I lifted my gaze to meet hers. “Is that why you came here?”

“What do you mean?”

“Did you come here to *kill* him?” I rose to my feet so that I towered over her. “Answer me! Was this your plan the whole time, to be part of the story?”

“Look, you just went through something deeply traumatic.” Zoe’s tone was infuriatingly calm. “You’re obviously feeling a lot of things.”

“Oh, am I? Is it obvious?”

“And it’s obvious you’re looking for someone to blame, who you can beat up like a punching bag. That’s fine. I can take it. What are friends for?”

The smugness in her voice made me want to slap her.

“Friends!” I stepped so close to her now that our noses nearly touched. “You thought this man was a bona fide serial killer. Based on nothing more than a group of online nerds. But you believed it. Which means you brought me to a serial killer’s cabin. On purpose. Without telling me. That’s not what *friends* do.” I gritted my teeth to keep from screaming the words. Tears poured out, and again I hated myself for crying, though they were rageful tears. “Even worse, then you provoked him! He attacked me and stalked us. And then you watched me . . .” I could hardly speak from crying. “You watched me kill a man. You watched me fight for my life!”

“I knew you were okay,” she insisted, but her face was white. A trace of guilt flickered in her voice. “I’d have never let him hurt you.”

I waved my bloody finger at her. “But you did! You’re a *liar.* I can't believe a single word you say anymore. You tricked me into coming here and you tricked me into killing a man!"

"Hold on now," Stef tried to step in.

I cut her off. "How can you think that any of this is justified? We were never meant to be any part of this story. *Zoe* just decided that for us. She inserted us into the narrative. And *you,*" I seethed, "you're nothing but a blind sheep. Following dumbly along, wherever she takes us. Even if it's right off a fucking cliff. Even if it ends in murder."

"That's not fair," Stefanie gasped. "We didn't plan—"

"Shut up! I'm not finished." I whirled back to Zoe, my voice low and shaking. "Be honest," I begged. "Be honest for one goddamn second of your life, Zoe. You came here to kill a killer—tell me I'm wrong."

"Obviously not!" Zoe cried. "I didn't plan for anyone to die! I came here to *catch* him, to see if *we* could. Yes, to be part of the story. Yes, to be a hero. Okay, are you happy? And I'll admit, things got a little out of control."

A little!

"But you want the truth? Fine. Here it is." Zoe's eyes narrowed, jaw set. "You love to hate me for all of your problems. And it's oh-so-predictable that you'd lay this at my feet. That's me being honest. Nobody made you stab him. That was you. *You* took the knife. *You* stuck it in him. Now you want someone else to blame. Typical Jade." She shook her head as though she felt sorry for me. "But I'm not going to feel bad that this sick monster is dead—and you shouldn't, either. He was a serial killer. He got what he deserved."

For a minute I was stunned, and a suffocating silence lingered between us. Any trace of guilt I'd seen on her face before was gone now. She folded her arms across her chest, self-righteous, defensive. She *really* wasn't going to take responsibility. She'd rather lash out at me than own her mistakes. Zoe never could stand being on the back foot.

For a flickering moment, I wanted to look to Stefanie to rally some support; surely, she wouldn't agree with this utter bullshit. But if she'd wanted to say something, to intervene, she would have by now.

"You've done a lot of fucked-up things, Zoe," I started, my voice hollow, "but this really takes the cake. It's the last straw. It is."

For a second, Zoe looked surprised. Surprised I wasn't just rolling over and playing dead? "I've had about enough of this," she hissed, cheeks pink with anger. "You're in shock. I get it, okay? You hate me now, sure, but soon you'll be telling everyone about stopping a psychopathic murderer from hurting anyone ever again. You get to be a hero, but don't make *me* the villain. I've just given you the best story of your goddamn life."

I could have hit her.

I'd never hit anyone before, but just then it was the only thing in the world I wanted to do. To let my fist fly and connect with her rosy cheek. To see the satisfying spray of her blood sweep the air. Stef must have seen the feral look in my eyes, and hobbled between us.

"Enough!" It was as forceful as I'd ever heard her speak. A break from her usually sweet, cheerful tenor. "C'mon, Zo, that was too far."

Finally! I thought I was losing my mind. My chest lightened. It was a relief to have Stef come to my defense, even if she had taken her sweet time.

"We've all been through a lot. And you and I can't even imagine what Jade must be feeling right now. After what she just . . . did. This has been really," she searched hard for the right word, "*heavy.* And yeah, I agree that at some point we'll all be able to look back on this with different eyes. But just let her fucking process it, yeah? She's got to feel her feelings."

Leave it to Stef to say it in the most diplomatic, therapist-like way. But still, the fervor of my rage dampened.

Zoe held up her hands in surrender. "Yeah, fine. Okay."

Far be it from Zoe to ever give me an apology. She'd give out meaningless apologies like candy for the sake of her manipulative games, like the one she'd played with Jeremiah. But this was as close as I'd ever get to one.

"It's like you said," Stef went on, eyes darting back and forth between us, "this has been traumatic. But we're going to get through this. We're safe now. I mean, Jade, you saved my *life.*" She leveled her warm brown eyes, full of gratitude, straight at me. "Now all we have to do is find a way home. We'll leave all this toxic energy here at the cabin, leave it all behind us. This fight and all the awful things everyone's said . . . it never happened. Everything is going to be okay."

It was Zoe's mantra parroted from Stefanie's lips.

I swiped the tears from my face and saw my hands still stained, wet with blood. "I don't think . . ." I sucked in a sobering breath. "I don't think I will ever get over this." I looked to Jeremiah's dead body. "This will never be okay."

Stefanie pulled me into a hug, and this time I let her. I wanted to cry into her shoulder, to surrender myself to this unbearable pain inside of me and let it all pour out. But if I started again, I didn't think I could ever stop. It was only when Zoe's arms wrapped around us both that I broke away.

Sunset had begun. Pinkish-gray light simmered in the distance, the sun disappearing behind the trees. The cabin was cast in a deeper darkness and the shadows growing behind my friends loomed like monsters. I thought I heard the sound of crunching dead pine needles outside.

Our eyes darted toward the front of the cabin, every muscle tensed.

"Did you hear something?" Stef asked.

Keys rattled at the front door.

My heart lightened, unburdened. "The ranger!" I exclaimed, hope swelling inside of me, filling me with something akin to joy but somehow even greater. "Finally!"

Zoe and Stef exchanged that look. That fucking look. Another secret they hadn't shared.

"Why would the ranger have a set of keys?" Zoe asked. "What if it's not him?"

"Stop it," I said. "Enough of your bullshit! Look where it's gotten us! The ranger is here and I'm going to tell him everything. We're going home."

It was only now that I realized the music was still playing. "House of the Rising Sun." The doorknob turned and gray light poured inside as the door squeaked open. I darted toward it, ready to throw myself at the mercy of this man. My nightmare was over. Once I'd told him what had happened, I had no doubt he'd call the police. But all the better for it. I was ready to answer for what I had done and let the chips fall where they may. This wouldn't be the justice that Zoe had pictured. But one way or another, justice would be served today. I was ready.

nineteen

A tall man stood in the doorway with a ring of light behind him. His face was obscured by shadow, but I could see dark sweat circles under his arms and around the collar of his pale blue button-down. His sleeves were rolled up to the elbow, revealing tan, strong forearms and a silver watch. I didn't care that he didn't have on a park ranger uniform. He was the picture of a hero in every sense. Complete with a goddamn halo.

Hallelujah, my sweet Little Savages. Our girl was saved.

"Good evening, ladies." His voice was deep, his tone calming. He scanned the room, left to right. Then his eyes stopped on Jeremiah's cold body, and shock swept across his face. His jaw twitched. He opened his mouth, but no words poured out. The silence was excruciating. Why wasn't he speaking?

"I can explain. . . ." I jumped in, fear and desperation bubbling inside of me.

"You got him," he finally whispered. He shook his head slowly, in disbelief. "I'll be damned. Someone finally got this son of a bitch. You have no idea how long I've been waiting for this."

Well, that was not the reaction I'd expected him to have. I teetered on a knife's edge, unsure of how to feel.

He turned his eyes to me. "So, do you want to tell me what happened, then?"

I blinked, unsteady, suddenly lost for words. "It was self-defense," I stammered, but the words didn't feel right rolling off my tongue. I still wasn't sure if I believed them, no matter what Stef and Zoe thought. Everything I thought that I was going to say when he first unlocked the door had now disappeared from my brain in a cloud of confusion.

"Who are you?" Zoe cut in. "The park ranger?"

Oh, so *now* she thought he could be the ranger. . . .

"No." He stepped through the threshold, farther into the house, away from the sunlight. Certain features of his face became clearer beneath the dim bulb in the living room. Stark cheekbones, strong chin, cutting blue eyes. "I'm not a park ranger."

I winced at this, annoyed that Zoe was right again. But there had to be a reasonable explanation for his arrival. His voice sounded familiar—so incredibly familiar. I examined him more closely. He could have been in his late thirties, maybe early forties. Around six feet tall, with broad shoulders and a muscled chest that filled his shirt, pressing into the white buttons, screaming "gym rat." His thick brown hair was longer on the top and short on the sides. A bushy mustache rested underneath an arrow-straight nose, perched above full lips. I stopped myself from exchanging a look with Zoe. His taste in facial hair was the least important thing in the world right now.

"So . . . I didn't speak to you on the radio?" I asked, nervous.

"No, ma'am. My radio is for official channels only. I'm with the police. Detective Bennett." He reached behind his lapel for a folded ID badge and showed it to me.

I snatched it, greedy, desperate. I traced my finger over the brass badge. It was real, so real I could cry. "Detective *Leeroy* Bennett?"

Zoe's mouth fell open. "You were on *Serial Killers USA* with Laurie Wolff."

"Oh Jesus, yes," the detective admitted, embarrassed. "I was feeling a little bit desperate when I agreed to that interview. Trying to stir some interest in the case. Not that it did much good."

"Oh my god, what are you doing here?" Stef gasped.

"Isn't it obvious?" Zoe said, her excitement growing. She pointed to Jeremiah. "He's the Bones Hollow Hunter, isn't he? It's him! It's really him!"

She craved validation. Her I-told-you-so moment. I didn't want her to have it. But at the same time, I *needed* to know now, too. If he was guilty, or if I had just killed an innocent man. Maybe knowing would ease the gnawing pain in my belly. Or maybe this would be a burden that would forever feel too heavy, that would suffocate me in my sleep. Either way, I had to know.

"I got pictures," Zoe continued, too eager. "He attacked my friends. Tied Stef up."

"Let's have a look." The detective held out his hand and Zoe pulled up the photo library on her phone before passing it to him.

"Was he really the Hunter?" I whispered, not wanting to absolve myself and yet desperate to all at once.

"That's him, ma'am."

My chest tightened, refusing to relax. I couldn't give myself over to relief yet, not until I was certain. "If you knew, why didn't you arrest him?"

"Well, there's knowing and there's proving. I could never get enough proof to warrant a search. Then, after Lars Brunner died, I was told to focus on other cases." He walked slowly over to the body and knelt by it. He gazed long and hard before rising, smoothing the creases from his black slacks. Even then, his eyes never left Jeremiah. "This man was the Bones Hollow Hunter, make no mistake."

I couldn't let this go. "But how did you *know*?"

"I had evidence, but let's just say it wasn't admissible. Obtained through less-than-legal means." His perfectly straight brows knitted together. "That was before Lars Brunner, even. I fucked up. After that, my boss didn't want to hear any of my theories. Then Lars came into the picture and, well . . . But I've always known it wasn't him. And I've never forgiven myself for my mistake and the lives it may have cost. That's why I still come around sometimes. I like to keep the fucker on his toes. Let him know he's being watched. But I guess you've made amends for me, and maybe now I can finally get a good night's sleep."

I waited for the knot to loosen. For the absolution to come, the pain in my gut to go away. I'd killed a murderer. It was self-defense. I'd done the world a service. But no release came.

Zoe had been right. I'd never again be able to utter those words out loud in her presence. But she was. I felt hollow, corrupted.

Detective Bennett flicked through the photos. Though I

couldn't see the pictures, the scene they'd captured replayed in front of my eyes all the same.

The memory of my words haunted me: "It's scary, honestly . . . how well you see me."

The detective side-eyed me as he scrolled through the unfolding event. "Looks like you played him all right," he stated coolly, and I could hear the stabs, the screams, reverberate through my mind. He turned the phone off, stuffed it into his pants pocket. Stared straight at me. "Well, you're the one I should be thanking, then. I ought to shake your hand."

A manic smile lit up Zoe's face. "I *knew* I'd find him here. I just knew it."

"Is that so?" Detective Bennett asked. "You girls came here on purpose?"

The same question I'd posed before. Except this time Zoe didn't look impatient or annoyed. Coming from the detective, it hadn't been an accusation; it'd been said with awe. The exact sentiment she'd been waiting for.

Zoe looked as proud as a gold medal winner. "That's right."

"Then I ought to be thanking you all." He reached his wide hand to Zoe's bloodied face like he might just cup her cheek, but then let it fall by his side. He looked to my bandaged finger, the gash on my head from where Jeremiah had cracked it against the kitchen counter. "Seems he really put you through the wringer."

"We're fine," Zoe said, speaking for us.

The blood and energy drained out of me, like someone had just unplugged my body from its power source. I felt light on my feet, woozy. I wanted to lie down and sleep for a hundred years. "I just want to go home now, Detective. Please."

"Of course you do. Please, call me Leeroy."

"Why do you have keys to the cabin?" I asked.

He frowned, ashamed. "Like I said, not all my means of investigation were strictly legal. I'm not proud." Detective Bennett ushered me to the couch with a hand on the small of my back. His touch felt warm, reassuring. "Can't imagine what you have been through. Here, sit."

I obeyed, having no drive to do anything but. It felt nice to finally surrender myself to safe hands. A wave of relief came, flooding me with soothing warmth. Finally, there was an adult in the room. We were saved and this nightmare could end.

Stef and Zoe squeezed in on the cushion to my left. I angled my body away from theirs because I still couldn't bear to look at them, especially Zoe. There were too many feelings to unpack here. But all I kept thinking now was that, even if they were right about Jeremiah's guilt, I'd still killed a man. For the rest of my life, I would be someone who had taken another life. I'd have to live with that every day. Go to sleep with it every night. Never again would I be the same. And that was all their fault.

It should have been Zoe who had wielded the knife. This had been her plan; not mine.

I looked to Detective Bennett's face, hoping to draw comfort from his calmness. Instead, the expression staring back at me robbed me of any newfound consolation. The detective looked worried. More than that, he looked grave.

Zoe and Stef seemed infuriatingly oblivious. They whispered excitedly to each other, planning for the interviews they were sure to give the media, trading taglines for Zoe's future podcast. Meanwhile, the detective paced back and forth between the front windows and the back. He was checking they were properly boarded.

I hesitated before speaking. "Is everything all right?"

"You said you spoke to a ranger?" But Leeroy didn't look at

me when he asked this. He was examining the front door lock now.

"Yes . . ." I flinched as he removed a handgun from his belt. "I told him that we'd been attacked. He said to head east downstream and that he'd find us there."

Leeroy checked the ammo clip, frowning. "Shit."

"Shit?" I felt horror return to my stomach, fluttering wildly like a bird desperate to escape. "What's shit?"

Leeroy paced back and forth and ran a hand through his dark hair.

"Are we okay? What's happening?" I asked.

Finally, Zoe looked up from their conversation, their ridiculous little daydream. "That wasn't the ranger she spoke to, was it?" But she didn't sound alarmed. She sounded smug. I wanted to hurl the skull ashtray at her head.

"What's going on!" I snapped. The dread flapping in my chest had now spread to wild terror. "What is it?"

"Stay calm," Leeroy finally said. He knelt in front of me, only feet away from Jeremiah's dead body, the pool of blood mere inches from his boots, so that his crisp blue eyes were level with mine. He took a breath before speaking, as if I was supposed to do the same, but my breath caught in my throat.

"Don't panic," he said, though tears crowded my eyes. "But that wasn't a ranger you spoke to on the radio. I believe that was Jeremiah's brother." He paused, the severity of his gaze deepening. "He's coming for you girls."

"What?" I hated how terrified I sounded, but I couldn't help it. My whole body had begun to shake. "But we're with you. We're going to be okay, right?" I felt like I already knew the answer to this question, and I didn't like it.

Zoe fist pumped the air. "I knew it!"

"Will you shut the fuck up!"

"So, what do we do?" Stef asked, worried. "You have a gun. You can protect us. Call for backup?"

"I don't have a full ammo clip." Leeroy shook his head when he spoke, his disappointment palpable. "And if I'm right and it's Jeremiah's brother . . . then that's very bad news. That son of a bitch is going to be heavily armed, like a one-man militia. He lives just outside Seattle, helps Jeremiah ship all this weird shit that he sells online. I've long suspected him to be an accomplice to the murders." He cast an eye to the various bone creations that littered the room. "He's been on the FBI's radar for some time. The number of guns registered to the brother alone is enough to stock a small army. Have you found any weapons here in the cabin we could use?"

The three of us shook our heads. "A bunch of knives in the kitchen. And that bow," Zoe said, the confidence drained from her voice. Perhaps the severity of our situation had finally begun to sink in.

"Shit," he said again.

"What do we do?" I gasped. "What are we going to do!"

He squeezed my knee. "It's going to be all right. Don't you worry now. I can radio for backup. But I'm not confident in my ability to defend our position here at this cabin. His brother will undoubtedly know all the ways in."

"How did you get here?" Hope briefly spread its wings in my chest. "You must have a car nearby?"

"No, ma'am, just a dirt bike. We won't all four fit." He ran a hand through his hair again. "We'll need a place to hide until then."

"Not here," I begged, panic rising. Jeremiah's dead body

pulled at my eyes, though I refused to look. The walls inched closer. "I can't stay in this cabin one more minute. *Not here.*"

"The basement?" Stefanie offered.

The blood drained from my body. The image of the stained mattress flashed hot in my mind. "Are you insane? I'm not going down there!"

"It's okay. Calm down. It's going to be okay." He put an arm around the back of my neck and pulled me into his strong chest. I pressed my cheek to his crisp white shirt and felt his lungs breathe in, then out. Then he sat me upright. "We don't have to stay here. But I will need to move you to a safer location. Somewhere I can easily defend, if need be." The detective stroked his mustache, thinking.

"Okay," he finally said. "I think I know just the place." He stood up, smoothing the crease from his black trousers. "Follow me."

He extended a wide hand and I let him help me to my feet.

And so, my Little Savages, our dear friend of the podcast, Detective Leeroy Bennett, had swooped in to save the day. Jade Edelman had found herself a new white knight. But she and her friends were not out of the woods yet. They were still being hunted.

twenty

I trailed the detective to the door, affixed to his shadow. Zoe helped Stef. Zoe's wounded leg must have been hurting her, too, though she didn't show it.

"Can you not walk?" Detective Bennett asked.

"I can," Stef assured him. "Don't worry."

I wasn't so sure about myself. Crippling exhaustion had seized my limbs. The emptiness in my stomach, the dryness of my throat, and the heaviness of my eyelids all felt like insurmountable obstacles. But Leeroy took my hand and I put one foot in front of the other, then again. I sucked in the cool, dusk air so moist that mossy earth filled my nose, distant sea salt on the breeze tickling my throat.

I would never set foot in that godforsaken cabin again. Every step I took was a step I'd never retrace. That hellhole's door had closed behind me forever. The comfort I drew from this reinvigorated my body; it gave me the physical strength I needed to hike on. But it still couldn't soothe my nerves. Another unseen assailant was hunting us, after all.

It was strange to hike without the weight of my backpack on my shoulders. I felt like a soldier slinking into battle without her armor. Vulnerable. Exposed. I clung to the detective's arm as we walked. Ashamed by how pathetic I seemed, how little-girlish. But I craved safety, security, and I had to get that from someone. It wasn't going to be from Stef or Zoe, not anymore.

Every once in a while, the handsome detective patted my arm or my hand reassuringly. "It's okay," he told me, knowing what I needed to hear. "It's all going to be okay."

It didn't sound like a bullshit platitude coming from him. I held on to him tighter.

We marched into the forest, surging forward through the dwindling light. We didn't speak. A few steps behind me, Zoe and Stef shuffled along. Their heavy breaths were rhythmic, in unison. Joined at the fucking hip, just like they should be. I knew they'd move faster if I helped them. Instead, I squeezed the detective's thick, muscled arm.

"You're safe." He put his hand over mine. "I've got you."

We must have been trudging through the forest for at least twenty minutes. With each passing step, I no longer felt that same comfort as I had before, the comfort of distance between me and that cursed cabin. Now I felt a new seeping dread. A dampness leaking through my boots, into my bones. I shivered. Why had we been walking for so long? Where was he taking us?

"How much farther?" Stef asked, pain blanching her voice.

The detective kept his tone hushed, just shy of a whisper. "Not far."

Goosebumps prickled the nape of my neck as I realized that the detective hadn't glanced at a map or compass even once. Though the sun had not yet fully set, it was already difficult to see under the canopy. Wherever he was taking us, it seemed to be somewhere he could feel his way to in the dark. He wasn't using the small flashlight clipped to his belt. It was clear he knew this forest well.

I tried to quiet my growing unease. There was nothing to be scared of. This man was a police officer. Not just any officer, but the detective from the podcast we'd obsessively burned through. I'd listened to his voice so much he felt like a friend. We could trust him.

Still, I had to ask. "Where are you taking us?"

Zoe and Stef tripped behind us and toppled. Stef yelped, muted, hand over her mouth.

"Here," Leeroy offered, "let me." Then he scooped Stefanie up in his arms. A true white knight.

I was being stupid. After everything that had happened today, of course I'd grown suspicious. But soon we would be safe. He would radio for help. And we would get out of this wilderness once and for all.

I wished I'd never agreed to come here. Never listened to that podcast. Never had to suffer Laurie Wolff rabbiting in my ears. Damn it, it'd been my turn to choose our trip this year! I should have *insisted* we hike the Camino de Santiago instead. But when Zoe set her mind to something, it was impossible to sway her. She'd told us this would be life-changing. If only I had known just how life-changing she'd meant.

I refused to make eye contact with her, though we now walked side by side. I could tell from her rigid posture that she was still annoyed with me. I hadn't accepted her as the hero in this twisted tale, hadn't fallen in line with her delusional narrative. And I never would. A couple of days ago, it would have torn me apart to know she was mad at me. Now the anger felt right. Suited me, even. Still, I couldn't help but surreptitiously scan her face and notice the way her eyes darted from left to right. Every other step, she glanced over her shoulder. Zoe was on edge, too.

"So where are you taking us?" I asked Leeroy again.

"It's a little hunting spot up ahead. We're close now. Keep quiet."

I guessed it was understandable that the detective knew this forest so intimately. He'd probably spent a lot of time hiking through here during his investigation, come to learn its nooks and crannies like the back of his hand. But one thing suddenly didn't make any sense and the question tore at my insides, plaguing me, a nagging doubt that needed resolving.

"So, how did you say you got a key to the cabin again? Public property shouldn't have a lock, right? Jeremiah must have installed it. And you just copied the key? Is that legal?"

The detective grunted, though whether it was from the exertion of hiking through a dark, muddy forest carrying Stef or because of my question, I didn't know. "I told you, I'm not proud." He shifted Stefanie, but didn't look at her when he spoke, instead directing his voice back to Zoe and me. "I can trust you girls, can't I? I can tell you these things, I hope. I think I can. Because what you did back there wasn't strictly legal, either. Makes me feel like we're in the same boat."

My stomach dropped. I knew it. I'd committed murder. I was going to prison.

"We all wanted the same thing. That monster wiped from this earth."

"We won't go to jail?" I asked, moving forward, desperate for comfort.

"Of course not. They ought to give you ladies medals as far as I'm concerned, and if I have my way, they will. You did good police work."

I cast Zoe a begrudging, fleeting glance. Her eyes had brightened. She tried to suppress her smile, but she still looked like a pig in shit. Of course she did. Getting complimented by the detective on this case was her wet dream. She was living her fucking fantasy.

It all worked out, I could practically hear her say.

It all worked out for some, was what I'd say back. *She* hadn't had to kill a man.

Darkness thickened around us. The shadows grew longer. "Is it much farther?" I asked, hugging my chest.

The detective stopped walking and set Stef down. "We're here. Look." Leeroy leaned over and picked up a thin wooden grate lined with vines and branches and leaves from the ground. It was so camouflaged I'd have never seen it. Underneath, there was a pit. A deep, dark hole. From where I stood, it looked like the mouth of a cave.

Girls who get led into caves deep in the dark, dark woods don't always come out again, Laurie Wolff warned.

I shuddered.

"It's a hunting pit," he said. "Animal falls in, breaks its leg usually. But you'll be safe, I promise. I'll radio for backup from here."

"You want us to get in there?" Stef hobbled back a step.

"It's perfectly safe. I'll grab a branch, lower you down."

"Won't the brother know about this spot, too?" Zoe asked.

"I can protect you a lot easier from this location." He held up his hands as if in defense. "Hey, you were the ones that didn't want to hide at the cabin. Are you saying you want to go back there now?"

"Maybe I do." I inched forward a step. The pit looked deep enough to be a mass grave. Too deep to crawl out of.

The detective walked toward me and I stepped back. "It's okay, it's okay," he said, palms still spread. "Whatever you want to do. You want to march all the way back to that cabin? His brother might hear us along the way. Track us. Harder to defend a moving position. But if you don't want to take my advice and hide here, where I believe you'll be safest, then I will pick up your friend and we'll start back. It's up to you."

Leaves crunched in the distance, somewhere to the left of us. Leeroy froze like a deer in the forest, ears perked toward a predator sound. He held up a hand for silence. My stomach clenched so tight I could hardly breathe. Zoe went rigid beside me. Slowly, our eyes met. My dread was reflected back to me, her face mirroring my alarm.

The sound came again, undeniable now. Footsteps. I stared into the shadows so hard my eyes grew sore, blinking in wide-eyed terror. I waited for Leeroy's instruction, for him to signal us to jump inside the hole. I would do it now, without hesitation. The detective's hand drifted to the handgun tucked inside his belt.

A yellow flashlight beam bounced toward us, emerging from behind a hill. A body, draped in shadow, came into view. Even from a distance, I could see the wide-brimmed hat. A ranger's hat, and a rifle slung around his shoulder.

Panic strangled me, a fist wrapped tightly around my throat. Leeroy motioned for Stef to get behind him. Zoe grabbed onto her shoulder, pulling her toward us. We huddled together, our bones clattering in unison.

"Hello?" the stranger called out, his voice deep but friendly. "Park ranger here. Don't be alarmed."

Leeroy removed the gun from his belt. I flinched at the sharp click of the safety going off.

"This is Detective Leeroy Bennett," he declared. "What brings you so far off-trail, Ranger?" With barely a glance behind him, the detective motioned for us to move toward the pit. "Get inside, girls," he hissed, raising his weapon to hip-height. "Before he shoots you. You're sitting ducks standing there."

I wanted to dive in headfirst or run and take cover behind the trees, but my friends remained still as statues and so did I.

"Been tracking a cougar. Got a few reports of some sightings a little too close to the trail," the ranger said, approaching. He sounded winded from a long hike.

"Don't trust a fucking word he says," the detective whispered.

"How about you, Detective? Long way from your jurisdiction. Or has there been a crime I'm not aware of?" The ranger shined his light onto our fear-stricken faces. "You ladies all right?"

"Everything is fine here," the detective said loudly. "I'm just escorting these girls back to the trail. They got a little lost."

The ranger's stocky shadow trudged closer, revealing a sturdy, formidable figure with broad shoulders and a neck thick as an ox. I shivered at each leaf that crunched beneath his boots. Leeroy slipped his gun to his side, out of sight, as the ranger clicked his flashlight off and tucked it back into his utility belt. His face became clearer now, no longer draped in darkness, revealing a twenty-something man with a wide nose and a cleft chin. He looked like a marine, nothing but hard lines and meaty muscle.

I looked to Leeroy for my cue. His posture remained rigid as a snake about to strike. I held my breath.

"Are you ladies sure you're all right?" The ranger lifted the brim of his hat, swiping the sweat from his brow as he closed the gap between us. His chipper voice didn't match his domineering physique and the contradiction was jarring.

Then again, Jeremiah had sounded charming, too.

"Looks like you all have seen some sort of ghost. Sorry if I gave you a scare. Can be a bit alarming running into folks this far off-trail, I know."

If this was Jeremiah's brother, he was a convincing actor. Maybe Leeroy was wrong. Maybe with a real ranger and a detective, we could finally be safe.

Or maybe Jade was so desperate to be saved she'd run straight into the arms of her killer.

When no one spoke, the ranger filled the void as though long silences made him uncomfortable. "You're welcome to travel back to camp with me tonight, if you like. It's very easy to get lost out here."

The ranger stepped nearer still. He was only feet away now. He sounded like a real ranger, but he could just be trying to trick us, to lure us from the detective. Stef's gaze floated from Zoe's face to mine and then back again. Our elbows touched. Uncertainty twitched through our bodies, from one into the next. We edged backward in unison.

"That's close enough there, buddy," Leeroy finally said. His gun remained fixed by his side, just behind his hip so that the ranger couldn't see. I watched his finger shift to the trigger, ready. "We know who you are."

The ranger chuckled, boyish, innocent. "I should hope so, Detective. I identified myself already. Didn't catch their names, though. Are you ladies registered on the trail?"

"Enough of the nice guy routine," Leeroy snapped. "Lower that weapon, real fucking smooth." He whipped his handgun out front now, too fast for the ranger to react. Stef yelped. A flinch rippled from my friends' bodies into mine. "Go on. On the ground."

"Whoa, whoa, whoa." The ranger lifted his hands, ten beefy fingers splayed wide. "What's going on here?"

"Put the rifle on the ground."

"I don't understand."

"Rifle! On the ground!"

"Okay, okay, let's just stay calm." The ranger eased the rifle off his shoulder and slowly placed it on the ground, then shifted back, hands still spread in the air. "Whatever's going on, I'm sure we can talk this through."

"On your knees."

Stef clutched onto Zoe. I heard a whimper catch in her throat.

The ranger lowered himself onto his knees, hands above his head. Gun still trained, Leeroy reached one hand into his pocket and removed a pair of silver handcuffs. "Don't fucking move," he said, edging nearer to the ranger. "Try anything and I'll blow your head off."

"L-look," the ranger stuttered, "whoever you think I am . . . I think you've made some sort of a mistake."

Leeroy stepped behind the ranger and shoved the gun nozzle into the back of his neck. "Shut up! Hands behind your back."

The ranger obeyed, trembling. "Please," he begged, slowly placing his hands behind his back. "I'm just out here doing my job."

"I said shut up!" Leeroy smashed the butt of the gun into his ear. "I've caught you now. The jig is up." The ranger whimpered as Leeroy cuffed his hands behind his back. "I've been looking for you for a long time, motherfucker. Now you're mine."

Tears rushed down the ranger's cheeks. "Please, I don't want to die."

The hairs on my body stood on end as Leeroy knelt behind the ranger and his face contorted into a vicious sneer. "Come on, big boy. Beg," he said. "Just like you made all those innocent girls do. Beg for your life."

"What girls?" the ranger wept, snot dribbling down his dimpled chin. "I don't know what you're talking about!"

"Cut the shit, Ranger Rick."

"You've got the wrong guy! My name is Holton! *Please!*"

Terror slammed into my chest. *Ranger Rick.* We hadn't given the detective that name. Had we?

But before I could think, the gun went off. The sound ripped through the air, exploding in my ears. I could hardly hear the three of us screaming, I just felt the rawness of my cries tearing my throat, could feel the horror bursting from my friends' mouths. The ranger's dead body slumped to the ground, blood gushing from the crater in the front of his skull.

Stef wailed wordlessly, her face gaunt with fear.

Zoe's body went slack. "He was unarmed," she whispered with horror. "You . . . didn't have to do that."

I couldn't stop crying. "You had him cuffed! You didn't have to kill him!"

"Girls, girls, calm down," Leeroy said, wiping blood from his hands onto his thighs. "It's okay. Take a breath."

Stef obeyed, silence gripping her. She threw both arms around Zoe's neck, burying her face into her shoulder. Zoe rubbed circles into the small of her back as I tried to temper the tears, swiping them away as they fell.

"I know I got a little carried away, but I've been hunting for that son of a bitch for years. Jeremiah's brother is gone now. You're safe."

But safe was the last thing that I felt. With a quivering breath, I finally stopped crying and gasped, grappling at a calmness that was out of reach. "W-why . . ." I stammered. "Why did you call him that?"

"What?" Leeroy asked, his gun still unholstered, hanging casually by his side.

"Ranger Rick."

Zoe and I locked eyes and I knew she'd caught it, too.

"We hadn't told you that's what Jeremiah called him," I said, turning back to the detective. "On the radio."

Leeroy smiled. He picked a glob of blood from his mustache and inspected it before flicking it to the ground. "Well, shit." The expression that he leveled at us now felt familiar. Smug, hungry, wolfish. "I told you I knew who Jeremiah's brother was. That he lived in Seattle. Obviously, I know his name."

His words made sense, logically. But they didn't register. I could barely hear them above the ringing in my ears. I could barely see anything but that wicked smile. Those lips spread wide across his cheeks; it was a smile I'd seen before. The smile of Jeremiah.

"You're not gonna believe me now, are you?" When he spoke now, it was with a mild Southern twang. All I could hear was Jeremiah. "I was hoping you wouldn't catch that little slip. But I can see we're not gonna be able to move past this." He chuckled, wistful now. "Ranger Rick was a code we liked to use."

Horror gripped me, cold and mean. "It was you on the radio," I whispered, moving backward, hardly able to believe my own words, let alone speak them with conviction.

"Fuck." Shock swept across Zoe's face; her voice wavered. "That's why they've never caught him. *That's* why they never investigated the fucking cabin."

"Wait, what's happening?" Stefanie asked. "He's not a real detective?"

"Oh, he's a real fucking detective." Zoe shook her head slowly, still in disbelief.

Leeroy laughed outright, a wolf howling at the moon. "I couldn't believe my luck when that ranger actually came over the hill! I know I milked it for too long, but I just couldn't help myself."

It was as if I'd been sleepwalking until now. The horrifying realization slapped me in the face, jolting me awake.

Jeremiah had been *one* Bones Hollow Hunter.

And Detective Leeroy Bennett was the other.

"*He's* the brother," I whispered.

The three of us had backed away from him in a crooked line. Leeroy stood by the innocent ranger's corpse, his smile leering in the dwindling light. He pulled Zoe's phone from his pocket, dropped it into the mud and crunched it with his boot heel.

"My brother and I, we protected each other," he told us, and for the first time I could see the rage he'd been bottling inside, words leaking through a jaw so clenched it shivered. "You took the one person I have in this world away from me." He raised his handgun at us. Its silver metal gleamed. "Believe me when I say," he looked straight at me, "you're going to die slow."

Zoe had always said that the three of us united together could take on anyone. I'd always believed her. I sucked in a deep breath, terrified, ready. This was our time—when we finally had to put action to those words. To make a stand, together. I had doubted her many times in my life, and rightfully so. But deep down, I'd always trusted that when the shit hit the fan, she would have our backs, as I would hers.

I looked to Zoe now, hopeful, ready for her to fulfill her promise, to make this all work out. Except there was something in her hazel eyes that I never thought I'd see. Complete and utter terror.

Then she did what I never believed she would. She tore herself from Stefanie's grip and ran.

"Zoe!" Stef cried.

Leeroy fired one shot at Stefanie. Shock stole the breath from my lungs as I watched it all in silent horror. She fell beside me, holding her leg, screaming.

"I'll be with you in a minute," he told her. Then he turned to me. "That just leaves you and me, baby girl."

Stef seized this moment, scrambling toward the trees, dragging herself away. Away from us, from me.

Leeroy Bennett didn't cast her so much as a glance. His focus was solely on me as he walked toward me slowly, gun ready. "I want you to run now. I like the hunt."

I spun around and raced into the shadowed forest.

twenty-one

"This has always been my favorite part," Leeroy called after me. "Jeremiah was the one that liked to keep the girls. Me? I liked to catch them. That was a bit ruined for me, with you at the cabin already. I was so glad to get y'all back out here."

Mud grabbed at me, as if the forest floor itself was pulling at my boots to slow me down. This wilderness worked for him. He knew these trees. He knew this terrain. I'd never outrun him; I had to hide.

I darted to the left, then zigzagged back to the right, weaving through trees, hoping to lose him. The graying darkness thickened, blurring the distant shadows into a darker black. I tripped on a rock, smashed my knee into another before hauling myself to my feet. Tree branches scratched at my eyes, but I kept going.

"You could never know the torture my brother endured so

that I wouldn't have to," Leeroy spoke steadily. From the sound of his voice, he did not run. His slow progression revealed his confidence. He didn't need to run. He knew he would find me.

My knees felt ready to crumple. My lungs blazed. I tripped over a hidden bluff, falling into a pile of dead leaves.

"I'm going to make you last for months, you stupid bitch!" Detective Leeroy Bennett howled. "Hell, maybe I'll even break our record, keep you going for a year. What do you think about that?"

He sounded far away, out of sight. Maybe he hadn't seen where I'd fallen. I scooped the dead leaves over me. I buried myself in moss and limbs and foliage, and tucked myself beneath the ferns. I hugged the slick, muddy belly of the bluff that had tripped me. Pressed myself deep into it, kissing the black earth, eyes closed, praying. Please, don't let him find me.

"Think I'm gonna toss you in the hole," his voice edged closer, "leave you there for a few days. You'll scream. You'll try to claw your way out. You may even make it to the top, but you won't get out. None of 'em do. Not until I want them to."

I clamped my hands over my mouth, squeezed my lips together until they trembled. Leaves rustled from his footsteps, floating down the bluff. They fell on top of my head. He was right above me.

"Sometimes I like to watch 'em try to run. If they run fast enough, maybe I give them a reward. But the ones that don't play, that don't give me a challenge, *well,* they're no fun. They don't get to stay around long enough to see my nice side. For you, the cunt that killed my brother . . . *ohhh,* I think you'll get to see sides of me that *no one* ever has. I'm gonna get real creative for you, baby. You killed the wrong brother. Jeremiah didn't even want to play this season. He said he might be done when I told him to take the mattress down from the attic. But I convinced him in the end; I always did. Jeremiah, he was the sweet one, the better man in every way. And I'm gonna make sure you have a long, long time to regret what you've taken from me."

I bit into my palm to keep silent. Blood tickled my lips.

Leeroy went quiet. The forest did, too. Not a bird chirped. Not a single leaf crunched. He might have been right above me, or right in front of me. I wouldn't know. I was too scared to open my eyes. Too scared to breathe, lest he see the fog from my breath.

The minutes were torture. I never knew time could move so maliciously slow. Finally, I heard a footstep. It started close, directly above me, but then the sound disappeared into the forest, moving farther and farther. I waited until the footsteps drifted out of earshot and then I waited longer still.

At last, trembling, I emerged from my forest bed. I picked my way through the darkness, opposite the direction I'd heard him go. I had no idea if I was headed toward the cabin or deeper into the woods. Perhaps I would simply wander through the night in nothing but my soaked T-shirt and shorts until finally collapsing from the cold. It seemed inevitable that I would die in this wilderness one way or another. If not from him, then from exposure. At least if I died from hypothermia, I would deprive him of his vengeance.

But then, I'd never have mine.

Zoe left us. I couldn't believe she fucking left us.

After all her talk, Zoe didn't stand by us. It wasn't the three of us against the world. She'd dragged us into this mess and then saved her own skin and left us to die. A punch to the face wouldn't be enough. I needed her to know, to really feel her remorse. To make her fall to her knees, apologizing. Maybe once one of us had actually died, that would be what it took. Maybe then she would finally admit she was wrong.

I wondered if that was worth dying for and I couldn't decide. It seemed there were worse reasons. If I had to die by a serial killer's hands, at least let it be for that glorious moment. The one in which Zoe fell from her pedestal.

Now *that* would be worth recording.

I didn't hear him coming. He was silent as a fox. One minute I was alone. The next, he was pressed behind me. His body firm, like a tree. A knife slashed across my lower back. The cold metal ripped through me and searing pain flooded my body. I screamed as he held me, cradling my face.

"Shhh," he whispered. "Don't worry. I know what I'm doing."

Leeroy wrapped his arm around my neck, squeezing the air from my throat. My windpipe constricted. My knees folded. He eased me to the ground.

His face hovered over mine as shadows grew, stretching dark fingers across his face.

"Don't worry," he said, wiping tears from my cheeks that I hadn't felt fall. "Daddy's got you."

Everything went black.

twenty-two

I woke covered in mud. Spitting soil and leaves from my mouth, I looked around. I was surrounded by earthen walls. Like I'd been buried, except above me I could see the mouth of the cavern. I was at the bottom of the pit.

Pain flamed across my shoulder blades and down the length of my spine. I pressed my hand to the gash on my back and blood wet my palm. My T-shirt was drenched; the back of my shorts, too. There was so much blood. I was going to bleed to death. I screamed, guttural, frenzied. Only silence answered me.

I was alone. My friends had left me and I would die in this godforsaken hole. I screamed and screamed until my throat was raw, until I couldn't breathe. I curled into a ball. Folding into myself, shaking with terror and with the might of my tears, I cried until I could barely open my eyes. This was it for me. This was the end.

"It shouldn't be me here," I wept bitterly. "It should be you."

I rolled onto my back and stared at the circle of dark sky above me. But wait—that was a circle of open sky. Leeroy hadn't put the grate over the top! That meant I had a chance. If I could climb to the surface, I could crawl out of here.

I scrambled to my feet, wiping the tears from my face with mud-caked fingers. The ferric scent of my own blood filled my nose, spurring me on. I was *not* going to die down here. This would not be my end.

It was fully night now and darkness clung to everything down here, deep in the belly of the earth. Trees' long, black arms swayed overhead, blocking the starry sky. The ground was soft from the earlier rain, cloying. My boot heels sank. I wondered if I could use this to my advantage; maybe I'd get better purchase for climbing. But the opposite proved to be true. The walls of the pit were slick as butter, and as I tried to dig my toe into the side, it slipped right down.

I burrowed my nails deep, clinging to the wall like a spider. My butchered finger throbbed, but I fought through the pain. If I could just grab hold . . . I pictured the gym rock walls that Zoe and Stef never invited me to climb. The walls upon which I killed myself to impress them whenever I insisted on joining. I never made it over seven feet off the ground. That was *with* a rope.

"You're terrible at falling." Zoe's words came back to me.

And she was right. Even with the rope, I always fell too hard. I never knew how to position my feet so that I didn't collapse, my back slapping into the ground. But I'd proven myself climbing in San Vito lo Capo with Stef as my cheerleader. I hadn't fallen once, which was just as well, since there was no padded mat to fall on that time and I'd have died if my ropes had failed. But I'd done it then and I'd be damned if I wasn't going to prove Zoe wrong again now. I'd claw my way out of this pit just to tell her I'd done it. I would hunt her down just to show her.

I dug my nails in and began to climb. Fire seared through my back, up my spine, but I didn't stop. I fell. And I fell. And I fell again. Each time, I pulled myself back up. This could not be the end for me. Not here. Not in some hole where no one would ever find me.

Grabbing hold of the wall with my hands wasn't the biggest problem. It was getting any traction with my boots. I carved handholds into the moist mud. Shaping the clay until it felt firm enough to latch onto, sturdy enough to place my boot on once I'd formed another handhold above. The first four steps worked. I was doing it! I was climbing out of this pit.

I pressed my foot down on my sixth handhold. There was enough air beneath me that a breeze whispered against my bloody back. I tested it with my toe. It felt strong, so I put my weight down. The mud slid away from me violently, my foot shooting into the air. My other foot lost its purchase and I hung from my hands alone. My left hand burned from the strain. I squeezed the slick earth, groping, pleading. Hold me. But it was too wet. The clay pulled away, my nails slipped, and I fell.

The flat of my back slammed into the ground, knocking the wind out of me. I rolled over, spluttered, and cradled my chest. It took me many minutes to recover, but eventually I wiped the tears from my eyes with muddy hands. I had to think of a new strategy. There was no one else here who would. No Zoe to turn to. No Stefanie. Hell, even Laurie Wolff had gone quiet.

I felt around me like a blind man, fingers stabbing wildly

into the pit for any stick or branch that I could use. My nails hit something hard buried in the mud, something smooth and circular and metal. I plucked it out and felt a button on the top. I clicked it and the case popped open, confirming even in the dark what it was. An antique pocket compass. *Florence's* silver compass.

Florence Marsh. She really had been the Hunter's victim.

Not only that, but she'd been here in this pit. God knows how long that monster had had her, torturing her.

Leeroy's words returned to me now, a shiver along my spine: *You won't get out. None of 'em do. Not until I want them to.*

No one came to save her. She died alone, in pain. I shed a tear now for Florence. For Wendy, Rae, Harper, Ginny . . . for all of them. No one came for them, just as no one would come for me. My friends had abandoned me. I was all alone and I would die as this psychopath's plaything.

There was nothing in my stomach, but still burning acid bile spewed from my mouth. Strands of spit dangled from my chin as I gasped for air, sobbing. There was no hope. I really would die here. Just like Florence. I was a fool to think I could be any different.

"Help," I whimpered into the earth. "Someone please . . . help me."

A twig snapped above. I froze. Was I too deep for predators to reach, or was I nothing more than a sitting duck for a hungry animal? Being eaten by a bear or a cougar was probably preferable to what Leeroy had in store for me. I didn't know if I should keep silent or call out to it, begging for the end.

My despair softened, my heartbeat a furious bird flapping, as a flashlight beam swept across the opening above.

"Hello?" I called.

"Oh my god, Jade!" Stef stuck her face over the edge. She whispered so faintly I could hardly hear. "Have you seen Zoe?"

"You've got to get me out of here!" I cried, softly as I could. "Find a branch or something."

She looked from left to right, frantic, until her eyes caught on something in the distance and she disappeared from view. Panic flooded my chest. I only breathed again when she returned a moment later dragging a dead tree branch. But it wasn't long enough to reach the bottom of the pit.

"You'll have to climb to it," she told me. "You can do it."

I flashed back to her coaching me, cheerleading me when I didn't believe myself capable. Revived by her presence, I summoned all my strength and followed the trail of handholds I'd already made. I would need to make at least two more if I was going to reach the branch.

"Hurry," Stef whispered. "I don't know where he is."

My foot slipped, but I did not fall. Pain racked my body and I shivered with cold; sweat dripped down my cheek. I burrowed into the mud for another handhold, shaping the clay.

"Hurry!" she hissed again.

My heartbeat quickened. I lifted myself up. The hold was just sturdy enough to set my toe on. I could almost reach. I stretched as high as I could. "Just a little lower." I could hardly speak from the exertion.

Stef lay on her belly across the branch and dipped the limb deeper into the pit. Just as I latched my right hand around it, my foothold collapsed. I clamped onto the wood with my left hand before I fell. Stef yelped, holding as tight as she could. We groaned in unison as my feet scrambled at the sides, flailing for purchase. I kicked the toes of my boots deep into the mud and managed to move my hands upward an inch. Then another. Stef held steady as, finally, I clawed my way to the surface. I emerged, gasping like I'd nearly drowned and now burst from the sea.

We held each other, shivering, for a heartbeat. We brushed the hair from each other's eyes, the mud from each other's cheeks, weeping into each other.

Finally, I looked down at the bullet wound in her calf, as if only just remembering. Even in the darkness, I could tell her leg was painted in blood. "Are you all right?" I placed a hand near her knee, but did not touch.

"I've been hiding in an empty fox den for hours, waiting till I was sure he'd gone." Stef was still panicked, breathing heavy. "I don't know where Zoe is. Do you think he has her?" Even now, Zoe was all she could think about.

"She left us, Stef. Zoe fucking left us."

"I don't believe that. If Zoe left, it's because she has a plan."

"Yeah, to let us die and save herself."

"She wouldn't do that!" Stefanie pulled at me, pleading. "You *know* she wouldn't."

"I don't know anything anymore."

"We have to go back to the cabin. That's where he'd have taken her, if he's . . ." Stef swallowed hard, sniffing back tears. "We can't leave her."

I didn't have the strength to argue. I also had no better plan. All our supplies were in the cabin, neatly stowed away in our backpacks. I was cold through to the bone. My fingers trembled, pricked with splinters from the branch Stef had extended. My head throbbed and the gash on my back pulsed with pain.

"Fine," I said. "We'll go find her. But only because I want her to apologize."

Stef laughed. It wasn't her usual infectious giggle. This was snotty and quiet, but a welcome respite all the same. "I think Zoe would probably rather die first."

"Great. She has that option now. I'm sure Leeroy would be happy to help."

Stef shined her phone light around the forest. "We came from that direction. Opposite . . . that."

She couldn't say "pit." I understood why. The word was a nightmare conjured into life. The reality of being inside it was much worse. A hunting pit, he had called it. It was a death hole. Where women waited to die.

Just beyond, the ranger's body was still visible, a shadowy lump in the moss.

"Turn that off," I told her. "The light. We don't know where he is."

Stef slipped her phone back into her pocket.

"How's your leg?"

"Well . . . my ankle is fucked and I've been shot in the same leg. So, you know, doing pretty good."

"Can you put any weight on it at all?"

"I don't have much choice."

She wrapped her arm around my shoulders, and together we hoisted ourselves off the ground. The extra weight of her leaning on me made the gaping slash across my back pucker. I yelped. Blood soaked through my shirt, dripping down my spine. But giving up wasn't an option.

"How about you?" she asked as we limped along. "How are you holding up?"

"Well . . . let's see, I got my head cracked into a counter, my finger chopped off, and I was slashed across the back. All before getting thrown into a death pit. So . . . yeah, pretty good." We shared a weak smile. For this fleeting moment, we could pretend we were back on the trail, comparing welts and blisters.

"Wonder what Zoe will have to contribute. Bet she outdoes us both, probably has two broken arms or something."

"That would be just like her," I said, grunting with the effort. "But I bet she's got something sexier. Like an eyebrow scar. Or a dislocated shoulder she'll have to slam back into place against a wall like some sort of action star. Show-off."

Stef giggled, muted, but closer to normal. It felt good to hear anything that touched on normal. "Hey, don't be mad at Zoe. I know it's gotten seriously fucked up, but . . ."

"Don't," I cut her off. "Don't defend her. I don't want to hear it." There was a fountain of anger surging inside of me, ready to burst forth. But now wasn't the time. I took a deep breath, pushing it back down. "I'll be honest, I thought you ditched me, too, when I saw you take off. What happened after he shot you?"

"You mean when he shot me and said he'd be back for me in a minute? You're fucking right, I ran. Well, as best I could. But not to leave you. I went to hide. And I bet that's what Zoe has done, too. She wouldn't leave us, Jade, and you know it."

I thought back to all the times Zoe had put me into crazy situations, circumstances I'd never have normally agreed to. I used to think she was helping me, like a gardener tending to a flower, helping me bloom, pushing me outside my comfort zone to realize my utmost potential. Now, I saw everything in a different light. Like a veil had been lifted from my eyes. What if she really *had* just left me in the corn maze that day, with no care if I found her or not. What if the man with the pool cue really had attacked us—would she have run?

What if my best friend, the woman I had idolized since I was in middle school, who I had worshipped, who I'd have followed through the gates of hell . . . what if she hadn't just fucked up this time? What if she wasn't who I thought she was? What if she actually wasn't a friend at all?

I swallowed the hard lump in my throat. It was like choking down a peach pit. "Before today, I knew my friends would never trick me into coming on some borderline-if-not-entirely-suicidal serial killer hunt. So, stop telling me what I know." She opened her lips to respond, but I spoke first. I couldn't talk about this anymore. "You found a fox den to hide in?"

"Yeah. I think that's what it was anyway. I'd gotten as far as I could, which wasn't very far, before I thought I heard him coming back. I tried to climb a tree."

"I knew that's what you'd do."

"But I couldn't with my leg. So, I lay flat underneath the ferns and fucking prayed. That's when I got lucky and noticed the burrow. I rolled in, hoping whatever was living there didn't come home. Then I heard you screaming . . ." tears tangled in her voice, "and I couldn't come for you. I was too scared. But, like, what could I have even done for you? I can't even walk upright on my own."

"It's okay, Stef," I reassured her. "You didn't leave me. You saved my life back there, getting me out of that hole."

"You'd have gotten out by yourself eventually. You're a better climber than you give yourself credit for."

Than Zoe gave me credit for.

And yes. Yes, I was.

I took hold of Stef's hand and squeezed it.

"Then I just waited. I didn't know what else to do. I didn't know if you were alive or dead. I didn't know if Zoe was. All I knew was he said he'd come back for me. So, I waited, hiding." She let go of my hand to wipe away a tear. "He started looking for me. I heard him, searching all around me for what felt like an hour. Stood above where I was hidden for so long; I could hear him breathing. I pissed my pants I was so scared." She tried a laugh; it came out like a cry. "Then he couldn't find me, so he left. But I was still so scared, I couldn't move. It wasn't until I heard you screaming again inside there. Knowing you were alive . . . that's what got me up. Otherwise, I don't know what I would have done."

I wasn't listening anymore. It felt so unlikely as to be impossible. He'd stood right above her, breathing over her, taunting her. Yet he couldn't find her? My heart sank.

"Stef . . ." I didn't want to say it. It sat on my tongue, a heavy pill I could not swallow.

My eyes darted left to right, but in the darkness I could see nothing but what was directly in front of my face. Crickets chirred and, somewhere distant, a wolf howled. Everything else was swallowed by the night. I motioned for Stef to stop, and we froze, two deer in an open meadow, listening for predators. She knew what I was thinking without my needing to say.

If Leeroy Bennett, the Bones Hollow Hunter, couldn't find a wounded woman leaving a blood trail in the forest, it's because he chose not to. He was watching us right now. A cat playing with his mice.

"Get low," I started to say, as if that would help.

I didn't hear the arrow fly. Not even a whisper through the evergreens. Stef collapsed into me, screaming. An arrow pierced her biceps, extending from her like a third arm. I couldn't hold her and we fell together, her on top of me.

"That was a warning shot!" Somewhere in the darkness, the Hunter's voice rang out. "I told you, no one gets out of the pit unless I want them to."

Stef screeched, staring at the arrow that went clean through her biceps.

"Come on!" I pulled at her. "We have to move!"

She scrambled to her knees, howling with pain. I wrapped her other arm around my shoulder.

"Time to run!" Leeroy called from somewhere, everywhere, all around us. "Shake a leg, ladies! I want to see how fast you go!"

We stumbled together and Stef cried out in agony and desperation, gritting her teeth, growling, dragging herself with one foot and letting the other trail behind as we staggered forward. Faster. Fast as we could.

"Come on!" I urged myself as much as her. I was the coach now. "Let's go!"

Stef leaned on me hard, so heavy I could barely keep upright. I squeezed her waist with one hand, her bloodied arm with the other. The gash across my back stretched, a mouth opening wide. My body was on fire. We tripped on a vine, crashing forward.

Stef started crawling now, on all fours. "I'm not gonna make it," she sobbed.

"I won't leave you! Come on!" I grabbed her under both arms and pulled her up. "Come on, Stef!"

The next arrow struck the back of her shoulder. The point went clean through, poking out the other side. We smacked the ground together, eating dirt and moss. "Get up," I moaned. "Let's move!"

Stef made no sound; her crying had stopped. I tried dragging her, a bag of bricks.

"Faster, girl! Come on!" the Hunter howled.

Furious rage burst from my lungs, echoing into the night, a body-shaking scream. I heaved her across the forest floor. Boots slipping in the earth, blood trickling down my side. I dug my heels in and pulled once. Then again. Inch by inch, we moved forward. Stef's eyes were closed and I didn't have time to check if she was breathing.

An arrow whizzed past my face from behind, piercing a tree in front of me. "I don't miss by mistake!" He cackled in the darkness. "I'm getting close now. You remember what I said about the girls who don't challenge me?"

He wanted me to run. To save myself. To be like Zoe.

"Fuck you!" I roared.

I hauled my friend another inch. I would not leave her. All I needed was to hoist her over my shoulders. If I could just get her over my shoulders, I could carry her. "Come on, Stef!" I cried, pleading, sobbing. "Wake up! Move!"

I set her down and snapped off both the arrows with my boot heel. Kneeling into the moss and winching her languid arms over my shoulder, I tried to maneuver myself so I could get one of her legs over the other. I would carry her on my back. It was impossible, but I wouldn't stop trying.

Footsteps approached and his voice grew nearer. "Next arrow goes clean through your Achilles' heel. I can do it, hon. I'm one helluva shot."

I stared down at Stef, sweating. Goddamn it, *goddamn it*! I shook her. She didn't flinch. I put my head to her chest, but heard nothing. She couldn't be dead. I refused to believe it.

Finally, her chest lifted, just barely. It pressed into my cheek before falling again. I waited another beat, to watch it rise and fall once more.

"That's it! That's my girl, Stef! You stay alive." I wept as I leaned down and put my lips into her ear. "I'm not leaving you. I promise. I will not leave you here." I kissed her cheek.

"You got five seconds," the Hunter called. "Tick tock, young lady."

I didn't know where he was. I couldn't see him. I lifted my middle finger to the sky all the same. Then I took one last look at my friend. "I'm coming back for you."

I raced on toward the cabin. It was the only direction I could think to run, the only place I thought that Leeroy might take Stefanie now. No doubt he'd get there first. He knew these woods better than me, was faster and stronger in every way. I didn't care if I ever saw Zoe's smug face again, but at least if she was there, we could rescue Stef together.

It's what Stef would have wanted.

twenty-three

I remembered Stef's vision board for this trip perfectly as I sprinted through the forest. She'd texted it to me the day before we left. Pictures of meditative serenity. A woman on a cliff top with her hands on her knees. A crackling campfire. The three of us laughing one Fourth of July, sparklers in hand. Each image was seared into my brain; pictures of warmth and light and love, the perfect adventure. That's what Stef had wanted for this trip. Or at least that's what her vision board had said.

She'd neglected to add images of serial killer cabins and torture. She certainly had forgotten to add death to her little manifestation collage. And there'd been zero mention of the podcast. Come to think of it, even Stef's vision board had lied to me.

God, what was I doing? Going back to the cabin was suicidal. That's assuming Leeroy would even take Stef there. With every forward step, I inched closer to my death. That cabin was cursed. Only bad things happened there.

Everyone knows that you never return to the scene of the crime.

Exactly. This was a mistake. Zoe had run. Stefanie was terribly wounded, maybe even fatally so. It was time to save myself.

But no—Stef wasn't dead. If there was any chance that she might survive . . .

"They suffered," Detective Leeroy Bennett said.

The thought of what he might be doing to her wasn't one I could live with. Apparently, Zoe could. But not me.

Jade Edelman was willing to die for the opportunity to get one over on her friend.

Hey, Laurie. There were worse things to die for. Also, what a cynical take. Any points for heroism? Friendship? Loyalty?

Jade wanted a medal for being a good person.

No. I just wanted to die knowing that I'd been different. That I hadn't been like Zoe. That I hadn't abandoned my sisters to save my own skin.

I scrambled over a boulder and dropped into a puddled trench that swallowed half my leg with wet, gooey mud. It took both hands tugging on my knee to yank it back out. I fell backward and whacked my elbow on the boulder. Fuck this fucking forest! I bit my hand so that I wouldn't scream with rage.

The forest was working against me. Every twig snapping beneath my running boot betrayed my location to the Hunter. Every tree limb that I had to move aside told him where I was. It was like the wilderness wanted me to get caught.

Maybe Stef had been right. Maybe there really was a sacred

burial ground in the Bones Hollow Valley. Maybe the spirits here were angry, spiteful of the living. Why hadn't *that* been on her vision board?

More people mysteriously vanished from the Bones Hollow Trail than any other in the Pacific Northwest. Those were among Laurie Wolff's first words to me, in episode one. We'd started listening to the podcast as soon as Zoe and Stef picked me up from my apartment six days ago. It'd taken two whole days to drive across the country to the Bones Hollow Trail.

"You've got to listen to this, Jade, it's wild," Zoe had said.

"When Zoe first sent this to me, I binged it in like one night." Stef had turned to me in the back seat. "I'm obsessed!"

I'd listened to Laurie Wolff's voice rasp through the crackling car speakers. Her message had sparked a sizzling, electric anxiety within me. But I had not heeded her warning. She'd said it loud and clear: *Do not go hike the Bones Hollow Trail, dumbass!*

I trudged onward through the black night. Without a compass, I could only pray I walked in a straight line. It felt like I'd been walking for an hour but it'd probably only been twenty minutes. Nighttime felt endless. An oppressive blanket chilling me to the bone. I stoked my anger to keep me warm, churning hot coals in my belly.

"Bloody Mary," Zoe had said three times all those years ago, so triumphant, so self-assured. Back when I thought she was the bravest girl in the world. So fierce as to ward off demons. Yet where was she now?

"Bloody Mary," I whispered, marching onward. Then a little louder. "Bloody Mary."

I was not afraid, not anymore. Did you hear that, Zoe? I didn't need you anymore!

Finally, I belted, "Bloody motherfucking Mary!"

Nothing happened. No demon appeared to swallow me.

I continued on, triumphant, proud. This newfound ecstasy sent a surge of warmth through me, radiating it from within like a tiny furnace. My breath plumed in front of me as I smiled ear to ear.

Something moved up ahead. A bush rustled. I froze midstep, making out a shape in the darkness. It stood, human height. Holy shit, I'd been wrong. Here she was, Bloody Mary, invoked by my call. Summoned to these woods.

I laughed. It started out as a giggle, but quickly morphed into something maniacal. A delirious squeal, pouring out of me. I bent over, clutching my side, unable to move. Tears squirted from my eyes.

"Shhh!" came a familiar voice. "Jade, is that you?"

It was her. My demon. The spell had worked. Bloody Mary had come to life. I fell to my knees, crippled with laughter. The figure approached. All those years ago I had thought it was Zoe's fierceness that had protected us from the ghoul, but now I realized it'd been her all along. She was the apparition.

It was Zoe. My Bloody Mary.

twenty-four

"Oh my god! I thought you were dead!" Zoe flung her arms around me. Warm tears kissed my neck, my shoulder; I didn't know if they were hers or mine. I realized my laughter had transformed into crying as she caressed my face with her muddy fingers. I could taste the dirt she spread across me. "I'm so glad you're okay," she said over and over.

"It's you," I muttered, delirious. The world felt hot, spinning. Like I was in a fever dream. None of this was real.

She dragged her thumbs across my tearstained cheeks. "Where's Stef?"

I shook my head. "He's got her."

"Is she . . . ?" Zoe choked back a sob.

"I don't know. He shot her twice with arrows. Told me if I didn't run, he'd shoot me, too."

"You did the right thing," she said, still petting me. "You did the right thing."

The right thing. I snorted. "Is that what you told yourself?"

Zoe stopped petting. Her hand froze on my cheek.

"You ran." I was no longer laughing or crying. My voice was grave as stone. "You left us."

"We all ran. It was the smartest move."

"You left us to die."

"I found you, didn't I?"

There it was. The usual Zoe adage: It all worked out.

It all worked out, so you can't be mad.

It all worked out, so shut the hell up.

"You didn't find me," I pointed out. "I ran into you."

"Look," she said, going back to petting me, "if I had rushed him, he'd have fucking shot me. Running away was the only option. The only way I stood even a little bit of a chance at helping you both."

She was probably right. I didn't care.

I needed to get back to Stefanie. I brushed Zoe's hand away. "We need to get back to the cabin."

"*That's* where you're going? Are you insane!"

"I told you. He has Stef and that's where he's going to take her."

Zoe grabbed my hand, but I ripped it away and continued walking.

"He shot her twice," she said slowly. "I hate to say it . . . but if she's not dead now, she will be soon." She pulled at me, but I refused to stop. "We have a chance to get away, you and me. We should take that. Stef would want us to."

"Oh yeah?" I halted, hard, and we almost collided. "Well, that's not what Stef said when she thought he had *you.* She insisted we go rescue you. Said it's what you would do for us." My laugh was bitter acid thrown onto her face. "She'll be lucky if she's dead. Not just because, thanks to special guest Detective Leeroy Bennett, we know that the Hunter doesn't kill his victims quick—*they suffer*—but because then she'll never have to learn the ugly truth about you. That you aren't who you've always pretended to be."

Our eyes met in the darkness. Stared hard into each other. I dug deep enough that I could see Zoe's shame, however fleeting. The flickering wetness of her pupils, like she might cry. She bit it back, swallowed it down with grinding teeth.

"Okay. Fine. Let's go," she relented.

It wasn't enough. I wanted her to collapse to her knees and grovel. To admit she was wrong. To fucking apologize. But there was no time for that now. No doubt the Hunter moved faster than us so we didn't have a moment to lose.

We have a special guest for you on today's episode, my sweet Little Savages. Detective Leeroy Bennett of the Bones Hollow Hunter investigation. Laurie Wolff's words replayed in my ears as I walked; thinking of her voice was almost muscle memory now. Hiking and Laurie Wolff went begrudgingly hand in hand. It dawned on me what a narcissistic psychopath Leeroy had to be to choose to speak on a podcast about himself. But then again, from what Zoe had told me about other serial killers, it wasn't unusual. They often wanted to insert themselves into their own investigation, and who could be better poised to do that than a detective on the police force? I remembered her telling me about the BTK and Zodiac killers, who sent letters to the media and police. I'd never thought it was strange how much Zoe knew about serial killers. Maybe I should have been more concerned.

This season of Serial Killers USA *is dedicated to the lost women of the Bones Hollow Trail.* But thinking back to that first episode, that first day in the car with Zoe and Stef, our backpacks stowed safely in her Oldsmobile's trunk, not a single bruise or blister yet to mar our bodies . . . I couldn't have guessed that this podcast was any different from the other true crime bullshit Zoe and Stef were always hooked on. I wondered now if there was a red flag that I had missed. A subtle clue I should have picked up on that would have warned me of Zoe's true intentions.

"This sick fuck," she'd said at the time, after episode one. "I can't believe no one's caught him." Should I have known that that was Zoe-code for "Hey, let's see if we can find him"?

"How did you even hear of the Bones Hollow Hunter?" I asked her now, breaking our beautiful silence because I suddenly had to know. This inexplicable need pressed into my chest, squeezed my ribs. "I never asked you."

"From my cousin Cheri."

"The tweaker that makes a big scene every Thanksgiving? I thought you hated her."

"I don't hate her," she argued. "She's my cousin—and she's clean now. But that's not even the point. She'd just done a leg of the PCT and said everyone on the trail talked about the Bones Hollow Hunter. Locals warned of him even more than Sasquatch. It was like he was a rock star."

Zoe had always wanted to be a rock star.

She grunted as she climbed over a dead tree. "I guess I just got curious."

Apparently, she'd never heard about what curiosity did to the cat.

"It was researching him that led me to the podcast. Which eventually led me to the group online. It seemed the answer was here, on the trail, but no one had bothered to find it. I just had to know." I didn't look at her face, but I could hear the pride seep into her voice as she said, "You know what I'm like once I sink my teeth into something."

Yes. I did. It was no longer an admirable trait. What had once felt like tenacity, the likes of which I could only dream of possessing, now felt animalistic, predatory. Zoe was a hunter, someone who chased down her targets with reckless abandon, no regard for collateral damage. I pictured her sharp teeth burrowing into skin, tasting blood, a death grip.

"And turns out"—Zoe wasn't going to say it; surely she didn't have the gall to fucking say it—"I was right."

I clenched my fists. My teeth. My whole body. I gritted every part of myself to keep from screaming. Even now, Zoe couldn't admit that she was wrong. It was as impossible for her as flapping her arms and taking flight. I would have had more luck expecting a pig to open its mouth and sing opera than I would waiting for this sick bitch to admit she'd done even one wrong thing.

When I could eventually control my breath enough to speak, all I could utter was, "Was it worth it?"

Zoe went quiet. Her breath grew heavier. Then she stopped abruptly. "Do you see that?"

Thinking of the Hunter with his bow aimed true, I hit the dirt. Zoe joined me, belly to the earth.

"Is it him?" I whispered.

"No, look." She pointed ahead. "Those figures."

I was scared to look, terrified I'd see two glowing blue eyes staring back at me. A Hunter, jaws open. "I don't see anything."

"You don't see that?"

My heart drummed in my ears as I stared into the blackness. Squinting, I could just make out two circular mounds between two trees in the near distance, but it was difficult to say. "Maybe . . . no. I don't know."

"They're tents."

My heart raced faster, too afraid to hope. "I don't think so."

"They are. I'm gonna go check."

"Zoe! No!" I grabbed at her ankle, but she was already up and moving past me. I watched her figure recede, but I refused to follow.

I couldn't make out what was happening. I heard the snap of leaves and branches. Then Zoe cried out. "Oh my god, help, please!"

Was she calling out to me? I hesitated before springing forward. For a split moment, I thought about staying still. Except then, I couldn't. Zoe was the one who ran to save herself—not me. I fumbled forward blindly, feeling for any large limbs as I went, anything I could use as a weapon.

A light came on inside one of the mounds. It was clear now they were tents; she'd been right. Even now I felt the twinge of resentment.

"Help us!" she called again.

Relief overwhelmed me. I stood beside Zoe, panting, out of breath. Finally, we were saved! I could have dropped to my knees with gratitude. "Oh my god, thank you, thank you, thank you," I whispered, and clenched my fists.

Whoever was in there would surely have a phone. Whoever was in there would surely call for help. At long last, this nightmare was over.

We watched together as the zipper rose up and down and the tent flap fell open. A scruffy head of hair emerged, then stood tall. A half-naked middle-aged man with enough chest hair to qualify as a shirt shined a flashlight in our eyes. I blinked white light.

"We're in danger," Zoe pleaded, voice hushed. "Please!"

"What's going on?" He cleared phlegm from his throat with a quick grunt and scratched at his balls. He wore woolly red flannel bottoms.

A second flashlight in the neighboring tent switched on. Another man with matching flannels and substantially less chest hair appeared from the opening. A round, almost pregnant-looking belly swelled beneath his wifebeater. "What in the hell?" he said. A rifle was slung over his bare shoulder.

These men were hunters. The utter relief I'd felt just moments ago gave way to something new. I didn't know if I should be worried now or grateful still, and felt myself fall somewhere in between, on the precipice of apprehension and joy.

"We need your help," Zoe said.

The hairy man rubbed sleep from his eye, then scratched his bushy beard. "Come again?"

"We need your help," Zoe repeated, grabbing him by both biceps. "Do you have a satellite phone or any way of calling the police?" she asked more urgently.

"Okay, let's stay calm," the second one said, bleary, annoyed at having been woken. "No need to sound so hysterical. Did you and your boyfriend have a fight?"

"We were attacked by the Hunter." I was so mad I could have punched him. "The *Bones Hollow* Hunter. He confessed to us. He took our friend. We need to get help!"

The men looked from each other to us, then back to each other. "Every hiker who hears a bump in the night thinks they've run into the Hunter. You girls just got turned around, didn't you? Spooked in the dark."

Why did everyone keep calling us girls? We were nearly thirty years old.

"You're not listening." Zoe still hadn't let go of his arms. "It was him. He murdered a ranger right in front of us! He's looking for us now. You have guns, right? You can protect us?" She made her voice soft, trying to appeal to their egos.

After a long, agonizing moment, the hairy one relented. He moved aside from the opening. "Come on. Get in."

The second guy looked to me like maybe I was meant to crawl into his tent. But there was no way in hell. I pressed in after Zoe. I hadn't realized just how cold I was until the warmth inside squeezed me tight like a hug. The tent smelled like feet; I didn't care.

Zoe spotted a bag of nuts next to the man's backpack. She didn't ask first. "I'm sorry, I'm starving," she said as she piled handfuls into her cheeks.

"That's okay." The man sounded hesitant, like he was still assessing us. "I'm Kevin, by the way. That's my buddy Tyler over there."

After a minute, Tyler appeared in the tent door with a jug of water. I grabbed at this and poured it greedily down my throat. "Thank you," I spluttered, drinking more.

Then I passed it to Zoe and she handed me the nuts. I ate almost the entire bag before I realized I shouldn't. Ruefully, I handed it back to the original owner. He looked more concerned than unhappy.

"How long you girls been out here?" Kevin asked.

"Three days on the Bones Hollow Trail," I said, still chewing.

"But we found his cabin yesterday and haven't eaten or drunk anything since."

I remembered the dry jerky Jeremiah had offered us and almost heaved. Best to never think about it again. To never wonder what—or who—the meat came from.

"Except for that god-awful moonshine." Zoe grimaced. "Tasted like rubbing alcohol."

"So, you drank with this guy," Tyler said. "Was that before or after he tried to kill you?"

It dawned on me with equal parts horror and fury: They didn't believe us.

Tyler sounded amused, even. "When exactly did he *confess* to being the Hunter?"

"Did you say cabin?" Kevin scratched his beard. "Shit, you must be talking about Jeremiah." He squatted so that his knees nearly reached his shoulders. His legs splayed wide, flanneled crotch on full display. He looked down at us like we were children gathering for story time. "He might seem strange to you. Stays there most months of the year hunting and making bizarre things out of animal bones. Has an online shop and does pretty well for himself. Hell, the missus and I even have a few of his wind chimes on our front porch. I can see why he'd give you girls the creeps. He's a hermit, all right, but I've known him for years. He's a good man."

Any relief I'd felt drained out of me. I had stepped fully over the precipice and was now free-falling into anxiety, on the way to despair. These men knew him. They liked him, thought he was a great guy.

Please, Zoe, whatever you do, don't tell them their friend is dead.

"A *good man*? Tell that to my face." Zoe pointed to her broken nose. "And he chopped off my friend's finger. Look!" She grabbed my wrist and waved my wound in their faces as evidence. My hand cast a strange shadow puppet on the tent wall. "Still don't believe me?" She sounded so self-righteous, triumphant even. "I have pictures of him attacking us." She felt for her pockets before remembering. "Fuck! He took my phone and smashed it."

"Jeremiah did?" Tyler asked, suspicious. He exchanged a look with his friend, eyes filled with doubt and disbelief. "And when exactly did he kill the ranger?"

This was spiraling nowhere good. To them, we were hysterical women. The kind that men like Tyler had filed away under the not-to-be-trusted category in his brain. We should leave. I tugged at Zoe's hand.

"No, that was his brother," she clarified. A mistake. She was only making us sound less credible. "Detective Leeroy Bennett. He's the one that confessed. *He's* the one that's hunting us."

"Thought you said that was Jeremiah." Tyler lifted a brow.

"No, Jeremiah was at the cabin." Zoe shook her head, frustrated, clearly seeing what I already knew but refusing to accept it. "Look, if you have a phone, we can call for help. The police will sort everything out."

Now Tyler's amusement was no longer veiled; he smiled openly. "We don't have a satellite phone. And regular phones don't get any signal. That's what most people like about being out here."

"Then come with us," Zoe urged, unwilling to give up. "Bring your guns. You'll see for yourself. He kidnapped our friend Stef."

"So, there were three of you?" Tyler shook his head. "Three girls drinking alone with Jeremiah, there's one for the books."

"Here's the thing, girls," Kevin cut in. "It's three in the morning. I believe that you got all shaken up about something, but I don't know what you expect us to do. We don't have a radio. And we can't go out there, guns blazing, in the middle of the night like a couple of cowboys. Best we can offer right now is a tent to sleep in. You can take mine. I'll move over to Tyler's."

Tyler groaned. "Ah, hell. Brought my own tent for a reason. Not to share farts with you all night."

Kevin shot him a look, then returned kinder eyes our way. "I'm sure this is just one big misunderstanding. We'll march down there to the cabin come first light and sort everything out. All right?"

I looked to Zoe with desperation. This was a bad plan. We couldn't trust these men to believe us. What would they do with their big guns when they found their friend Jeremiah dead tomorrow—who would they blame?

But, most important, we couldn't waste any more time. We couldn't leave Stefanie alone with Leeroy.

"We should go," I whispered. "Stef . . ."

Zoe took both my hands in hers and squeezed. "We cannot help her like this. We need rest. At least an hour. Then we'll go back, I promise."

Her promises weren't worth much anymore. But suddenly a weariness hammered into me so hard I could barely sit upright. My limbs felt heavier than lead.

"Just an hour," I conceded, already leaning back, unable to stop myself. "Then we're leaving."

Tyler and Kevin zippered the tent flap shut behind them, grumbling to each other. Then a black, dreamless sleep embraced me.

twenty-five

Birdsong woke me. The sun was not yet up, but the darkness had thinned now to a milky gray. I had no way of knowing what time it was, but I felt certain it'd been over an hour.

My furious heart battered my chest. I shouldn't have slept so long. Stef needed me.

My back throbbed and every bone in my body felt brittle like frost. But I sprang upright, shaking Zoe. She was slow to wake, as always. She could have slept through the Blitz. Once she was asleep, she was gone to the world. I shook her again, harder.

"Come on," I hissed, not wanting to wake the hunters in the neighboring tent. "Let's go!"

Zoe lifted her head, rubbing her eyes.

"I don't want them to come," I whispered.

"What? Why not?" she demanded blearily.

"They knew Jeremiah. They're *friends.* They're not going to take our side when they see what's happened to him—what *I* did."

"That won't matter. They're going to find Stef with us, and then they'll see we're telling the truth. We need them; they have guns."

"Who's to say they'll use them to help us and not *the detective*? We can't trust them."

"We don't have to. Just trust me." I was so sick of her saying that. Zoe reached for my hand, but I pulled it away. "More witnesses can only be a good thing. Especially since he destroyed my phone."

"Except if we don't find Stef and then our witnesses testify on behalf of the dead guy's stand-up character."

"We need them," Zoe repeated, firmer. "We can't get her back on our own. That's if we can get her back at all."

"Don't talk like that."

A pained expression swept her face, but still she shook her head. "We have to be practical."

Bodies shuffled outside the tent. It was too late; the men were already up. My stomach coiled in on itself, writhing like a snake. Zoe unzipped the tent and the flap fell open. The first thing we saw was Tyler's pimpled back. His wifebeater exposed long, curly strands of hair on his shoulders. He was standing beside his green camouflage tent, hands at groin level, head tilted up to the sky as a stream of urine jettisoned into the ferns. He glanced behind at Zoe as she emerged, gave himself two shakes. Grunted a greeting.

I checked behind me before exiting. The blood from my back had left a thick crimson stain on the tent floor, a line the length of my torso. Normally, I'd have felt embarrassed and apologized.

Now I was glad to see the blemish. These men wouldn't be able to pretend that we hadn't been here, that they hadn't seen us. If they didn't help us, as I was almost sure they wouldn't, then it was good that they carry this stain. I hoped it would never wash out.

Between the two tents, Kevin had readied their stovetop. A package of pre-cooked breakfast sausages waited on the ground beside his dirty stockinged feet.

"No, no, no," I pleaded. "Please. We don't have time to eat. We have to go *now.*"

Kevin smiled. "Relax. We'll get to the cabin soon enough."

"You don't understand," I said. "God knows what he's doing to her!"

Tyler and Kevin traded looks. "Look, hon," Kevin said, "we need breakfast. We can't go without eating."

"I don't go anywhere without eating," Tyler added, offended at the mere suggestion.

I realized this was my chance to leave them behind. "Okay, that's fine. You stay and eat breakfast. We'll go by ourselves."

Zoe pulled at me with her eyes. "Jade . . ."

"We can't leave Stef with *him.* It's already been too long." I could hardly speak from the sudden onset of tears. I gritted my teeth, struggling to hold them back. Zoe tried to take my hand. "No!" I yanked my hand out of reach. "We have to go. If you won't come with me, I'll go alone."

"What makes more sense?" Zoe used her disarming, sensible tone. "Charging off half-cocked into the woods with zero sense of direction, getting lost, and taking an extra hour to get to the cabin? Or waiting ten minutes to nourish ourselves, recharge for the fight ahead, and then following two men—with guns—who actually know where they're going?"

My lips downturned, teeth chattering with rage. Damn it, she was right. Words could not express how angry I was that she was right. I couldn't bring myself to say it to her. I simply looked away and discreetly wiped a tear from my eye.

Kevin and Tyler took their sweet time with breakfast. I thought Tyler dragged his feet on purpose. After eating, he went to the woods for a shit. At least this act of excretion was done out of sight. Zoe kept Kevin talking, and I knew she was trying to endear us to him. If he liked us, then he'd be more likely to help us, to believe us. But it was hard to listen to. It was hard not to take affront at her tone—our friend was probably getting tortured and here she was making small talk. My foot tapped in anticipation, bouncing off the earth, desperate to move. I gnawed my thumbnail to the quick. I only stopped once I tasted blood.

I didn't realize Kevin was speaking to me until Zoe nudged my boot with hers.

"I could take a look at that, if you want," Kevin repeated. "Dressed my fair share of field wounds." He was looking at the gash on my back; my T-shirt flapped open, exposing my wound to the moist, cool air.

I shook my head. I didn't want to waste any more time.

"Tyler will be at least another ten minutes, hon. We've got time," Kevin said reassuringly.

I still wasn't sure, but Zoe nudged my boot again. Urged me with a tilt of her chin.

I glanced at my backside and saw it was smeared with dried blood. The top of my pink hiking shorts had been soaked through; my ass cheeks doused with red. I felt woozy looking at it. "Yeah, okay," I finally gave in. "Thank you."

Wincing, I lifted my tattered shirt and slowly peeled it away from my skin, over my stiff shoulders. I held the cloth around the front of my chest. I already felt guilty. Who was seeing to Stef's wounds? How many more had she endured in the time we'd been apart? Here I was waiting to be doctored, and she was probably hog-tied on that sleeping pad—that cursed mattress that would haunt me forever.

Zoe squeezed my hand. She'd read my mind. "You need this," she said. "It's okay. You'll be more help to her if you're patched up."

Kevin disappeared into his tent and returned a moment later with a first aid kit. "Here we go, now. Let's have a look, kiddo." He was a dad. In the light of day, I could see this about him. As he unzipped his medical pouch and displayed the stainless-steel bounty of tweezers and neat rolls of white bandages, it was obvious that he'd done this before. Not just for himself or his hunting buddies, but for his kids. He had a calm warmth that felt achingly paternal. The way his full cheeks pillowed when he smiled, his whole face upturned. It made me miss my dad. I bit back the tears, wondering if I'd ever see him again.

Kevin whistled at the wound when he saw it. "Something got you good."

"Not something," Zoe was quick to correct. "Some*one.* Leeroy Bennett."

"Okay, okay." Kevin still sounded unsure, like he couldn't decide if he believed us. "I got a scar on the back of my shoulder from a tree branch slashing me, that's all. This forest can be vicious. So, here's the deal. I could clean it and bandage it, but that won't last you long 'cause you definitely need stitches. This cut is pretty wide, deep, too. Glue would be the best way, if you ask me. I've got some with me. But it's whatever you want."

"You should," Zoe told me.

Resigned, I nodded my consent.

First, Kevin dabbed it with alcohol and I growled to keep from crying. Then he pinched the edges of the wound together. I burrowed my nails into my thighs, trying to distract myself. If something else hurt, I could focus on that pain instead. He swiped the glue over my skin and held it tight. He told me he would do this a few more times and then repeat the process all the way down. "This cut's gotta be about six inches long, at least."

"Look at me," Zoe said, trying to be my coach. "You got this." But I wouldn't meet her eyes.

I spoke to Kevin instead. "Do you have any kids?"

"Three." His smile warmed.

"I thought so," I said, teeth gritted with pain.

"Yeah, you've got that dad energy," Zoe agreed.

"So . . . boys, girls?" I asked as he pasted another layer.

"Two boys," he said. "One girl. They're all grown now. Like you."

"Grandkids?" Zoe asked.

Kevin beamed with pride. "Baby girl on the way this fall. My daughter's pregnant with her first."

I grimaced as he pinched my skin. "Congratulations."

"You must be so proud," Zoe added, watching him work with a keenness that was more curious than it was concerned. "Bet you've patched up your boys more times than you can count. Look at you with that glue; you're a pro."

The way she said "your boys" was my clue. Zoe was leading up to something.

"Oh yeah, they played college ball, both of them." His pride practically glowed from within. "When you don't have insurance, you learn to get handy with things like butterfly bandages and superglue. One time, my eldest came back with a three-inch cut right down his arm. Not a single hospital bill, though. So, I know what I'm doing."

"Could have been a doctor in another life," Zoe said, stroking his ego. "Or wait, are you a doctor?"

"I own an auto parts shop," he said proudly, applying another glue coat.

I cringed, but this time not at the pain. I knew what was coming next. Zoe could talk cars with the best of them. She'd lovingly named hers Ethel, and liked to speak of her old girl like she was a vintage Stingray, not a beat-up Oldsmobile; loved the phrase "real thing of beauty." I needed to stop her before she got going, but Zoe beat me to the punch.

"Tell me more about your daughter," she said—a happy surprise.

"My daughter? Oh, she's got me wrapped round her lil' finger of course. I bet it's the same with you two and your dads."

Zoe and I exchanged a weak smile. Both of us were closer to our dads than we were our moms. It was something we'd always bonded over.

"Is she excited to be a mom?" Zoe asked.

"Over the moon. Won't stop sending us articles about all this gentle-parenting crap. Like we were planning on spanking our grandbaby. Like we'd ever spanked that girl once in her damn life. But, hey, it makes her happy. So, I read them." Then to me, he said, "This should be the last coat. Almost done now; you're doing great."

"Did she travel much?" Zoe asked. "Before getting pregnant, I mean."

Finally, I had an inkling of where she was going.

"She's done a few girl trips with her friends. Spring break in Florida, Cancún, that sort of thing."

Zoe's hazel eyes twinkled, a cat with a bird in sight. "Has she ever run into any trouble?"

Kevin bristled a little now, unsure of where this was headed, or perhaps he could see it, too, the iceberg ahead. "No. Thank god."

"Not that she's told you," Zoe corrected.

Kevin pinched me a little harder. "She would have told me. She tells me everything."

"Because you believe her."

"Of course I do."

"And if she was in Cancún and some guy, god forbid, attacked her . . . and she ran to some other man for help, you would hope he'd believe her. Right?"

Kevin stood upright. He wiped his hands on his jeans. "I see where you're going with this." His brows knit together. At last, Tyler was returning from his deep woods defecation. Kevin grabbed a bandage from his medical kit and slapped this onto my wound. "Let's just leave my daughter out of it. Okay?" His body was stiff, rigid in the shoulders. But I could tell she'd gotten through to him. Zoe had planted the seed.

"Thanks," I told him. "For patching me up."

He nodded. "Let's go pay Jeremiah a visit."

• • •

What will the noble rescuer do when he goes to the cabin and discovers his friend has been murdered? Stay tuned for the next episode to find out, here with Laurie Wolff.

This was such a terrible plan. Should I try to explain myself to these hunters before they found Jeremiah's body? Or should I just let them find it? If I told them now, I risked anger and violent retribution. If I waited till they saw for themselves, I risked anger and violent retribution.

I couldn't make up my mind. So I kept my mouth shut and followed them into the forest. Though this felt like a suicide mission, it was also immediately apparent we would have been lost without these men. I had assumed the cabin was in an entirely different direction from the one we took. I would have probably wound up back at the pit, for all the sense of direction I had. I'd have fallen right in and snapped my neck. That would have been an ironic way to go.

Mist settled into the fern leaves, cool and thin. Walking behind the men, all of us silent, stalking, I felt like a hunter myself. I could taste my iron heartbeat pulsing on my tongue. When a fox scuttled by, I half expected Tyler to shoot it. Instead, the fox scraped over a dead tree and turned to look at me with knowing, beady eyes. Then it was gone.

It took us what felt like an hour. When I finally heard the bubbling stream, every hair on my body stood on end. We were close. The trees started thinning. Through them, I could see the clearing now. Then, there it was.

The cabin.

twenty-six

"We need to get into the basement," I said to Zoe, voice low. "That's where I think Stef will be."

She nodded. Finally, something we could agree on.

"What's all that whispering?" Tyler snapped his head back at us. "We're here now. We'll see what really happened."

"And Jeremiah's got a radio," Kevin said. "We'll be able to call the rangers, if that's still what you want." He gave me a nod that was meant to be reassuring. "Everything will be all right. You girls are safe."

"What are you going to do?" I asked.

"We're going to knock on the front door," Tyler stated plainly, like I was the dumb one.

An uncontrollable chill shivered through me as we stepped into the clearing around the cabin. The familiar crunch of pine needles beneath my boots felt like teeny-tiny bones. Delicate, feminine bird bones. Coming back here was a mistake. I couldn't stand face-to-face with Leeroy. Feel the heat from his devil-blue eyes beating down on me. I'd escaped him once. Now I was about to knock on his front door and . . . What? Just invite myself back in? This was suicide.

The basement was the sanest option. Zoe and I should sneak in through the cellar doors and look for Stefanie while these hunters kept him busy talking. I tugged at Zoe, pointing at the side of the house with my lifted brows, praying she would understand.

Zoe took my hint and slowed. The two of us fell a few paces behind the men.

Tyler turned and noticed. He stopped, one thumb under the rifle strap across his shoulder. "Where do you think you're going? You're coming to the front door, too." He snorted and spat a wad of phlegm into the grass.

We walked reluctantly toward the front porch. The dead deer still hung from the banister. It no longer dripped blood, but a coagulated pool had formed on the porch underneath its head like a halo. Panic surged inside me and I dug my heels into the earth, unable to take another step. "I can't. I can't go in there. He tried to kill us! I can't do it!"

Kevin put one hand on my shoulder. "It'll be okay," he said, taking me by the elbow. "Don't worry."

"Please, let us wait over there," I begged, pointing at a faraway cedar.

"We won't leave," Zoe tried. "Just don't make us go to the door, man. Please."

"C'mon, now." Tyler pulled Zoe forward by her arm. "You look a man in the eye when you accuse him of something."

The front porch groaned beneath our feet. I quivered between the two men as Kevin rapped his big knuckles on the door. There was a lingering, brutalizing pause. Then footsteps creaked inside. A lock unlatched, and slowly the door opened. I tried to turn and run, but Kevin held me fast by the elbow.

Numbing terror filled me. There he was. Detective Leeroy Bennett. The Bones Hollow Hunter. His mean blue eyes glittered at me like ice in the sunlight. "What can I do for you?" he asked, as if he didn't recognize us. All traces of his Southern accent had vanished.

Tyler and Kevin looked surprised to see Leeroy and not his brother. They exchanged an embarrassed, awkward glance, like they'd imposed upon the wrong man. My stomach clenched with fear. Any second now, they would learn the truth about Jeremiah. They would see his dead body and then it would be all over for us.

Leeroy looked at Zoe and me, at the blood smeared across our faces and bodies. A smile flickered in his eyes, fleeting, and then a worried expression knit his brows. "My god, are you two all right? What happened?"

Kevin cleared his throat. "Well, these girls say they were attacked last night. By a man in this cabin."

"Actually, we said two men," Zoe said boldly, rediscovering her courage as she stood beside two men with guns. "It was *both* of them. Him and his brother. There are two Bones Hollow Hunters."

"I don't have a brother, ma'am, and I only arrived an hour ago; you clearly have me confused with someone else. But I can see you ladies have been through something awful." Leeroy's concern looked terrifyingly convincing. "The cabin was empty when I arrived this morning, but there's evidence of a recent break-in. You say you were attacked by the Bones Hollow Hunter here last night?" He turned his attention to Kevin and Tyler. "I'm a detective."

My blood went cold as he groped his pockets for his badge. Leeroy was loving this. He found his badge in his breast pocket and handed this to Kevin casually, offhandedly.

"What brings you out here, Detective?" Tyler sounded intrigued.

"I'm here because there's been another recent sighting reported, of the Hunter. From another young woman who got away; she's safe, in police custody right now. Another very brave girl, just like you two. So, I want you two to know that I'm taking you very seriously," he continued. "Did you get a good look at your attacker in the dark?" He patted down his pants pockets and withdrew a notepad, staring directly at Zoe and me. "Let me take your statement so we can file an official report."

The killer was taunting his prey.

I wanted to puke all over his shiny shoes.

Leeroy glanced at Kevin now, who examined the metal badge closely, as I had last night. It was as real as the thumb he brushed over its metal edges. Anger surged at the back of my throat, knowing the relief Kevin must be feeling. The same relief I had felt to be in the presence of a certified detective.

"He's full of shit!" The words exploded from my lips. "See?" I tapped at the badge in Kevin's hands. "Detective Leeroy Bennett, just like we told you. *He* is the Hunter! You have to believe us!"

"Sounds like you're in shock." Leeroy frowned. "I can only imagine what you've been through. Trauma does wild things to the brain, to memory. I once arrested a man who'd just murdered his wife and he looked straight at me and called me 'honey,' thinking I was her. We see this sort of confusion all the time."

Kevin ran his finger back and forth over the badge. He chewed on his bottom lip for a moment before returning it to Leeroy. "If you've never met these girls before, then how did they know your name?"

Yes! Yes, Kevin! Thank you!

Leeroy pretended to wonder for a second. Then he smiled again. It was a wolfish smile. The smile of his brother. The smile of a hunter. "Well, shit, I bet they've listened to the podcast I was on."

And so it all comes back to me. Your host, Laurie Wolff.

I fought back a scream. It would only make me look more traumatized, *hysterical.*

"I did an interview for a popular podcast about the Hunter, trying to stir up interest, for all the good it did. It was a low moment for me, to be honest. Those sorts of podcasts are all about entertainment, weaving stories out of loosely strung-together facts to titillate bored housewives and wannabe investigators. That Laurie Wolff is just telling a tale; some of us are out here living it. Unfortunately, the only thing my interview stirred up were the crazies, fanatics who come to the woods looking for trouble. If you listened to that podcast, then I'm guessing that's what brought you ladies to the park in the first place, isn't it?"

I boiled in my rage. Not just because he made us sound so uncredible—thrill-seekers who got more than they bargained for—but because even while he lied through his teeth, he was still right. My friends *had* come looking for trouble and they'd found it; I'd just been unwittingly along for the ride.

"No, we came to hike the trail," Zoe claimed without missing a beat.

She lied so easily, and I hated her more with each subsequent word she spoke, knowing she was feeding them the same fabrication she had fed to me, and knowing that she absolutely could not admit the truth—because it was psychotic. If they knew that we'd come here on purpose to hunt for the Hunter, they'd leave immediately.

"We detoured to find a waterfall," Zoe went on, "and Stef broke her ankle. We found this cabin and asked for help. His lunatic brother, Jeremiah, took us in and when we found out he was the Hunter, he attacked us. Then *the detective* showed up and tried to kill us, too. And he murdered a park ranger!"

"This is getting crazy complicated. Look, he's a policeman," Tyler said to his friend with an impatient sigh. "They need the police. Sounds like we've gotten them to the right place. Let's just go, Kev." His bored expression said it all. He wanted to get back to his hunting. This was their *boys' trip* we were interrupting. Their guy time. "What's more likely? That a detective is the Bones Hollow Hunter? Or that these girls have gotten confused after going through some shit? You've seen his badge; he's legit. Let's call it a day, man."

Kevin wavered, bushy eyebrows furrowed, unsure. I could practically hear the thought reel playing through his head: Leeroy was a detective, a bona fide man of the law. We were just two crazy girls he'd met last night who had clearly been traumatized. We probably hallucinated the park ranger for all he knew. What the detective said made sense. What his friend said made sense. It was time to go.

But then I could see Zoe's message wiggling around in his brain. If this had been his daughter . . .

"Look, I don't know what to believe here," Kevin finally said, clearing his throat. "I don't know anything about this park ranger business, but someone obviously attacked these girls. That one's missing a fingertip and she's got a gash six inches long that I patched up myself. I know the man who stayed here. And I don't think Jeremiah would do something like this, but . . . I also don't know what else could have happened. Where is Jeremiah?" He scratched his beard. "You said there was a break-in?"

"Oh yes, multiple points of entry. But there was no one here when I arrived."

"So, maybe there was a couple of drifters." Kevin turned to Zoe and me. "Nights are pitch black in this forest. Cabin's not well lit. It's possible you were mistaken, right?"

"We know what Jeremiah looked like," I said. "He has a scar down his cheek, right?"

The gap between Kevin's eyebrows closed in confirmation. But he still seemed unconvinced. "Okay, so you met Jeremiah. And maybe he is the man that attacked you. Who am I to say? Your story has been hard to track, but I've tried my best. You said a second guy came along later—the one that confessed to you—and it would have been dark. You might not have gotten such a clean look, is my point, so we can't know for sure who that man was. But we do know that this man is a real detective. One that you said you've listened to on a podcast. So maybe, in all the trauma and confusion, you girls got a little mixed up. There's a chance, right? In which case, this detective is the exact man you want to see."

"They're in very safe hands, I promise you." Leeroy nodded, a dutiful civil servant.

"If you leave us with him," Zoe told them, "he will kill us. Our blood will be on your hands."

And my blood will be on yours, I wanted to say to her, for bringing me to this cabin in the first place.

"You're here now." Zoe took both Kevin's hands and squeezed, staring into his eyes earnestly. "Don't leave us with him." I knew the way her hazel irises glittered without seeing them. He wouldn't be able to say no. "Not yet. Our friend is somewhere inside. All we are asking is for you to look around for her. That's it. Then you can go."

"I've searched the whole house, guys," the gallant detective said, palms up in apology. "I'm sorry, I can tell you with certainty that your friend isn't here."

It dawned on me now that finding an as-yet-unmentioned dead body in the living room might look even worse for Leeroy. After all, he'd had his chance to say there was a corpse inside. He hadn't taken it.

Tyler looked to his friend with insistent, tired eyes. "Come on, Kev. Let's you and me still catch some of this day while we can. You heard the detective; they'll be all right."

"Just another ten minutes of your time," Zoe urged Kevin. "Please."

Kevin looked encouraged by Zoe's suggestion, relieved. She'd offered him a simple solution. He turned to the detective. "Seems like an easy enough way to clear this up, don't you think?"

Zoe squeezed his arm, Daddy's little girl. "Thank you, thank you!"

Leeroy sniffed. He thumbed one nostril, inspected the results, and flicked it aside. "Like I said, I already searched the property. But if that'll make you feel better, then that's what we'll do. We'll have another look together." He extended a hand to Kevin, the same one he'd used for his nose. "Didn't catch your name, pal."

"Kevin." He reluctantly shook the detective's hand.

"Tyler," his friend grunted.

"Pleasure to meet you both. You're doing a good thing. I completely understand. We, on the force, appreciate men like you."

The men moved toward the door. I knew that I had to go in. I *had* to find Stefanie. But when my feet touched the threshold, my body rebelled, a survival instinct setting in. I shook my head. "No, I can't go back in there . . . I'll wait outside."

Kevin and Zoe receded into the cabin's dark mouth. Tyler latched onto my elbow and pulled me closer. "What are you whining about?" he demanded. "You got your way. We're doing this for you." Tyler dragged me into the cabin's shadows, into the belly of the beast.

I looked frantically from left to right. There was no sign that Stef had been here. No sign that we'd been here, either. Our backpacks were gone. As was Jeremiah. His body had been moved and the blood cleaned away. I shuddered in both horror and relief, and looked up to find Leeroy staring right at me. Hungry, keen.

"What was your friend's name again?" he asked.

I wouldn't speak to him. Zoe answered, her voice stiff. "Stefanie."

Leeroy tilted his head back to the ceiling. "Stefanie!" he called, one hand to his mouth to amplify the sound. "Stefanie!"

If Jade had had a knife right then, she might happily have gone down for murder.

Kevin meandered around the space, clearly familiar with it. He'd probably shared a beer with Jeremiah on that disgusting deerskin couch. I bet that was what he was dreaming about right now, a nice cold one. He probably couldn't wait to get back to his campsite and crack open a fresh brew and put this day behind him. He looked tired and disinterested. Leeroy was putting on a convincing act, after all.

I scanned the room for any other discrepancies, any small sign that my friend had been dragged through this living space. Ripley's silver handle caught my eye; it gleamed on the bookshelf near the couch. "There!" I pointed. "That's ours."

I pulled away from Tyler and this time he let me go. I picked up the closed blade, all folded and sanitized, like it belonged here on this shelf. Like it had always been here beside the snake skeleton and the vertebrae that had been fashioned into a coaster. I was disturbed by how clean it was. Blood flashed in my mind, pouring off the metal, painting my hands. I blinked and it was gone. My hands felt dirty.

I showed the knife to Kevin and Tyler. "This is ours."

Zoe smiled in that way that told me I'd done good finding this, that she was proud of me. In that way that now made me feel sick. She held out her hand for Ripley, but I slipped it into my pocket instead.

"No one doubts you were here," Kevin said, and I couldn't tell if this was meant to be reassuring or admonishing.

"There's a cellar with this creepy fucking sleeping pad, here through the kitchen." I pointed at the kitchen door, hoping no one could see my finger quivering. "We need to check down there."

I led the way, grateful to put three bodies between the Hunter and me. The kitchen had been tidied, too. The hutch no longer blocked the door and had been replaced on the far side of the kitchen. All the blood on the counter had been wiped away. Every shard and sliver of glass was gone.

The killer had been a busy boy.

The cougar still lay on the kitchen table, dead eyes unwavering.

Tyler whistled, impressed. "Now, there's a beaut."

"So where's this basement?" Kevin asked, losing patience.

I pointed to where it'd been, but the hutch was there instead. Positioned over the top of it. A rational thing to do if he was trying to block anyone from getting out. My heart catapulted forward.

"Here! See? He's moved this over the door. Stef!" I barged my shoulder into the heavy wooden furniture, ignoring the pain scorching my body. But it wouldn't budge. "Help me!" I said to the others. "Stef! Stef, we're coming!"

Zoe found space beside me and Kevin took the other side. Together, we shuffled the hutch away. It dawned on me as I dove down the cellar steps that the Hunter might have boarded up the broken window and the cellar doors already as well. In which case, he could easily trap us now. Four mice in the lion's den. We'd be swallowed whole. But I wouldn't leave Stefanie behind.

"Stef!" I called. There was no answer. No doubt he'd gagged her, left her bleeding, unconscious. "Stef!"

The Hunter's voice echoed mine, a mockery. "Stef! Can you hear us?"

I blazed into the shadowy cave, darting left to right, not leaving any corner untouched. The cellar window was still thankfully unfixed. A tiny pool of light poured through, illuminating only half of the basement. I charged deeper, making my way to the mattress. When I came to it, my horror didn't quite sink in. It was like a blurry photograph coming into focus. I didn't want to believe my eyes; I wanted them to be a lie.

Stefanie was not here. The bloodied, urine-stained sleeping

cot was empty. As haunted as before. I stared, wondering if any of the stains were new. The dark marks swirled in my vision. I pictured the dozens of wounds that left them, the torture that had inflicted those wounds. I gagged and turned away, unable to look anymore. Zoe was with me now, rubbing circles on my back. I shrugged her off.

"There you have it," Kevin said reassuringly. He clearly hadn't even noticed the cot, just that there were no women held captive down here. "She's not here. Do you girls feel better now?"

I wished he would stop calling us that.

"I told you," Leeroy said from the darkness. His face was obscured by shadow, but I could feel him beaming. "Satisfied now? There's a radio I found upstairs. Let's go bring in the cavalry, okay? I can have choppers here searching for your friend in a couple of hours."

"He's put her somewhere else," I insisted to Kevin, desperate. "I know he has her. You have to believe me!"

"The shed! It's locked, out back," Zoe broke in. "Have him unlock the shed for us. He has the keys. Check his pockets."

"We're not gonna check his pockets," Tyler said.

"Here. Be my guest." The detective stepped forward from the shadows and turned his empty pockets out. "I don't have any keys."

"Please just check the shed," I begged. "It's the last place she could be."

"We're wasting daylight here," Leeroy chided. "If you want any chance of finding your friend and catching the monster that did this, I ought to be radioing in for help."

Tyler looked to Kevin with a sigh, done indulging us, ready to get back to his planned hunt. Kevin's head hung low between his broad shoulders.

"You asked us to look in the cabin," he said, not quite meeting our eyes, "and we've done that. You asked us to look in the cellar and we've done that, too. There's no sign of your friend. I think it's possible you've gotten this man confused, after all you've been through. But I really think you're in the best hands here with him."

Zoe was running before I could blink. Her body a shadowy blur cutting through the men, toward the cellar stairs. I raced after her, heart hot in my throat. Tyler tried to grab my wrist as I whizzed by, but I managed to pull away in time. Zoe was already to the steps. I couldn't hear anything but my throbbing lungs. It felt like all the shadows had arms reaching for me.

My boots hit the first step. I looked up to the light raining down from the kitchen. The light that was shrinking as the hatch door started closing. "Wait!" I screamed, bursting out the opening.

Zoe slammed the door down behind me. Then she was at the hutch, putting her whole body into it, pushing it over the top. Below us, Tyler raged, cursing and roaring like a wild animal. I rammed my body into the hutch beside Zoe. Our shoulders touched. Anger filled me up, gave me strength.

"You were going to lock me in there with them!" I growled, pushing with all my might.

"Don't be stupid." Zoe grunted into the hutch. "I knew you were right behind me."

Finally, we squared the furniture over the hatch door. The force of their pounding fists reverberated through the wood. They rattled the floorboards.

"Let us out, you bitches!" Tyler pounded the door.

"Come on now!" Kevin shouted. "This isn't right. Let us out!"

"We have to find his keys," Zoe said, rushing out of the kitchen.

Underneath my feet, the Hunter spoke in a low, hushed tone. No doubt he was reassuring the others that they could escape through the cellar doors on the other side of the basement. Even if it was still chained, Zoe had hacked a narrow opening in it already. The men couldn't fit through yet, but they had plenty of tools down there to help them widen it. They'd be out soon.

Zoe was right, damn it. We needed the keys for the shed. And we didn't have much time to find them.

twenty-seven

"You check over there, I'll look here," Zoe said as we burst into the living room.

Zoe still thought she could give instructions.

"You literally just tried to trap me in a basement with a serial killer," I spat back. "Do me a favor. Don't fucking talk to me. Like ever again."

"God. Fine." She started on the right side of the room, working her way around quickly. Her fingers flew across the surfaces as she muttered under her breath. "You'd think a life-or-death situation might finally force you to grow the hell up. But I guess not."

I stopped searching the left side of the room and glared at her. "What was that?"

"I asked if you saw his motorcycle," Zoe said, loud, pointed. Like I was a deaf person in an old people's home. "I haven't seen where he left it, but it's got to be close. Do you know?"

I shook my head. I actually did have an idea of where the motorcycle might be. When the Hunter had pretended to be the ranger on the radio, he'd told me he was coming from the east. His plan was to catch us there if we'd escaped. So, I figured Leeroy had parked his bike somewhere east along the stream, far enough away so as not to be heard. But I wasn't going to tell Zoe that.

This was the sort of moment when Stef would usually cut in, to try and keep the peace. She'd interject with a "remember that time when . . ." A little trip down memory lane, something to lighten the mood, to unify us again. But Stef wasn't here. And I had no desire to close the cavernous gap between me and Zoe.

I looked underneath a table, getting eye level with the floor to see if any metal clumps stood out.

"Where do you think he's hidden it?" Zoe asked.

"If I knew where he hid the keys, I'd have found them by now."

"No. The bike." Zoe said it like I was stupid.

"Not really my priority right now."

"It should be. You should be thinking of our escape plan. What happens if we don't find Stef—what happens if we do? We need a way out of here."

"Thought you had a route mapped back to the car." The words were bitter on my tongue.

"Yeah, well, that seemed a lot more tenable before the killer had a motorcycle to chase after us on."

It was as obvious to me now as the skull paperweight atop this table. Zoe wasn't looking for the keys to search the shed.

She wanted the keys to his motorbike. If she found them first, she'd be straight out that door. It wasn't even a question in my mind if she'd go check the shed for Stefanie first. It was only a question if she'd give me enough time to hop on the back of the bike before speeding off. But even that didn't feel like much of a mystery anymore.

Just a few short days ago, this train of thought would have been inconceivable. But maybe it shouldn't have been. Once again I was faced with the chilling thought: Maybe this was always who Zoe was, and I'd just never wanted to see it. But none of that mattered now.

The only thing that mattered, in this moment, was that I found the keys first.

My fingers flew across the desk with the radio in the drawer, feeling every inch just in case there was something my eyes had missed. The keys weren't in here. I raced down the hall. Zoe had come to the same conclusion as me and was only a step behind.

She tried to slip around me in the hall, but I wouldn't let her. I thrust out my elbows. Every time she tried to push by, I blocked her.

"Come on, hurry up!" Her foot snaked around mine and I nearly fell, but caught myself against the wall.

"Did you just try to trip me?" I threw my elbow back. It knocked her in the chin.

"What the fuck!" Zoe snatched a fistful of my hair and yanked me backward. "I wasn't trying to trip you! I was trying to get past you because you're so fucking slow and I don't want to die!" She scrambled around me. I grabbed her by the back of the neck and we tumbled into the bedroom together.

I don't know what I'd pictured. When Stef and Zoe had described pulling a trunk out from under a bed, I guess I'd pictured some queen foam mattress atop an ornate wooden headboard. I'd pictured every "rustic" cabin getaway on Pinterest. But this room was bare bones. A boarded-up window allowed trails of light, just enough to illuminate a simple wooden frame where a sleeping pad rested. A dusty sleeping bag was placed on top of this, no pillow. Underneath the bed frame was a wooden trunk. The chest of drawers against the wall was the only other item in sight.

The only article of sentimentality was a small, dusty picture frame resting atop the dresser. It appeared to be a faded photo of two young boys sitting on the dilapidated porch of a farmhouse. This must've been Leeroy and Jeremiah as children. Even from where I stood, I could tell that neither of them was smiling.

Zoe was the first one to the dresser. She flipped open drawers so hard they flew onto the ground. My heart raced, and a part of my brain urged me to join her in this ferocity. But another, rational, part of me slowed for a minute. I took a breath. Downstairs, the men were hacking at the cellar doors. They would be out soon. I needed to calm myself and think. When I lost my keys, I retraced my steps and I usually found them in a pocket or on a counter I'd forgotten passing by. So where would the Hunter have gone? I needed to think like him.

After a long night terrorizing three women and with one of the injured victims safely stashed away, the Hunter returned to his lair, tired. He needed to rest.

I dashed to the bedside. The sleeping bag was slightly parted. The nylon fabric was gritty to the touch as I patted it down. My fingertips felt soiled. Then they felt wet. The bag was soaked through at the feet. I withdrew my hand quickly in horror, expecting to find it smeared with the first thing that came to mind: blood. I was relieved to find my nails dipped in black mud instead.

The Hunter had felt so besieged by exhaustion, he hadn't bothered to take his boots off before crawling into his bed.

If he hadn't taken the time to take off his boots, he probably hadn't taken the time to empty his pockets, either. A bulky key ring may have fallen when he sprawled himself here. I looked to the floor.

Bingo, Jade Edelman.

Tucked into the shadow of the wooden chest, underneath the bed, there they were. The keys had fallen, and then perhaps later been inadvertently kicked. Now they waited for me, better than any prize. I reached for them and Zoe was instantly by my side. I snatched them first. Winner.

"Great job! Give them here." Zoe held out her hand, expectant.

"Hell no." I held them away, out of reach. I was taller than Zoe. For once that was a good thing. Normally, I hated my height when compared to my friends. Stef was tall and elegant. Zoe was petite and nimble. I was just the completely average one between them both. But today, I was grateful for my extra inches.

The chopping sound downstairs was rhythmic. My heart drummed in time.

"Why not?" Zoe demanded. "It just makes more sense. You know I'm faster than you."

Not today, you weren't.

"I know," I replied. "And you'll be faster to save your own ass."

"I'm trying to save us both!" Zoe reached for my arm, but I still held the keys too high.

"Uh-huh. That's why you were going to trap me in the basement with them." I shoved her onto the bed and then raced out of the bedroom and into the hall. "I've had enough of your shit!"

Zoe trailed behind me, a tiny dog biting at my heels all the way to the front door. "Oh my god, I'm so sick of *your* bullshit drama—I didn't try to lock you in the basement! How many times are you going to make me say it?"

"I'm fucking done with you, Zoe. I mean it. I really am."

"Oh, what, like you're going to stop being my friend?" Zoe scoffed. "Grow up."

"Me, grow up? I'm not the one playing with her friends' lives! I'm not the one who put us all in danger!" I stopped. The hacking noise downstairs had silenced. "Wait, do you hear them?" I looked to Zoe. "Downstairs. It's gone quiet."

"I don't know. All I know is those hunters are buying us time to get away and that's exactly what we brought them here for."

I blinked, stunned, as a chill ran through me. Even now, Zoe could still shock me—horrify me. "I thought we brought them here to help us." I searched her face for any trace of remorse, but all I saw was blunt impatience.

"That *is* helping. Any distraction buys us time, so let's stop wasting it."

"That's why you asked them to come, to *buy us time*? To be our decoy? What happens if they die?"

"When are you going to stop being so naïve?" Zoe said. "The only thing that matters right now is survival."

She flung open the front door and we charged outside. Fresh air kissed my face and I drank it deep, grateful to taste anything but the stale, smoky cabin air.

"Let's find the bike," Zoe ordered, making one last grab for the keys.

"No! The shed." I didn't wait for her to try and persuade me. I darted around the side of the cabin toward the shed. I ran smack into Kevin's red-flanneled chest.

The three hunters waited for us here. Leeroy leaned against the shed door.

Tyler aimed his rifle. He spat onto the ground. "You bitch."

The detective placed his hand on the gun's nose, lowered it. "Let's not get too hasty. I think everyone's blood is running a little hot."

"They locked us down there!" Tyler said, spit flying. "That's got to be, like, assault, right? Kidnapping? There's got to be something we can charge them with!"

I looked up into Kevin's big brown eyes. Disapproval stared back at me.

"I've got the keys," I said, meek at first.

Zoe, who had been hot on my heels, pressed up against my back. But she wasn't here for support. She was trying to get close enough to make one final grab for the keys.

My voice strengthened, became an order. "I'm opening that shed. You two guys can go. Press charges. Whatever you want. But I am going to find out if Stefanie is in there. And none of you are going to stop me." I stared deeply into Kevin's face, imploring him with my eyes. "I need to know."

Kevin's anger dissipated slowly. It was still there, but diluted by a renewed cloud of concern that slackened his shoulders. He sighed. "Fine. We'll have a quick look. Open her up."

Tyler growled, glaring at us. "You've got to be fucking kidding me." But he stepped aside from the shed door.

Leeroy, however, didn't budge. He leaned against the shed

with one knee bent, his shoe flat on the door. It was a cowboy pose. He looked like Jeremiah.

"Come on, man," Kevin said. "I know it's been one hell of a morning. But, like you said yourself, these girls have been through it. All they want is to open up the shed. They have the keys. Let's just do this and be done. Then we can all go our separate ways."

Leeroy picked his teeth with his thumb. "You sure you want to do that?"

"Do what?" Kevin asked, tired.

"Are you sure you wouldn't rather just go back to your hunt?" Leeroy made eye contact with him now. "You've already wasted half the morning here. If you leave now, you can still get some game in. Not go home empty-handed."

Kevin furrowed his brows. He placed one hairy hand on his rifle. "Step aside."

Leeroy smiled, ear to ear. His white teeth glistened. "As you wish."

I stepped to the shed door. The Hunter puckered his lips at me in a subtle kiss. Then he walked a few feet to the right, giving the trio of onlookers a wide berth. Instinctively, Kevin didn't like this. Now, both his hands were on his weapon, one finger poised on the trigger. His eyes flicked from Leeroy to the shed and back again. Tyler, unsure of what was happening, followed suit, trigger finger ready, eyes twitching left to right.

Zoe nudged closer to me, her breath hot on my neck. I didn't turn to meet her eyes, but I felt her fear pulsing through her body, permeating her sweat. It coated the air, salty on my tongue. Leeroy stepped farther away still, edging toward the cabin.

"Stay where I can see you," Kevin ordered, a vague tremble to his voice.

Leeroy lifted both hands. "Oh, I'm not going anywhere."

"This is such a mistake," Zoe muttered only for me. "We should have run while we had the chance."

"Run now," I whispered back. "No one's stopping you."

"Just open the fucking shed."

There were four copper-colored keys on the ring and one silver. I pushed the silver one into the lock first. It didn't fit. My hands shuddered, keys jingling, as I tried the second. Then the third. I almost dropped them readying the fourth. Zoe tensed, a cat ready to pounce; she'd have snatched them in a second if I let them go. I steadied my hand.

It was the last key on the ring that unlocked the door. I thrust it into the hole and shivered when it turned. I dropped the padlock to the ground. The dead pine needles by my foot crunched beneath its weight. The shed door swung open slowly, teasingly.

"Now," Leeroy sang, "don't you wish you'd just gone back to your hunt, boys?"

My sweet Little Savages, this time Jade wasn't afraid to admit that Zoe had been right. They should have run while they still had the chance.

twenty-eight

I couldn't tell if it was me or Zoe who screamed. Maybe it was both of us. Our voices twisted together as one, trumpeting into the forest.

Kevin stuttered, fumbling on words that were just a series of consonants. I wondered if his eyes were caught on the tools, like mine. Metal tools dripped down from ceiling hooks like stalactites. Silver teeth and razor-sharp points glinted in the sunlight, winking at me. I was hypnotized by them. I didn't want to look down.

The smell hit me next. The ripeness, dried blood, caked and rich and festering. Tyler threw up behind me. My eyes traveled down to the floor, just for a moment. Just long enough to see her purpled skin, the bruises she wore like a blanket. The red gouges and wounds that decorated her body. Long enough to see that she was naked. To see that her mouth gaped open, like the cougar with its lolling tongue—and her top left canine tooth had been ripped out.

Blinding, searing rage crashed into me. It pummeled the air from my lungs like a tidal wave. One thought surfaced through the suffocating emotions. It bubbled up to the top and then replayed, on a loop, again and again: This was Zoe's fault.

I turned to her, keys in hand. The look of horror on her face was unlike any I'd ever seen. I didn't know it was possible for Zoe to look so afraid. But there was no shame in her anguish. Not even a flicker of guilt in those wet hazel eyes. Zoe didn't feel bad; she was scared. She was scared for her life, for *herself.* The one and only person she truly cared about. Zoe stared at the repercussions of her actions, at our butchered best friend, and all she could think about was her fucking self. If she had a phone, no doubt she'd be taking pictures, I thought viciously, focusing on my anger; I couldn't bear to let myself feel anything else.

Kevin pulled himself from his trance. "What . . . what is this?" he finally managed to say.

What the fuck did it look like, Kevin?

It looked like we were right and you were wrong, *Kevin.*

Kevin swung his rifle around to shoot Leeroy. It was only then that any of us realized he had vanished.

Zoe lunged inside the shed. Jeremiah's fully clothed corpse was propped against the shed's back wall alongside the dead park ranger. Beside their boots was a pile of clothes that Zoe had clearly noticed. She dived onto Stef's clothes in a feverish, practically rabid state. For a minute, I thought she must be in shock. This was her desperate attempt to cover our friend, to restore some of her dignity. But Zoe rifled through her pockets, then tossed the clothes aside.

She found what she was looking for on the narrow workbench. Next to the bloodied instruments of torture that Zoe somehow paid no mind to, sat a neat pile of Stef's belongings. Her SPF lip tint. Her charm bracelet. Her earbuds and a single mint. And, of course, what Zoe was looking for so frantically. Stefanie's phone.

"What the fuck are you doing?" I demanded.

But then it was obvious what Zoe was doing with it. Exactly what I'd suspected. Taking pictures. Of Stef's dead body. Of Stef's red-flowering wounds. Of Stef's missing tooth.

Zoe was a monster. This person who used to be my friend was a soulless monster. I did not know this person. I never had. The keys shivered in my hand and I clenched them, a fistful of tiny knives. "Stop it!" I screeched. "Get away from her! Just stop it!"

Suddenly, Tyler had me by both shoulders and he dragged me away from the shed. "Where the hell has he gone!" He shook me. Vomit dangled from his chin like silly string. "Look at me! Where would that bastard have gone?"

Zoe sprang back out into the yard, eyes crazed. "Come on, we have to go!"

She was only saying that to me because I had the keys. If she had them, she would have dashed away without a word. I would've gladly slashed them across her face if she'd gotten close enough. But she stayed at arm's length, waving me along. "Come on!"

"We have to stick together," Kevin stammered. Fear poured from his eyes. He and Tyler had formed a border around us, encircling us, rifles at the ready. They aimed at the trees, at nothing, eyes flicking back and forth.

"Let's move to the cabin. There's a radio inside," Kevin said, recovering some resolve. "We can board up the busted window so he can't get in. Probably not even necessary anymore." He cleared his throat, encouraged by his own wishful thinking. His bushy eyebrows relaxed, unfurled into two distinct caterpillars. "He's most likely made a run for it, if he knows what's good for him. But better safe than sorry."

A little late for that now, Kevin.

"Good idea," Zoe said.

She dragged at me with her eyes, trying to grab my attention, but I refused to look at her. Little by little, she fell behind the two men as they marched forward. My footsteps slowed with hers. We allowed the hunters to get farther ahead of us. The gap between us widened.

It killed me to stand alongside Zoe. To smell her sweat so close. I couldn't bear to be anywhere near her. But these two hunters were sitting ducks now. Decoys. It's what Zoe had wanted, what she had planned. I felt disgusted abetting her, but it was already too late for these two men. Leeroy wasn't going to let them live now that they'd seen what was inside the shed. Their time was running out, and to be anywhere near them would mean my death, too.

The first arrow stabbed through Tyler's throat. It came from above. I scarcely had time to glance upward before the second one went through Kevin's belly, poking out the other side. He fired his rifle at the upper window of the cabin, but the Hunter had already slipped away.

This was our chance. Our distraction. The men's final purpose served, to *buy us time.* But I'd be damned if Zoe would get to capitalize on this.

I wrenched the compass from around Zoe's neck. Then I punched her. My fist connected with her already broken nose and red sprayed, blooming like a flower. Pain surged through my knuckles and my wrist. Then I shoved her as hard as I could, hurling her to the ground. The only thing in the world I cared about now was getting to that motorbike first. It's exactly what Zoe would do if she had been in my shoes, if the keys were in her hand. It's exactly what she deserved. Better, in fact. She *deserved* to be lying in that shed, not Stef. Maybe soon she would be. But unlike Stefanie, at least she had something of a chance.

I raced as hard as I could toward the southward trees.

"Come back! You bitch!" Zoe screamed, her voice not far behind me. "You think you can outrun me? You think I can't catch you?"

I charged through the stream. The cold water kissed my shins, soaking my boots. I clambered up the muddy side and snatched up a fallen tree branch as thick as my arm. I hid behind a long-armed cedar beside the bank and listened to Zoe splash through the water. She surged out of the stream, and I swung. The branch struck her chest, snapping in two. The blow knocked her back and she fell into the bubbling water.

"I will never *ever* forgive you for this!" I screamed with every ounce of my anger.

Zoe coughed, spluttering, pulling herself up. She snarled, furious. "I am so sick of your shit!" When she emerged, it was with a large river rock in hand. "Get back here."

I picked up a small rock by my feet, the first I could find, and launched it at her head. I knew I wouldn't hit her. I just needed to make her duck, which she did. Then I ran south and quickly zigzagged east. I hid behind another tree. If I could lose her, then I wouldn't have to try to outrun her.

I pressed my body flat against the gruff, mossy trunk. Moist pine filled my lungs. I listened to Zoe trudge out of the stream, cursing, growling. Her wet footsteps squelched southward. She stopped walking, looking around.

"This was what Stefanie wanted, too!" she shouted into the trees. "It wasn't just my idea to come here!"

Bullshit. Stef agreed to every one of her suggestions. Her mind had been a blank, trusting canvas where Zoe could paint her ideas. Slowly, I peered around the edge of the trunk and saw her, a little southwest of me. She couldn't see me.

She called into the void, grasping at straws, hoping I would answer. "Stef would have wanted us to get home and tell everyone what we saw. So that she didn't die for nothing!"

Dying for a podcast was worse than dying for nothing. I clamped down on the inside of my cheek to keep from shrieking this at her.

"We have to get out of here, you and me, while we still can!" Zoe still clenched the rock in her hand. "I can still fix this! I can . . ." Tears garbled her voice. "I can make this mean something."

I couldn't bite my tongue any longer. "There is no fixing this!" Her head whipped around searching for me, but I didn't care anymore. I couldn't stomach one more word of her self-important bullshit. I emerged from behind my tree. "Everything is not going to work out all right. You can't turn this into one of your fucking stories!"

"Okay, okay." Her impatience was palpable, though she tried to sound calm. "I misspoke. I'm sorry. Now will you please come on? He won't be distracted by those guys for much longer. We have to get out of here."

"I'm not going anywhere with you," I snapped. "And if you thought you were going somewhere with me, you wouldn't still have that rock in your hand."

Zoe stepped closer so that we were a few yards away from each other now. I edged backward, nearly tripping on a small mossy boulder.

"You're the one who hit me with a log," she spat.

"It was a branch, but okay."

"I need to defend myself. We do still have a sociopathic serial killer hunting us."

"And whose fault is that?"

"Jesus, fuck! Okay! You have seriously made your point! I'm a piece of shit. Everything is my fault." She inched closer as she spoke, rock still in hand. "We wouldn't be here if not for me. Stefanie would be alive if not for me. There, have I said my penance enough?" Tears rushed down her face, but I didn't believe them. Nothing that came out of her mouth was genuine. "Now, please, for the love of god, you can whip me more at home, but let's get the fuck out of here. Okay?"

We were an arm's length away from each other now. The keys trembled in my fists like sharp, uncertain claws. Zoe squeezed the river rock and tried a smile, the same one that normally disarmed people—that had talked me down off a dozen cliffs—but it just looked fake.

Zoe and I stared at each other. Our legs were smeared with mud. Our clothes were tattered and torn, our hair disheveled. Her pink streak was earth brown. Blood stained her cheeks.

"You can keep the compass," she offered, rock in hand. "Just give me the keys."

"No," I said. "I'm carrying them."

"I don't trust you," Zoe shot back. "You're going to leave me here."

"You only think that because it's what you're going to do to me."

"I wouldn't *do* that."

I sneered. "Ha."

"Fine," she said. "Keep the keys. But I won't let you leave me behind."

I gritted my teeth till I thought a molar might shatter.

"Let's go," she said. "You have the compass. Lead the way. Do you think he came from downstream? It's where you were headed."

"Yeah," I said, reluctant. At this point I was wasting time. The two hunters' bodies would only keep Leeroy occupied for so long before he came looking for us. "From the east."

I was eager to take the lead for once in our lives. Desperate to be in charge on some ridiculous internal level. I stepped in front of her. That was my mistake. Zoe's foot hooked around mine and I didn't catch myself this time.

I pitched forward. My face crashed into the mossy earth. Twigs stabbed at my face, just missing my eyes. My left knee cracked open against a rock.

Zoe leaned down to my ear. "That was for my nose, bitch. You didn't think we were all cool for that yet, did you?"

But I hadn't dropped the keys. That's what she'd really wanted. Any minute now, she'd probably bash my skull in for them. I grabbed a small fist-sized rock with my free hand, and when I turned around I smashed it into her shin. She screamed and kicked my ribs.

I pulled myself up just enough to bite her leg. Blood pooled around my teeth. She roared, stomping on my chest with her other foot. All the air whooshed from my lungs and I coughed. Zoe straddled me now, one knee on each side of my chest. She reached for the keys, but I had just enough wind in me to hide them beneath my body.

"I don't want to hurt you," she panted, raising the rock above her head. "But I will if I have to. Give me the keys."

I thrust my hips up hard. She lost her balance and I threw her off me. She tumbled down a small, muddy slope. I scrambled to my feet, gasping. She clawed after me, like a zombie pulling at my legs. I kicked her and swung at her head, but she managed to drag me back to the ground. We wrestled, each of us biting and kicking and scratching. She sunk her teeth into my shoulder. I slashed the keys across her cheek. We rolled and tumbled.

"I fucking hate you!" I screamed.

"Yeah? Well, I fucking hate you, too!" Zoe lifted my head by the hair and smacked my face into a rock.

Blood wet my temple, head spinning. When she lifted me again, I managed to swing my elbow back. It connected with her tooth, which I felt loosen.

The unmistakable sound of a human whistling stopped us. It cut through our rageful fog, clean and clear like a scythe. We froze, heads tilted to the wind, listening.

A constant rustling of leaves filled the air, overpowering the methodical crunch of footsteps. It was a dragging sound. Occasionally, the whistle became strained, but its tune always remained merry. The dragging stopped nearby. The whistling continued, jaunty, like a sailor at sea. Then came the unmistakable smacking of a spade hitting the dirt.

I realized now just how close we still were to the cabin. We had obviously gone back on ourselves. The stream was only a few yards down this slope and I could see the shed across from that. I felt for the compass with my free hand, the other still clutching the keys for dear life. It was gone, lost in the tussle. Never mind. I could remember which direction was east, and if I followed the stream, I would find the bike. Hopefully.

The digging sound grew more fervent. Leeroy's whistling stopped. He must be working up a sweat now. I crawled on my belly down the slope toward the stream to get a better look. Zoe pulled at me, silently begging me to go the opposite way. But what was the point? We'd obviously just been making a shit ton of noise fighting each other. This was the Bones Hollow Hunter we were dealing with; he knew we were here.

I crossed the stream as quietly as I could and hid behind a cedar within view of Leeroy now. I was only a few yards from him at most. Not far from the shed, along a row of perfectly distributed grassy mounds, he had begun to dig a fresh hole. His shirt was unbuttoned, a sweaty sheen glistening in the sun as he thrust the spade again and again into the earth. Behind him lay the four bodies he had dragged. He was digging their graves.

Ice rattled my bones when I saw her. Stefanie. Even from this distance, I could see the bloody slashes and shapes he'd carved into her body. Now he was digging her a hole. A pit that he would dump Stefanie's lifeless body into. *Our* Stef. I couldn't let myself cry, but I found that I couldn't stop myself, either. I wiped the tears away as quickly as they fell.

Zoe was next to me now, shoulder to shoulder. "Holy shit, they *were* graves." I detected the faint hint of pride in her voice.

Don't say it. Don't you dare fucking say it. I will kill you if you say it.

"I was right."

twenty-nine

The heat of Ripley in my pocket burned a hole through my thigh. Fury bloomed in me, unfurling its blood red tendrils. Exploding through my body. Taking over my soul. I turned on her, ready to unleash it all.

"Y'all can come out now. Fun time is over." Leeroy's singsong voice cut through my rage.

My heart galloped against my ribs. Zoe and I looked at each other and our eyes mirrored the same message: *This is all your fault.*

"What should we do, genius?" she hissed.

"I promise, it'll be a lot worse for you girls if I have to *make* you come out." His Southern accent had returned. "I'll give you to the count of three. One."

The saliva evaporated from my mouth.

"Two."

My lungs burned with fear. I slipped my hand into my pocket for Ripley and drew strength from its metal as my fingers wrapped around it. I came out from behind the tree just as he started to say, "Three." Zoe was a step behind me.

"Excellent," he said, wiping the sweat from his brow. "I brought you both a shovel. Even got you started, because I'm nothing if not a gentleman." He stretched his shoulders back until his spine cracked. Then he extended one of the shovels to me. The other lay on the ground. Next to the bodies.

Next to Stef.

Leeroy reached into his pocket and withdrew a single key on a ring. He swung this around his finger. "Heard you ladies fighting an awful lot over some keys. Hope you didn't think those were to the bike." He smiled and tossed the key into the air. It spiraled in the air, glittering, before he caught it and replaced it in his left pants pocket. "Okay, chop-chop, now. It's going to be a busy day!"

Zoe trembled beside me. I thought I heard her whimper, but surely not. When neither she nor I had moved, Leeroy clapped his hands together so hard we both jumped. "Come on, now! Or do I have to wave my gun in your face?"

I walked forward slowly, eyes trained on the ground away from Stefanie. Don't look at her toes. Her blue-painted toenails that glittered in the right light. Don't look at the ankle where she planned to get a cedar tattoo to match Zoe's. I kept my eyes away from this. One hand in my pocket, I accepted the shovel.

I glanced behind me. Zoe wasn't looking at the bodies, either.

Zoe had frozen, scared stiff. Her bottom lip wobbled and she bit down on it hard, but it still wouldn't stop. She had always looked so brave in the face of adversity. More than brave: cool. Stefanie always thought she was the ultimate badass. We both did. She was our role model. But now, she was unrecognizable. Urine trickled down her trembling legs.

I couldn't help but smile. At least if I was going to die, I'd seen her nosedive from her high horse first. Her chickens had fully come home to roost, and I got to be here to see it. I could die happily with that.

I realized now that I was nothing like Zoe, and that was a good thing. She wasn't the person I thought she was. She wasn't a brave hero, or our righteous defender. She ran away. She was a coward. Someone who would do anything and sacrifice anyone to save herself. I was *nothing* like her. I could finally celebrate that.

This trip had been good for me, after all. Look at my *growth.*

I took the shovel with both hands and plunged it into the hole the Hunter had started. He lit himself a cigarette while he watched. "Go on," Leeroy said to Zoe. "Get a movin'. You each gotta give me two holes. Whoever finishes last, well . . . you don't want to finish last. She got a head start on you. So if I was you, I'd shake a leg."

Spurred by this, Zoe picked up the spade and struck the earth. Then again. She sniffled, face blotched and red. It was obvious that she had given up hope. She would only cry like that if she thought this was truly the end. If there were no more cards up her sleeves, no more tricks left to play. But I wasn't like her—I didn't plan to die today.

"Hey, Zoe," I said after a minute. "Remember that time you had Stef and me dig a grave? How old were we—fourteen?" I grunted, striking the moist churned earth. The smell of soil was pungent in the misty air. "It was for our math teacher. He was a real dick," I said to Leeroy, who listened with amusement. "And Zoe made us go to the school at night, with shovels," I stabbed the dirt with my spade, "and dig a grave. She didn't do that much digging actually, come to think of it. *Someone* had to be the lookout, after all."

Zoe ground her teeth. Her jaw skated back and forth.

"Anyway, this reminds me of that. Though," I said with a laugh, "it's nice to see you break a sweat for a change."

I know she wanted to curse me. Maybe even to hit me with her shovel.

"So, I guess we know now what the Hunter does with his special ones," I said, breathing heavy with exertion. "He digs graves. She thought you mounted them on your wall. The truth is always kind of disappointing, isn't it?"

"After that poor fuck Lars, we had to stop leaving our toys around for others to find," Leeroy stated, matter of fact. "Now our girls are just more missing hikers, like all the others who disappear in this park. People believe whatever helps them sleep through the night. Or whatever story that podcast bitch feels like peddling."

"Well, Zoe would know all about that. She is the Bones Hollow Hunter expert," I explained. "She's the one that brought us all here."

I watched Zoe as she shook her head, grinding her teeth. Anger was dwarfing her despair.

"Oh yeah. She must have listened to that podcast over a dozen times. Knows your case backward and forward."

Leeroy stared at her as he exhaled smoke. His shoulders tensed. "Is that right?" He sounded every bit like his brother.

"So hey, tell us, were you sacrificing women to the spirits of the Bones Hollow Trail? That was another one of Zoe's theories."

I watched her stew. Any minute now she'd open her big mouth. Even overcome with fear, she wouldn't be able to hold back. Her fury was rising.

"She's the one who planned everything. Came up with this whole elaborate lie about a waterfall to lure me off-trail to the cabin. It was so clever." I dug hard, sweat dripping. "I didn't even know we were coming here. But Zoe had it all mapped out, like she always does. What was it you said before, Leeroy? A fanatic who went looking for trouble and found it. Yep, that's her."

Zoe's jaw quivered so hard I thought her teeth might shatter.

"Is that right?" Leeroy said again, a hungry twinkle in his cold blue eyes.

"Your brother is dead," I said, thrusting my spade into the moist clay, "because of Zoe. All because she wanted to hunt the Hunter. Thought she could be a big hero."

His mean eyes blazed like the cigarette ember he flicked to the ground.

Finally, Zoe snapped. "Will you shut the fuck up already!"

Slowly, Leeroy withdrew his folding knife from his pocket and flicked it open. Two inches of metal gleamed in the sun.

Zoe knew she couldn't outrun him, not from this close. She squeezed her eyes shut. "Jesus, oh Jesus fucking Christ . . ." She shuddered, frozen, as he moved toward her. "It was her fault! She's the one who stabbed him! You saw it for yourself. It was her, her, *her*! Please . . ." she begged.

Leeroy walked closer. His back was to me. He pressed the tip of his blade to her chin.

"Please, oh please, for the love of fucking god, I'll do anything. Just don't kill me."

I looked to Zoe. I looked to Stef. Finally, gazing for a moment upon her pale face, I stepped out of the hole I'd been digging. I moved slowly, quietly, as soft as the earth herself. I lifted the shovel.

"I'm going to start by stripping the skin from your cheeks," Leeroy Bennett, the Bones Hollow Hunter, said to Zoe. "Then I'm going to fry it up like pork rinds. Feed you some."

I struck the back of his skull. Brought the spade down so hard it sang. He grabbed at his head, spinning around. I raised the shovel to swing again but he pummeled me hard in the stomach. I doubled over, breathless. He waited until I caught my breath before he punched me so hard in the center of my chest, I flew backward.

I heard Zoe scrambling away. No doubt she would try to run. Now that she could use me as her decoy, to *buy her time* to escape. But then, that's exactly what she'd just done for me, in a manner of speaking. She'd been my distraction. But not to get away. Unlike Zoe, at least I was smart enough to realize that running was futile. This monster would hunt us down, no matter how far we went. He was the Bones Hollow Hunter; it's what he lived for.

If I didn't kill him now, I'd be the next in that hole.

Gasping, I crawled across the grass, belly in the mud and the dead pine needles. Leeroy snatched my ankle and dragged me back close. "Why'd you go and do a stupid thing like that?" he snarled. "You know I want to keep you around. Don't go," he punched me in the spine, "making me," then he smashed my head to the ground, "kill you," and smashed again, "yet."

He flipped me onto my back, so that my bloodied face was pointed to the clear sky. I coughed, choking on the blood that filled my nose and poured down my throat. My ears were ringing, or maybe it was just the birdsong trickling through. The Hunter's face loomed over mine. Nice and close, so close I could almost kiss him. He smiled that hungry, wolfish smile.

Then I headbutted him hard, right between his blue eyes, cracking the bridge of his nose. Blood rained down over me. His eyes flinched shut for just an instant. It gave me time to reach into my pocket. It gave me time to unfold Ripley before he punched my cheek. Two teeth popped out of my mouth. Blood burst from my lips, spluttering forth in red ribbons down my chin.

I squeezed Ripley's handle. Then I thrust her blade into his throat, to the hilt.

Leeroy stared at me, blinking, blood dribbling down. I yanked the knife out and blood sprayed, blanketing me in its wet warmth. Leeroy gargled, hand to his throat. He tried to speak but choked on his words. I stabbed him again, this time in the chest. I hoped it was the heart. I wriggled out from under him, knife in hand, before he fell. Before he trapped me beneath his weight like his brother had.

Jade's second murder. She was learning.

Adrenaline coursed through my body as I shivered from head to toe. My eyes felt burning red, radiating heat. I pulled myself upright and swiped the blood and sweat from my blurry vision. There she was. I blinked with disbelief, Zoe's figure slowly coming into focus. I hadn't expected to see her here, so certain she'd have run. For half a heartbeat, I wondered if she had changed her mind and come back to help me, save me.

But then I saw it: the phone in her fucking hand. She'd been recording.

"What?" Zoe asked.

I squeezed the knife that I'd once been afraid to touch.

I was nothing like Zoe. I wasn't going to pretend that everything would be all right.

epilogue

Welcome to a breaking news special of Serial Killers USA: The Bones Hollow Hunter. *I can't believe I'm saying it, but the case is* solved. *Take a minute to breathe that in. Finally, there is justice for the Bones Hollow Hunter victims.*

Now, the situation is still unfolding, but I had to make sure my Little Savages had all the juicy details, courtesy of a few friends of the podcast.

A park ranger—whose name has not yet been released by authorities—went missing in the forest last week. The search party couldn't have prepared themselves for the gruesome scene they would discover.

Deep in the forest, they stumbled upon a secluded cabin. At first glance, it appeared normal. It was an old structure that had been used by park rangers and hunters for a time, now seemingly abandoned. But its furtive purpose was far more sinister.

Because these walls had been home to true evil: Detective Leeroy Bennett.

The Bones Hollow Hunter.

That's right, my Little Savages—our guest on this very podcast, and one of the officers charged with investigating the disappearances of eight women. I had always believed the Hunter was still at large, but the fact that I actually met this monster in the flesh, here in this very station . . . The thought alone gives me chills.

When the search party arrived at the cabin, Leeroy Bennett was dead—lying beside a series of unmarked graves, and most horrifyingly of all: the bodies of new victims. One was reportedly his own brother. Inside sources speculate that he had caught Leeroy in the act of burying these new victims and confronted him. Evidence suggests there may have been a violent struggle. More details will surely come soon.

What we do know is that, based on early forensic evidence, Leeroy had murdered the missing park ranger along with two as yet unidentified male campers. Perhaps they'd sought shelter at his cabin, only to discover the damning evidence inside. Maybe this was why Leeroy Bennett couldn't let them live.

One body does fit the profile of the Bones Hollow Hunter victims: a woman in her late twenties who has been identified as Stefanie Alcott. Information has been trickling out about Stefanie, and according to her wilderness permit she had been hiking the Bones Hollow Trail with two friends—Jade Edelman and Zoe Burroughs. When and how Stefanie became separated from her group we don't know, but the crime scene suggests that she had been brutally murdered not long before the search party arrived, tragically too late.

Now, you may have already heard bits and pieces of this situation from the mainstream media, but I have a spicy detail that has not yet been released to the public, a piece of insider intel that will no doubt help us fill in the gaps of our story: We have a survivor. She's been battered and brutally maimed, but one victim was found alive.

Jade Edelman, Stefanie Alcott's best friend, was discovered in the forest near the scene of the massacre, dehydrated and traumatized after spending an estimated three days waiting for rescue. Had she tracked Stefanie to the cabin, only to find her already dead? Whether or not Jade came face-to-face with Leeroy Bennett, we can only imagine the horrors that she witnessed.

Only Jade can tell us what happened to the missing member of her party, Zoe Burroughs, whose whereabouts are still unknown. Did Zoe run for help and get lost somewhere in the woods? Did she manage to escape the Bones Hollow Hunter? Or was she his final victim?

I've been informed that Jade hasn't said much to investigators yet. From her social media, we can see that she had been friends with Stefanie and Zoe since childhood. It's apparent just how much she loved them. Clearly, this was a friendship for the ages, one I'm sure she would have died for.

God only knows what trauma that poor girl has gone through. But I'm sure with time that she'll be eager to shed light on the terrible series of events that unfolded. She'll want her side of the story to be heard—and what better place to share than here with us?

Thank you for following me on this journey, my sweet Little

Savages. It's been one hell of a ride, but this isn't the end. There is more to uncover here, and that's just what we're going to do. Make sure you subscribe to get the next episode—and you never know, maybe even an exclusive interview with Jade Edelman herself?

That's all for now. I'm your host, Laurie Wolff, signing off. As always, thank you for listening.

Cue end credits track: "I Think We're Alone Now" by Tiffany.

acknowledgments

Wow, where do I even begin? So many people have supported me on my journey here.

Thank you to Rebecca, for taking a chance on me, and for always *getting* my writing. I couldn't imagine a better agent to work with. I hit the jackpot with you.

Thank you to Tilda, for being an absolute dream to partner with on this book.

Thank you to Wendy, for your incredible enthusiasm and creative insight.

Thank you to my dad, who has always been my first reader and critique partner, from those very first weird, dark stories I wrote in elementary school all the way till now. You inspired me to be a writer and showed me this beautiful world of creativity. Thank you for always believing in me, and for your endless encouragement, wisdom, and support. I could write a book of gratitude just to you.

To my husband, who I cannot thank enough. You have always been my biggest cheerleader, uplifting and supporting me in every way. I'm so grateful for the countless hours of reading and feedback. Thank you for talking me down off all my mid-draft anxiety cliffs, and for being my sounding board, listening to my crazy ideas late into the night. I thank my lucky stars every day for you.

Thank you to my brothers, for always being there.

Thank you to the rest of my family for always cheering for me.

Thank you to my forever beta reader, D—even though you didn't get a chance to look at this one, you've read everything else I've ever written, and your feedback gave me the confidence I needed to submit my first query. I'm so grateful that you reached out and asked to swap reads for those first novels.

Thank you to all the people I've met traveling; from the lasting friendships to the fleeting bonds, you have inspired me in ways you'll never know.

Finally, thank you to my friends, who have rooted for me and dreamed with me and indulged me in all my craziness for all these years.

And to those of us who were on the mountain, thank you for still being my friends, even after I almost got us all killed.

ABOUT THE AUTHOR

Eliza Jabore began globetrotting at seventeen and spent the next decade devoted to traveling. She met her husband abroad and, after many years of adventure, finally planted roots back in her hometown in Iowa where she has two kids, two cats, and a dog. *Backstabbers* is her debut novel.

Instagram: @elizajabore_theauthor
X: @KupcakeProse

ABOUT THE TYPE

This book was set in Warnock Pro, a typeface designed by Robert Slimbach and commissioned in 1997 by Chris Warnock as a tribute to his father, John Warnock, one of the cofounders of Adobe Systems. Warnock Pro was released by Adobe in 2000 and features an array of state-of-the-art character sets, such as Latin, Cyrillic, and Greek. Warnock Pro is a contemporary update of classic old-style yet contemporary typefaces that features sharp and wedge-shaped serifs.